T. A. Cotterell read History of Art at Cambridge University. He was a freelance writer and now writes and edits for the research house Redburn. He is married with three children and lives in Bristol.

WHAT ALICE KNEW

Alice has a perfect life. A cool job, great kids, a wonderful husband. Until he goes missing one night. The phone rings and then goes dead. Unexpected gifts appear. Something isn't right.

Alice needs to know what's going on.

But when she uncovers the truth, she faces a brutal choice. And how can she be sure it *is* the truth?

Sometimes it's better not to know . . .

T. A. COTTERELL

---◆---

WHAT ALICE KNEW

Complete and Unabridged

CHARNWOOD
Leicester

First published in Great Britain in 2016 by
Transworld Digital
an imprint of Transworld Publishers
London

First Charnwood Edition
published 2018
by arrangement with
Transworld Publishers
Penguin Random House
London

A catalogue record for this book is available
from the British Library.

ISBN 978–1–4448–3705–6

FLINTSHIRE SIR Y FFLINT	
C29 0000 1218 723	
ULV	£20.99

For my family

1

A portrait is a quest for the truth. It spares no one.

I was painting the portrait of Julie Applegarth. She was sitting in a high-backed chair covered in crushed scarlet velvet in the drawing room of Applegarth Park. Julie had golden highlights, the green marble eyes of an alley cat, and was beautiful in the way of a woman who was not yet handsome but no longer a girl. Her dress was too tight, her hair too big and blowsy, and her caramel tan spoke of Monaco and Mustique, but she was more Harlow than Hollywood.

It had not been an easy sitting. I had hoped we would finish before tea but the demon time had marched too fast. Julie had tried but concentration was not her forte and she wasn't used to being told what to do, at least not by anyone other than her husband. Certainly not by another woman, particularly as I was only a hired hand — for what is a portrait painter if not literally a hired hand? She couldn't sit still for longer than it took to have her legs waxed without calling a friend or making a hair appointment. She fidgeted. She wriggled. She posed like a tragic actress. She gave the impression she had important business to think about, but that was a fiction. Julie played at business as she played at being chatelaine of the park, yo-yoing between self-assured entitlement and the fear she'd be rumbled.

1

She had been sitting, with breaks, for nearly five days in her high-backed chair. I had been standing at my easel looking directly at her and thinking about her, thinking around her, painting the idea of her, for almost five days. Mine, by some distance, was the more interesting task. It demanded full concentration. I don't like talking while I work. I pick up everything I need to know in the breaks and the meetings I have before a sitting. These are always more useful when the sitter is female. Men — successful men as my sitters invariably are — are always positioning themselves as something they're not, nicer perhaps, more generous or more cultured, better connected, and they have to flirt, it's a power thing. It all finds its way into the painting.

As we neared the end of day five, an unscheduled but necessary extension into Saturday, Julie seemed bored. She'd been through the usual stages: the early excitement, wallowing in the attention, pretending being painted was just another inconvenience of her in-demand life. Then the novelty and self-obsession wore off and the hard grind of sitting with nothing to do but thinking began. Yet still sometimes she refocused, gathered herself around the attention and basked in the hot eye of an artist paid a not inconsiderable sum to do nothing other than capture her beauty for the benefit of posterity and her husband.

At the far end of the room the double doors opened simultaneously. They were painted a spirit-sapping mustard, a colour that could only have been chosen by a very expensive interior designer. I'd tried, not entirely successfully, to avoid looking at them. Sir Raymond Applegarth — 'Call me Ray, darlin'' — entered with the anticipatory air of a man who had two ladies and a drinks cabinet to hand.

'Ah, there you are the both of you. How's it going, Jules?'

He pronounced her name with two syllables, 'jewels'. Somehow he managed to sound surprised to find us exactly where we'd been for the best part of a week. Maybe he'd expected me simply to take a photo and disappear, or to finish the painting *en plein air* like some latter-day Monet. Ray had a shiny skull with a band of grey hair semicircling his head like a slipped halo and eyes that absorbed the light. Even in his sixties his body was packed tight in his camouflage of combat trousers and wheat-coloured shirt. Most people over the age of eight who wear combats are children's TV presenters or lone gunmen — and Sir Raymond was not a children's TV presenter. His nose was wide and broken, the result, he told me, of park rugby in south Ipswich where he scrummed down on Sunday mornings until his early forties with men who didn't believe in rules.

Julie twisted a band of hair into a rope. Her calves tapered impressively, expensively honed in gym and pool.

'I think we're nearly done here . . . ?'

Her voice registered an octave higher for her husband than for the friends she gossiped with on her mobile during breaks. She told him what he wanted to hear, tilting her head, offering a coquettish smile. He nodded briskly and looked

3

at me. I glanced at my palette. The ochre needed replenishing. It was Julie's portrait but my reputation. Art was little more than decoration for the Julies of the world, an expression of wealth and status, acquired culture. As I looked for the tube on the trolley I said,

'The rest of the day to be really done.'

Julie rolled her eyes at Ray. He pulled a face — the little boy denied his toys — walked round and stood beside me. Julie twitched in the chair as if momentarily tempted to follow. Ray had checked on my progress regularly since the first morning, as if he had not only paid for the portrait but for the right to watch it painted. He always stood too close, smelling of aftershave and the spearmint gum he chewed to stop smoking. Ray gazed at the portrait with a cyclopean eye. There was still a bit to do but I could see my way to the end. Eventually he nodded, the self-made dealmaker satisfied he'd got more than he paid for, and said,

' 'S'great. Looks just like her.'

'Thank you.' I hoped it did rather more than that.

'It's definitely Jules but . . . ' he paused, searching for the right sentiment in an unfamiliar language, ' . . . at the same time it's somehow more, there's something extra.' He tilted his head and squinted down his nose at Julie as if he was the portraitist. 'Sort of like you've painted her as she really is.' Julie frowned, uncertain whether it was a compliment. 'Don't get me wrong, you look great, babe. Alice here has done you proud. You wanna look?'

She shook her head. Julie had said at the start she didn't want to see the painting until it was finished. She thought it might bring bad luck. I preferred it that way too. I like the drama of the moment when the sitter finally sees their portrait, the adrenaline rush of all that hope and expectation and fear and vanity squeezed into a single second, the first impression.

Ray said, 'Oh come on, babe, just a peek,' but Julie shook her head again.

He looked at me as if maybe I could persuade her but I shrugged helplessly. Ray continued looking at the portrait. He didn't want to seem disappointed, though it was obvious he couldn't wait for them to look at it together, to rejoice in her youth and beauty and his money, the age-old combination that had made it possible. Ray winked at her tenderly. The way the old bruiser did it I could have forgiven him anything. Julie wrinkled her nose at him fondly but didn't move.

I took a step back and scanned the portrait sitting on the easel. Not bad. It might have taken a day longer than expected but it had been worth the extra time. Perhaps I had been more forgiving than I should have been with the age of the hands and the womanly strength of her shoulders. Ah well. These little generosities cost nothing and they bring such pleasure. They didn't affect the final portrait. I had caught the determined flexibility of Julie's character. That, after all, was how she came to be sitting on a crushed velvet chair looking mournfully out over Applegarth Park when women no less pretty and certainly no less intelligent were scrapping for braising steak in blue-lined bags in Tesco. The great Joseph Mallord William Turner painted light; I had painted a faux-girly voice and a belief in the redistributive power of shopping.

But that was only the surface. I had also painted the subterfuge. This was a portrait of someone stronger than they seemed, wilier too, someone apparently shaped by a powerful man but who had everything she wanted. I had painted the tug-of-war between a rich, pug-faced older husband and his younger, seductive wife. I had painted the fragile interplay of power and beauty, money and youth, age and mobility. I had painted the portrait of a second marriage.

★ ★ ★

When finally we had finished, Julie disappeared to fetch Ray. He had retreated to his study, a room the size of a runway where he barked orders into a pair of phones and kept callers stacked up like planes above Heathrow. I wandered over to the floor-to-ceiling windows and looked out across the park. The grass stretched away under a blank sky towards the lake. Away to the left a speckled fawn appeared at the edge of the trees, paused, sniffed, and disappeared back into the protective darkness. I half expected to see a Cuyp cow nosing around the water-meadow or Constable's lad flat on his stomach, drinking from the stream.

I pulled my mobile out of my smock. There was a text from Nell saying Ed wasn't back yet but everything was OK. Translation: she'd eaten cereal straight out of the packet and Arthur was plugged into the TV and therefore not bothering her. She didn't ask what time I was getting home or say what she was doing. She didn't have to. Like every other fourteen-year-old girl in the world she was texting. I couldn't be on the phone when Sir Ray reappeared to survey his investment so I simply replied that work meant I was going to be late back but I couldn't wait to see her. Hugs and kisses. They knew the form. Art doesn't always work nine-to-five. Ed had texted that he would see me 'at Pete Spurling's' but he was 'totally boxed' and wouldn't stay late. Oh God! I'd completely forgotten about the party. Peter Spurling was Ed's protégé. He'd just passed his final obstetrics exams, the MRCOG IIs, and was having a party to celebrate. I replied saying the portrait had taken longer than expected and I wouldn't be back in time.

He signed off with three kisses. For a moment I wondered how Sir Ray signed off his texts to Julie, and whether it had changed now she was his wife rather than his lover. She would be the first to notice. The second wife, particularly of a rich man, is intimately attuned to these things, I imagine, her antennae always fizzing. Uneasy lies the head that wears that crown. By contrast, Ed's three kisses were as predictable as sunrise and I loved every one. The double doors swung open and Sir Raymond barrelled into the room, Julie a step and a half behind. I felt a surge of confidence in the reception my work would get and secure in the knowledge I was about to head home to wrap myself around my wonderful

7

husband and kiss the cheeks of my sweet sleeping children.

* * *

It is a long drive from Suffolk to Bristol, particularly as I try to avoid motorways. They're as interesting as processed cheese. If I'm alone in the car I stick to A or, better still, B roads wherever possible. I'm happy to swap the time for the nuance. The drive seemed even longer that night as there was nothing on the radio worth listening to — politicians bickering, luvvies loving, the distant crackle of Texan property prices misbehaving. No matter. I was in a good mood, feeling alive and optimistic, a sure sign the portrait had gone well. At a remote Edward Hopperish service station where the cashier fingered her phone in a bright desolate booth and even the oranges were in cellophane, I bought hazelnut yoghurt and a smoothie with disingenuous bonhomie on the carton. Passing a sign to Cambridge, I was reminded of my tutor's ginger goatee, his elegant study with its floor-to-ceiling bookcases and tall windows looking down King's Parade, Jerry Streeter jumping off Clare Bridge naked except for a dinner jacket and a smile as wide as the Cam, and I wondered, as everyone does, how I had got from there to here. Soon after, I swung right and headed towards Oxford and the west, white lines unfurling in front of me, buried memories unearthed by stray signposts.

I find driving at night wonderfully therapeutic,

alone in my car, the darkness warm and silky, headlights sweeping the road, the thrum of the engine the only sound in the silence, no family to fuss over, no food to cook, no clothes to wash, no tables to clear. No sitters to satisfy. It's like being at sea.

It is even better when I'm driving home through the night from a job well done and I can luxuriate in the warm glow of another sitter understood and represented, a creative impulse temporarily stilled. It is the best feeling in the world. I don't know how people get through life purely as consumers, never needing to scratch the creative itch or to leave their daub. They breathe in but they never breathe out.

He may not be an artist but Ed will leave his daub. Not on canvas but on the thousands of lives he has touched at birth and the not inconsiderable number of babies he has delivered and saved. He doesn't need the consolation of art; he has the consolation of life.

I was passing the sign to Bicester when my mobile burst into song on the passenger seat, 'Home' backlit in the rectangular screen. I glanced at the digital clock on the dashboard, 23.48, slowed down and scanned my rear-view before picking it up.

'Hello?'

'Mummy?'

Nell. I had expected Ed, startled awake by exhaustion and the still-empty bed, the lamp switched on, wondering where I was, checking I was OK, eager to know what time I would be back.

'Nell darling, what is it? Why aren't you in bed?'

'Mummy, Daddy hasn't come home.'

It was a child's voice again, stripped of the teenage ennui of her text.

'Have you tried his mobile?'

'Yup. No answer. I left a message.'

'St Anthony's?'

'They said he left about eight and hasn't been back.'

'And there hasn't been any emergency call-out?'

'Not that I know of.'

'OK, well I know he was going to Peter Spurling's party. Maybe he stayed on later than he expected?'

'Maybe. Only . . . '

'Only what?'

'Only he rang before he left the hospital and said he was really tired and would be back by nine thirty at the absolute latest and it's . . . '

'Late. I know.'

'And he was working all night last night. Though he did come back for literally five minutes to check we were OK around suppertime.'

An all-nighter? We'd agreed he would never do all-nighters when I was away, barring a life-and-death. He was as insistent about it as I was, maybe even more so. It wasn't fair on the children. They were too young to be left alone all night, even if it was just about legal. I was going to pick up on it but now wasn't the time. Besides, I should have been there. It wasn't the

10

first time my work had taken precedence.

'Mmm . . . OK, maybe he ran into someone he hadn't seen for ages at the party?'

Silence. She'd picked up the doubt in my voice. I couldn't blame her. It would be completely out of character for Ed to stay late at a party or to renege on a promise he'd made to the children.

'Is Arthur awake?'

'No. He's at Mikey Sutton's.' She left a telling pause. 'Remember?'

'Sorry, yes, of course. Well look, why don't you go back to bed? You can get into ours, if you want. I'll head on to the M4 so I'll be quicker. I should be back in about an hour and a half.'

'OK . . . '

'Yes? You sound unsure?'

'Do you think everything's OK?'

'Of course it is.'

'Because it's not like Daddy to — '

'I know. But, darling, don't you worry. There'll be some totally ordinary explanation.'

I truly believed it. Ed was the most reliable man I had ever met. I don't mean reliable in a Health & Safety, two-pens-in-his-breast-pocket way — he was too sharp for that — but in a family-means-everything way that made us all feel secure.

'Don't you worry, my darling.' I put on the 'there we go' voice I used when she lost a school hockey match. 'Everything will be fine. He'll probably be back before I am.'

2

The moment Nell clicked off I started scanning the roadside for somewhere to stop. There was no sign of a lay-by so I pulled on to the gravel in the dark mouth of a private driveway, angling the car as near to the gate and as far from the road as possible. It wasn't ideal but I had to call Ed. His mobile tripped into voicemail. I rang St Anthony's. An automated receptionist apologized that reception was unstaffed and gave me the number of the Bristol Royal Infirmary to ring in the event of an emergency. This was an emergency, but it wasn't that type of emergency. There was no one else to call. All his colleagues would be at Pete's party. I wrote a text, 'darling, hope all OK, when u getting home, i'll be c/1.30am, love you loads Ax'. I waited a couple of minutes in case there was an immediate reply before heading back out on to the road and wheeling the car in the direction of the M4.

The advantage of being on a near-deserted motorway after midnight is one can drive on autopilot and think about anything other than driving. The disadvantage of being on a near-deserted motorway after midnight is one can drive on autopilot and think about anything other than driving. So . . .

Ed had been called out to an emergency?

Unlikely on the back of a thirty-six-hour shift.

He'd stayed late at the party?

Unlikely bordering on inconceivable, given he was dog-tired and Nell was home alone. Ed never lingered at parties, particularly those filled with junior doctors. He knew they liked to let off steam, which is rather harder to do when your boss is across the room nursing a glass of fizzy water.

He'd been in a crash?

Pete's apartment was somewhere by the river. It would only take five minutes to drive home, half an hour tops if you walked, and you can't crash on that road, it's practically a straight line. Besides, if he had, the police or a hospital would have been in touch by now.

Heart attack?

At forty-six? A fit, virtually teetotal, never-smoked, tennis-playing forty-six? It would have been a cruel fate if he had. Anyway, again, surely someone would have been in touch?

Fallen for another woman?

I was more likely to sleep with another woman.

Drunk too much and was weaving home right now?

We are talking about the same Edward Sheahan?

★ ★ ★

I woke with a start, instantly remembering, and reached across the bed to feel for Ed. It was empty. Four forty-seven. There was no chance of getting back to sleep. Why hadn't he come home? I felt for my mobile on the bedside table

13

and switched it on. There was one message. I jabbed at the message icon and the text sprang into life. It was from Vodafone, telling me — oh, who cares what it was telling me? There was nothing Vodafone could tell me that I wanted or needed to hear. I slumped back on the pillows, my heart pounding as if I'd run a marathon rather than simply woken in the night, head spinning with a single question.

He must have been called out to an emergency home delivery — but after a thirty-six-hour shift? Maybe he was the only one still sober at Pete's party when the call came? But why hadn't he texted? It wasn't possible to be anywhere in the western world for twenty-four hours without access to a phone, let alone in a city in the south of England.

I decided that if he wasn't back by nine I would call Pete. That was as early as I reasonably could, the morning after his party. If that didn't throw anything up I would ring St Anthony's. It wasn't ideal. Pete's discretion was assured, but St Anthony's? A provincial town is the Aussie outback when it comes to the bushfire of gossip and nowhere is as tinder-dry as a hospital, where doctors and nurses put in long hours, mainly on the patients but sometimes on each other. You can't blame them, given the proximity, the pressure, the tension, the shared experience. Who else knows what it's like to tend to a car-crash amputee as they wake from the operation or spend a year watching a cherubic six-year-old who doesn't understand what is happening to him die of a brain tumour? Maybe

14

the real surprise is that they're not all at it round the clock. Maybe they are? I lay back on my pillow and the demons swirled in the darkness.

Eventually I switched on the lamp. I wasn't up to reading fiction, or poetry, or anything that required brain engagement, so I picked out from the bedside table the book of Pierre Bonnard paintings that Ed had given to me for my birthday. I tried again to decipher his inscription on the title page but Ed's handwriting was worse than Guy Fawkes' *after* he was tortured.

Bonnard painted his wife Marthe, a miserable shrew by all accounts, 385 times, and continued even after she died. As an unbending act of love his devotion to painting Marthe always seemed to me to be, if in a lower key, on a par with the great ones: Romeo and Juliet, Tristan and Isolde, Bonnie and Clyde. So I lay in bed leafing listlessly through the pages and looking at the paintings of Marthe-not-Marthe and found myself wondering: if Ed didn't return, would I be able to pull things together again?

★ ★ ★

Edward Sheahan was my opposite and we were instantly attracted. He came from a humble background. I don't mean that snobbishly, because I loathe snobbery. Old money was new money once and all that. I mean humble intellectually, educationally. Not that you would have known. Through sheer hard work and his extraordinary talent, Ed had become a celebrated obstetrician, a citizen of the world, in demand, first-class travel, top-dollar conferences, flashy hotels, all that jazzmatazz, but his dad was a postman and his mum a school dinner lady. They were a sweet old couple who'd had Ed late in life — they were already nudging their seventies when I met him — and lived in a tiny bookless house in that no man's land where South London blurs into Surrey.

By comparison, my upbringing — well-off, intellectually curious, Cambridge — was a shiny bauble. Not that it matters. It didn't exactly make us happy. I don't want to sound like Holden Caulfield but I hate all that class stuff, I really do, especially when it's snobbery kidding itself that it's talent. Who cares if your maternal grand-father was a direct descendant of Charlemagne? It's what ends up on your own canvas that counts.

Ed was totally unfazed by the difference in our upbringings. He was totally unfazed by anything beyond his work and, oh, it was so refreshing. Having read English at university I was outside the trendy Goldsmith's/YBA scene which dominated (or paralysed, whichever you prefer) art in the late 1990s. It was considered antediluvian to want to paint real people, to want to try to understand humanity and to commit it to canvas. I might as well have joined the tax office. But I knew what I wanted and I was prepared to work like a longshoreman to get there, and so was Ed. I found his absolute belief in what he wanted to do and his refusal to compromise a hugely powerful aphrodisiac.

Meeting Ed was like entering a whole new

16

world, one pregnant with possibility. He seemed so real compared to the people I had mixed with at school and university, where everyone was obsessed by the witty put-down and who knew who. His bolted-to-the-ground common sense was just what I needed. He was calm and rational and his wry humour made me laugh out loud. He had this solidity which made me feel everything I had done up to that moment was like a piece of Conceptual Art, one which looked clever and sounded interesting but which had nothing tangible to hold on to. I would prefer to sit in a toll booth on a busy bridge than to be a conceptual artist.

Ed Sheahan was obsessed by obstetrics. Other than playing guitar badly and hitting a tennis ball as hard and as flat as he could, obstetrics was what he did. If he ever had spare time we would head out to Chiswick and walk by the river. We talked about everything — ambitions, families, politics, the past and the future — and refused to agree about which was more important, medicine or art, giving life or making life worth living. He said art was an adornment, not a necessity. I said babies had been born without obstetricians for thousands of years. He said that's why so many died. I said he was responsible for over-population and insufficient resources. He said, I said. We argued, we laughed, we agreed, we disagreed. We were together.

He didn't sleep with me because I had cheese-wire cheekbones and a Camden loft. He didn't sleep with me because I knew the difference between Duchamp and De Stijl, or because I painted bowls of apples you could imagine crunching into and tasting the juice when you did. In the beginning — damn him — he barely slept with me at all. He was too knackered by his hundred-hour weeks and wretched medical exams.

★ ★ ★

I only got back to sleep as a sheet-metal dawn crept between the curtains and didn't wake until after nine, still exhausted after the four-hour drive, the broken night, a shadow of fear stretching across the empty bed. I reached for my mobile. No missed calls, no messages. I speed-dialled Ed but again there was the irritating click and his voice, deep and reassuring, saying, 'You have reached the mobile of Edward Sheahan . . .' I heard him out and left another message, trying not to sound too concerned. I wrote another text — 'darling, where r u? call me xx'.

I rang Pete before I got up. I suspected there would be no answer but he picked up on the second ring. I apologized for calling so early after his party but he said he'd been clearing up for an hour and he sounded cheerful enough to be telling the truth. Pete was confident and polite. He knew where he was heading and that Ed could help him get there. I asked my question.

'Ed?' My hope died on his tone. It was too quizzical. 'What do you mean?'

'Well, he hasn't come home and he's not answering his phone. I was just wondering if you knew where he might be.'

18

'No. I'm afraid I don't.' His voice was businesslike but with the perfect hint of concern, enough to empathize, not enough to frighten. Doctors deal with the world as they find it. They work in the grain of its imperfections. 'To be honest, I haven't been around much. I was on a course at Guy's last week and had yesterday off to prepare for the party. We talked a bit at the party but not about work or that sort of thing. Have you tried St Anthony's?'

'Not yet. I'm about to. I thought he might have been, well, you know, called out from the party or . . . '

'Not as far as I know.'

'Did he stay late?'

'Um, yes, he did actually, surprisingly late. He seemed to be having a very good time. I don't think I've ever seen him have a drink before, let alone several.'

'He was drinking?'

'Yes, he was. Not like Ed at all, I know. In fact he was flying.'

'Great.'

I tried, perhaps not entirely convincingly, to sound positive. No one needs to know their husband switches from teetotal medic to all-in party animal the moment they're not around. Pete gave a little cough.

'Obviously I'm not suggesting that when the cat's away . . . '

Ed had always said that not only did Pete have all the clinical skills, he was also as smooth as ivory.

'Of course.' I matched his lightness of tone. I

19

meant it too. The last time Ed looked at another woman was the day before he met me.

'I'm not sure what time he went. I didn't see him leave but he wasn't there at the death. Last I saw he was talking to a girl who's an art student down here, Araminta Lyall, and a man who's a picture dealer in London. It all looked quite involved. Do you want me to do some digging?'

'Um, no, not yet, it's fine. There's bound to be some perfectly simple explanation.'

'OK, well, whatever. I'm sure there is. Just let me know if you want me to.'

'Thank you. Oh and well done on your exams. You must be delighted.'

He was, but typically he was far too sensitive to be triumphant when I was stressed. He brushed it off and moments later he was gone. I dialled St Anthony's. A receptionist with a warm Dublin lilt answered. No, as far as she was aware there had been no sign of or word from Ed since he left yesterday evening, sometime after seven.

As we signed off my eye caught a photograph of Arthur on holiday in Spain when he was six. He was grinning malevolently, lolling in a plastic canoe, all skinny legs and arms, sharp angles, like an insect. Beads of water glittered on his lightly tanned skin. He had leapt in it as Nell crouched at the poolside, lining it up for sunbathing. Little did he know — and it didn't show in the photograph — Ed was underwater behind him, about to surface and tip him out, turning Nell's out-of-shot rage into the triumphant cackle of justice. Where was Ed now? Was he about to surface? Nine thirty-five. I would call the police in two and a half hours. I lay back on his side of the bed and watched the slanted light move across the ceiling.

★　★　★

When someone disappears unexpectedly you can't help the most outlandish possibilities entering your head. As I hopped out of bed it occurred to me that maybe Ed had for some reason gone straight from the party on one of his trips, either to a medical conference or to do pro bono work in the Third World. But if he had, why hadn't he told me? Could I have forgotten? I do have history. I once worked through a dinner party having spoken to Ed at seven and said I would finish a corner of a painting and meet him there. The next time I looked up from the easel it was midnight and he was standing in the doorway of my studio. Could that have happened again? I had been working ferociously hard for the last three weeks, racking up sixteen-hour days in my studio as I touched up Jean-Dominique Laborde for the BP Portrait Award (Monsieur Laborde having unhelpfully cut short his Paris sitting to fly to Singapore), completed my still life *Peach, Knife, Dead Rose* for the RWA show, and researched and prepared the Applegarth portrait, which was more work than one might have thought because to paint Julie I also had to understand Ray. So it was possible — just — that Ed had told me he was going somewhere and I simply hadn't taken it in.

Of course, if he had gone on a business trip he

would have taken a suitcase and clothes. So I went to the cupboard where we kept the bags and suitcases. There was, as usual, a pile of holdalls, backpacks, rucksacks and sausage bags reaching back into the darkness. I pulled them out one by one and there, glimpsed before I held it, was his travel bag. I let out a long slow sigh because he never travelled without it. There was no business trip.

I looked in his wardrobe but it was impossible to tell if any clothes were missing. Ed had so many shirts it was like a scene out of *American Psycho*. What else could have happened? Something at work? Something I've missed? Our marriage isn't always perfect — whose is? — but without tempting fate, we have it pretty good. Everyone is healthy. Ed and I communicate. We both know you have to love your partner *for* their faults. Anyone can love someone for the good bits. And he's just not the sort of man who chucks everything in to reinvent himself as a rare book seller in Baton Rouge or stream-of-consciousness poet in Popocatépetl. I got dressed and headed down to the kitchen.

Waiting for my toast to pop up and the coffee to filter, I convinced myself I was getting worked up over nothing. There was bound to be a perfectly straightforward explanation. It wasn't unknown for Ed to be called out to an emergency. Some could last twenty hours, life-and-death stuff under conditions that didn't always allow him to stroll outside to make a leisurely call. That sort of labour didn't punch the clock. It was also possible the Irish girl on the desk was new, or hadn't known, or had only just come on duty, or simply wasn't at her sharpest on a Sunday morning. I clicked on my mobile: 9.57. Two hours and I'd call the police. Then I'd wake Nell.

★ ★ ★

To kill time, and to take my mind off worst-case scenarios, I walked up to Clifton Village to do the mundane jobs I had been putting off. It was a low grey day, the clouds slouching like hooded teenagers, the air warm and damp. As I walked through the village, through shoppers with no cares beyond finding the best cut of sirloin, the ripest avocado, I could only imagine unlikely explanations and plead with higher beings I didn't even believe in for one more chance to complain about Ed playing the same song three notches too loud, three thousand times too often, or leaving dirty sports gear in a pile in the bathroom. I saw him everywhere: darting into shops, disappearing around corners, hair swept back, pink-cheeked, eyes soft and grey and amused, his self-reliance bordering on solitude. I bought mushrooms and asparagus in Reg the Veg to make his favourite risotto for lunch. But all the time I was checking my mobile and the tightness was growing in my stomach, gnawing away at the idea I should have heard from someone.

At 10.52 I was wondering whether I should go to the Clifton Cobbler to pick up Arthur's school shoes or to the flower shop on Waterloo Street to lose myself in the beautiful colours and

23

arrangements, when a voice said,

'Alice?'

I turned. A slight woman of about my age was standing under the faded awning of the jeweller's. She was wearing dark-blue dungarees and calf-height Doc Martens. Her hair was short and dyed peroxide. An Oxfam bag hung from her shoulder.

'Alice . . . ?'

'Yes?'

'Hi! Lucy Rennell. From school. You remember?'

The moment she said 'Lucy' I knew who she was. Even though her face was thicker and her cheeks more rounded, a cartoon rat that had become a mouse, she retained the waif-like figure and wary look I remembered. Lucy had been in my dormitory. We were never close but always friendly.

'Lucy Rennell! What are you doing here?'

Even as I said it I was praying she wouldn't say she lived in Bristol. I hadn't kept up with anyone from school, not because I disliked them but because my life had taken a different route. The last thing I wanted was Lucy Rennell living a hundred yards away, taking me back into my past. As an artist, if you're not moving forward you're moving backwards.

'I'm visiting my niece. She's just finished her first year at Bristol Uni.'

I nodded, trying to keep my relief from showing, which only made me remember Ed and realize that until he reappeared from wherever he was there was no possibility of relief. 'What are you doing here?'

24

'I — oh . . . ' I'd lost concentration. You do when someone you haven't seen for twenty years asks a question while you are wondering why your husband has disappeared.

'Do you live here?'

I clicked back into the present. 'Yes . . . yes I do. Just down the hill.'

'That's great. Married?'

I nodded. Having established she was only visiting I could afford to be friendly. We ran through our respective lives, twenty years of hope and love and work concertinaed into bite-sized images. Lucy worked in charity in the world's hottest spots. She had always wanted to do the right thing.

Lucy still saw girls from school. She reeled off names, girls I remembered but hadn't thought about for years. If you spend most of your life abroad your English life freezes the moment you leave, in Lucy's case the day she left school and headed out to work for MSF in Niger. I made inquisitive noises. My old school friends had become teachers, nurses, bankers' wives, mums, small-time entrepreneurs, artisan bakers, floppy-hatted Sunday-afternoon painters, boutique owners, amateur jockeys. Even as the names rolled off her tongue I steeled myself for her inevitable question, 'Do you still see anyone from school?'

'I don't really.'

I frowned as if struggling to understand why this should be.

'Except Marnie Latham.'

'Marnie Latham? I *definitely* don't see Marnie Latham.'

Her face clouded.

'Never?'

'Never.'

'That's funny.'

'Why?'

'Because I ran into her a couple of years back in London. We were hailing the same cab. As we were going in the same direction, we shared. She was very friendly, as though nothing had happened, yet she was still, I don't know, a little bit odd. Apparently she's successful in fashion somewhere up north . . . ' She cast a sweetly self-deprecating glance at her dungarees. 'Anyway, she said she hadn't kept up with anyone except you.'

'Are you sure?'

'Definitely. Because I remember being surprised given what happened. She was the one who told me you were an artist.'

'Well, that's odd because I can promise you I haven't seen her since the day she left. We didn't exactly part on great terms.'

Marnie Latham. Should I derive some tiny pleasure from the fact she still thought of me or feel weirded out by her false claim? I hadn't spoken to her for twenty years.

Lucy pushed her hand up through her hair. It spiked like a punk.

'That's really weird then, but somehow . . . '

'Somehow?'

'Well, I guess somehow it fits. I mean, that's how I remember her from school. She always was a little liar.'

26

★ ★ ★

By 11.17 I had slid out of Lucy's enthusiastic offer of coffee — 'I'm afraid I have to pick up Arthur, but if you're ever in Bristol again . . . ' — and was sitting in Coffee #1 squeezing a lemon and ginger teabag against the rim of my cup with a teaspoon and counting down the minutes. At the table next to me a man with straggly hair and hippy-beads was on his mobile asking a succession of people if they wanted to join him for Chai Latte and telling them about his new life split between Bristol and Glastonbury. 'I have my Glastonbury reality and my Bristol reality,' he repeated to each of them. There were no takers. I was beginning to tire of his Bristol reality when my mobile rang. I looked at the screen and had to stop myself shouting out loud.

I put the phone to my ear. There was a silence. Wherever in the world he is calling from, I know by the soft, velvety nothing-sound that always precedes Ed's first word that it is him. It's a silence that contains multitudes — expectation, recognition, arrival — like the gaps between the tracks on old LPs, each scratched moment instantly recognizable, almost as if it was part of the chord to come.

'Darling! Where are you? Is everything all right?'

'Yes.' He sounded exhausted.

'But where are you?'

'On my way home.'

'From where? Work?'

27

I wanted to ask a million questions, but none mattered any more. He was safe.

'Yes and no. From Stokes Croft.'

'Stokes Croft? How did you end up there?'

Stokes Croft is the gateway to St Pauls, a neighbourhood where they let off fireworks all year, horizontally, usually towards the police. It is home to artists' studios and vegan cafés, squatter collectives that sprout in disused buildings, all-night clubs, wraith-like dealers, protest groups. Stokes Croft is as far from Ed's natural habitat or the broad terraces of Clifton as it's possible to be, geographically or culturally.

'Well, I made a bit of a mess of Pete's. I don't really know what happened. I guess I was just completely exhausted and it was all so . . . so unexpected. I mean, I didn't know anyone at all.'

'No one?'

'Not one person. They were all arty types down from London. Miranda, Pete's girlfriend, is a stage designer. I guess Pete knew them through her.'

'So how come you stayed so late?'

'I guess I was sort of wrong-footed by the whole thing. I'd always assumed Pete lived in the usual scuzzy digs — '

'Last cleaned by Hippocrates!' I was happy again. Ready for humour.

'Exactly. But it wasn't even a shared house. It was an enormous apartment in one of those warehouses over-looking the river. There must have been a hundred and fifty people there.' I imagined Ed surrounded by the arty-glitterati, men and women who disappeared to the loos

28

and reappeared, conversation faster and more inconsequential. I imagined flutes of champagne, abstract art, jet-black cocktail dresses. Soho transported to BS1. Ed would have been like a child entering a forest in a fairy tale. 'Anyway, I was about to slip away when Pete cornered me and started introducing me to everyone as his 'mentor' and 'the best obstetrician in the world' and — '

'It went to your head?'

Beside me, Bristol — Glastonbury was taking his own pulse. His lips were counting, his eyes closed.

'No, well OK, maybe a little bit.' He could hear the teasing in my voice. 'Everyone was really nice, early thirties, and they all wanted to know what Pete was like at work and some had heard of you and when I said I was leaving they said not to be such a bore and I don't know . . . I guess I suddenly had my second wind, and because it was all so different and I'd had a drink to keep me awake I . . . I just sort of lost track of time.'

Surprise mingled with embarrassment in his voice. I knew from personal experience how his shy, serious demeanour could prove seductive, exotic in its difference. Ed had welcoming eyes, stanzas of grey, a wide kind mouth with soft lips, a clockmaker's fingers and a hank of unruly blond hair he was forever pushing back from his forehead. He was five ten, well-built, and exuded a quiet but unshakeable confidence. Ed was a man women trusted with the most precious thing in their lives. I couldn't be annoyed.

'Don't worry, my darling, it's called drinking.

29

Most people do it most of the time.' I came over all casual. I could afford to. 'So: Stokes Croft.'

Ed grunted, as if appreciating for the first time the calamitous weight of a hangover.

'God knows. Five or six of us went back to this girl's flat. I can't remember her name. Annabel someone. The moment I got there I knew it was a bad idea.'

'So why didn't you just get a cab home?'

'I tried, but the driver drove off while I was saying goodbye and there weren't any others around. I'd left my mobile at work, which meant I had to go up to her flat to call one, and of course they persuaded me to stay for a drink, which I wouldn't have if I hadn't already been completely plastered. Next thing I knew I was waking up in a chair with a head full of pig-iron. That was about half an hour ago. I cabbed to work, picked up my mobile and now I'm walking home. I'll be back in twenty minutes — and I think I'll have to go to bed!'

He signed off with a kiss and a groan. I pictured him walking past the Highbury Vaults, his head protesting, trying to work out what had happened.

I felt good. Nothing had happened. He would soon be home. Outside, the man selling the *Big Issue* crossed the road from his pitch beside the Lloyds ATM to his pitch outside the Co-op. He worked long hours and wore the same clothes every day, summer and winter. As I watched him chat to a passer-by whose thick eyebrows and full-sheen dark hair reminded me of Peter Spurling, I suddenly realized I had never asked Ed *why* he had gone back to Stokes Croft.

3

I was climbing up to my studio after dropping Nell and Arthur at school on Monday morning when the phone rang in the study. I paused, wondering if I could leave it, but I was alone in the house. I have avoided answering the phone if possible since I was a child. I don't like having to pick it up and say 'hello' all bright and breezy without knowing who is on the other end or what they want. For that second, or as long as it takes for whoever it is to introduce themselves, it's as if I'm hanging from a tall building with a crowd below. I feel too exposed. I would never sit for a portrait for the same reason, which may seem hypocritical, but there you go. I hate being looked at. I hate feeling vulnerable. Certainly I would never sit for myself. Being painted is like standing in front of a firing squad. You are in the light. The guns, the witnesses, the artist, they are sheltered by the darkness. There's nowhere to hide.

'Hello?'

Silence. I dangled like a marionette. Finally a woman's voice, youngish, cut-glass.

'Is Dr Sheahan there?'

'No, he isn't at the moment. Can I take a message?'

'Um, no, no thank you.'

The voice was haughty, as if I was hired help.

'Can I tell him who called?'

'Um, no, no worries. Do you know where I might find him?'

We occasionally get these calls, pregnant women ringing Ed at home. They are not supposed to. Most obstetricians don't give out their number, but Ed is not most obstetricians. I tried to keep the sarcasm out of my voice.

'At work?'

'Oh, of course, I'll try him there. I'm sorry to have bothered you.'

'Are you one of his patients?'

Pause. 'No.' Longer pause. 'I work for a charity. A medical charity. I've been given his name specifically as someone who might be able to help.'

'Which charity do you work for?'

'Oh, it's only a small one, nothing you would have heard of.'

Normally I wouldn't have pursued it but there was a cadence in the woman's high-handedness and well-bred vowels and evasiveness that made me curious.

'Try me.'

'No, it's nothing, don't worry but thank you anyway, that's great, I'm sorry for disturbing you at home. I'll call Dr Sheahan at the hospital. Goodbye.'

I was about to say 'goodbye' but she had already put the phone down, leaving me with nothing to say or think other than it was unusual for someone working for a medical charity not to know that doctors revert to 'Mr' when they become surgeons. It was even more unusual for someone who was asking for a favour to be so brusque.

★ ★ ★

That afternoon, when I got back from picking up the children, someone had left a bouquet of lilies propped up by the front door. An empty-handed Arthur thoughtfully walked past them while I was hauling heavy groceries out of the car. The card only said they were for Ed, from 'ML xxx'. I took them into the kitchen to put into a vase.

Our house was always full of flowers because they bring such colour and life. I often bought them in the village to draw or paint when I wasn't preparing for a commission, or just to remind me of Highlands, the remote house on the edge of Dartmoor where I grew up. Or a new mum or proud dad might send flowers if they knew us or there had been complications. It was unusual, though, for the sender not to add dewy-eyed and humbling messages of appreciation and joy. It was also unusual for people to hand-deliver flowers and then to leave them outside. After all, if someone bothers to buy *and* hand-deliver flowers it is generally because they want to thank Ed, The-Man-Who-Gave-Life, in person.

ML xxx

They couldn't be from Marnie Latham, surely? That would be too much of a coincidence. Nevertheless, so soon after meeting Lucy the initials catapulted her back into my mind. It was unsettling to know she had been thinking about me but not getting in touch. For a time at school she

33

had been my absolute best friend. Marnie heightened my experience of the world with her fierce intuition and refusal to kow-tow. Her energy lifted me like a dancer at the peak of her powers.

For years afterwards I would see a flash of black hair in the street, glimpse snake-hips or Roy Lichtenstein-lips, or hear a Manchester accent and I'd have to check it wasn't her. It never was. The moment I saw the eyes, I knew. Marnie could change anything except her eyes.

★   ★   ★

I poured a splash of Côte de Beaune we had been given by a brand-new father into a bubbling Thai curry that didn't deserve wine of such quality, turned round and said,

'I had an epiphany today.'

Ed was sitting in the orange-check armchair in the corner of the kitchen, a mug of tea with four Warhol silkscreens of Marilyn balanced on its arm. He raised a laconic eyebrow. I didn't have epiphanies about clinical science. I wasn't about to announce I'd found God.

'About Jackson Pollock.'

Ed's eyelids flickered as if I was a wayward child.

'Well, I suddenly realized Pollock was the man who embodied a particular moment when everything changed. For a thousand years artists had put their canvases on easels and looked past them to paint the world that they saw. Even Picasso and the moderns, they were all looking for different ways of depicting the visible world.

But Pollock wasn't. He wasn't interested in painting physical reality. He was only interested in painting his psychological reality. So he took his canvas off the easel and put it on the ground — after all, he didn't need to look at anything — and dribbled and flicked the paint on to it. He literally poured his soul on to the canvas. It was as if he was saying: 'Don't paint what you see, paint how you feel; don't look out, look in.' Anyway, what I realized was that was the moment art became about the self rather than society. And so, this is my point, you can draw — or drip! — a line from that moment down through Salinger, Kerouac and the hippies all the way to Tracey Emin's bed and the selfie and the me-me *X-Factor* culture of today. It captures the atomization of society, the breakdown of the family and so on.'

There was a pause, Ed waiting to see if there was anything else. When he realized I was done he knitted his eyebrows as if testing the thesis from every angle. Ed cheerfully tolerated what he considered my random theories and enthusiasms but he was far too practical to engage. Had art theory ever done anything useful?

'Does it explain the breakdown of your family?'

'Stop it! I'm being serious.'

Arthur appeared in the doorway.

'Mummy?'

'Not now, darling, I'm just talking with Daddy. Be with you in a minute.'

'But — '

'In a minute.'

Arthur disappeared.

'No, it's interesting, I like it.' His mouth creased into a laconic smile. 'Good to know you haven't wasted your day.'

There were times when it could be incredibly frustrating being married to Ed. Those were the times when it would have been nice to be married to someone who would have grabbed an idea with both hands and stayed up all night smoking untipped Gauloises and drinking cheap Rioja. But how many of those types would also have had the generosity to help me fly? There were times when Ed's unflappability made me want to yelp like a coyote, but it was precisely those qualities that enabled him to do his job, to cope with the things he saw. I accepted the ending implicit in his drollery.

'By the way, did someone from some charity call you at work today?'

'Someone from some charity?' His tone was light and ironic. 'No. Not that I know of.'

'That's odd. She sounded very keen to get hold of you.'

'Maybe she spoke to someone else at St Anthony's?'

'I suppose so. Though she seemed very keen to speak to you.'

'What did she sound like?'

'Youngish. Well-spoken.'

Ed shrugged.

'How long till supper? I've got a call I need to make.'

I glanced at the curry. 'Ten?'

'The perfect ten.'

He kissed me on the temple. I felt a smudge of

warm air from the open window and watched the fat cushion he'd been sitting on slowly inhale. Ed plucked the phone from its stand by the fruit bowl and headed down to the basement to make his call.

★ ★ ★

'Can't sleep?'

I looked up from my easel. Ed stood in the doorway of my top-floor studio leaning against the jamb. He was wearing pyjamas striped red and white like toothpaste and holding a glass of water. I knew those slate-grey eyes better than anyone. When we started going out he sat for me whenever he could, which wasn't often. It was through painting Ed I learnt you paint the light in the eye rather than the eye itself. I could see he was exhausted but unable to sleep and didn't know how to cope because he wasn't used to it. I smiled sympathetically. I often worked in the middle of the night when I had ideas I couldn't get out of my head, but from the day I met him Ed had slept like a baby.

'Uh-uh.'

'Me neither.'

He looked around the room. Ed rarely came up to my studio. He considered it some sort of magician's cave and felt any intrusion might disturb the delicate ecosystems or unfathomable alchemy that occurred within. This was where, as someone once put it, my mind was made physical. My studio was always untidy, if not a Bacon-level slum. Ed's eyes roved around the room in one long panning shot from where I stood at the easel, taking in the paint-splattered sink, the metal trolley holding my palette and brushes in jam jars, oil paint, tubes of acrylics, the bookcase piled with monographs and catalogues raisonnés, fiction, short stories, Salter and Fitzgerald, Carson McCullers, sentence-makers and picture-poets, the 'resting' (*never* abandoned) canvases leaning against the wall, the wood-framed *Artist with a Coiled Rope*, the first selfie I ever painted, postcards of heroes — Rembrandt, Goya, Velàzquez, Motherwell, masters of black — a Van Gogh-style wood-and-wicker chair minus his pipe and tobacco, and back to the easel, where I was picking out the early contours of a still life in pencil, a decorator's swab of experimental colour behind.

'Nice flowers.'

'They were left by the front door. By someone called ML.'

'Emel? Emily?'

'M-dot, L-dot, no message, that's all it said. And three kisses. Any ideas?'

Ed frowned.

'Pass.'

'Well, who's had a baby recently who begins with L?'

'Um . . . let me see — the Langtons, maybe?' He gave a confirmatory nod, as if shoring up his own conviction. 'Must be the Langtons. Jeremy and Jemima. They've just had a baby boy. Jules. That's who it'll be. You wouldn't have thought they needed another 'J' in the family.'

Jemima Langton. She had been on our table at

a school charity quiz night we'd been roped into. She had been the designated driver, her husband in chalk pinstripes and commercial property, drunk. She introduced herself as a patient of Ed.

'Why ML?'

'Mima. She calls herself Mima.'

He picked out a brush and stropped the bristles against his palm.

'And why hasn't she signed it from both of them? Or all of them? She could have just done one big 'J'.'

Ed shrugged. 'How should I know? Maybe she forgot. New mothers often do. Or have you forgotten that?'

★ ★ ★

Wednesday night was book club night. I picked Arthur up from Richie Railton's birthday party and gave him and Nell tea. As it was the first half-decent evening of the summer I left Ed, who had texted to say he would be running late, some cold chicken and a tomato-and-onion salad and headed up to Sion Hill. It's so peaceful in the golden-green sunlight of a West Country evening, lying on the grass overlooking the bridge and the gorge, the Georgian houses with their tall black windows and wrought-iron balconies. I took a Cy Twombly exhibition catalogue because I felt like wallowing in his roses. Ed had worked late on Tuesday night too and therefore reneged on his offer to cook supper. When he did get home he'd simply disappeared into his study. I also wanted to find some space away from Arthur. He'd been in trouble at school and was being a pain. He'd pushed Alfie Warburton into the pond. There was a lot of 'he said, I said, he did so I did' (Arthur the innocent party in his telling, as usual). I didn't listen. Alfie Warburton is a trouble-maker but Arthur has to learn that violence begets violence and punishment. So I decided to get out and to lie on the grass luxuriating in the evening sunshine and the evanescence of Twombly's brushwork until it was time to walk across Christchurch Green to book club.

There were eight in the book club, including me. They were an odd crew, with more men than is typical. Don't ask me how they'd got together. I was a late joiner. It was the sheer randomness of the group that attracted me. John was a retired prep school headmaster. Neil did something in software. Peter used to be someone in the City. Fiona was obsessed by fitness and talked incessantly about the musclebound Greek, Costas, who put her through her paces in a Redland gym. Sarah, whose Farrow & Balled Gloucestershire-gastropub-styled kitchen we were sitting in that night, was a bored housewife with a husband who was in London half the week and children away at school. Geraldine was a no-nonsense Scottish GP. Diana was a successful retailer, which meant she talked about 'sales densities' and 'click and collect' rather than old-hat stuff like selling things people wanted. She wasn't there that night. And then there was *moi*.

Sarah provided scalding soup with bread and cheese, olives, brownies, and a warm Côte du Rhone. The soup was pea and ham, the colour of

40

floodlit grass. There was a blue-veined Dolcelatte riper than Gielgud's Hamlet. It reminded me of Granny Querry's ancient hands as they warmed themselves on her sherry glass in the drawing room at Highlands, the silk curtains behind stained by her smoke, an ornate gilt mirror speckled black in the corners where the reflective silver had disappeared. Neil turned to me, leaning too close as he always did, his breath smelling of cheese, and said,

'I saw Ed earlier.'

He stared at me through his blue-tint aviator glasses. I simply said 'Oh' because I hate it when people invade my space.

'On Stokes Croft. At dinnertime.'

I was thinking this wasn't the most inspiring conversation I had ever had when it occurred to me that if Neil had seen Ed it was the second time he'd been to Stokes Croft in less than a week. Was that surprising? He hadn't been there for years, at least as far as I knew, but presumably there was a straightforward explanation. There always was with Ed.

'Was he . . . was he doing anything?'

'No. Just walking. I was in the car. I recognized him as I drove past.'

'I see. And?'

Neil licked thin lips. His tongue was nicotine-yellow. I wondered if he was trying to tell me something.

'Just it seemed a . . . a funny sort of place to see him.'

'Maybe he was going to see someone?' I thought about reaching for a brownie but

41

decided against. I'd been working too hard to take much exercise. 'They have babies there too.'

'Just he looked a bit out of place. You know how it is down there. Don't expect to see a man in a suit walking.'

'It's not Texas.'

I meant it as a joke but Neil gave me a sour look. He was ridiculously thin-skinned. If ever I took a different stance on a book we had read, and I often did, he always took it personally. I'd given up minding. There are some people who never connect.

'Just saying, you know,' he said peevishly, but before I could say anything Fiona drummed her fingers on the table and said,

'Who would like to start then?'

It was an old joke. John always started. He's the headmaster. Plus, we'd been reading an unpublished manuscript written by his nephew. He looked around gravely, as if lecturing junior assembly on why you shouldn't run in the corridor. Headmasterly hairs grew out of his ears and nose and oval leather patches covered the elbows of his tweed jacket. He wore black lace-up Oxfords, each as shiny as the bonnet of a new car, and owned a holiday cottage in Padstow.

John outlined the plot of the novel — he always did, even though we had all read it — and suggested various themes. Fiona rejected his interpretation, as she always did. Peter agreed with her, as he always did, for no better reason than to wind John up. Neil scratched notes in green ink. People who use green ink often see themselves as mavericks. They are usually a pain to be around. I bet Oscar Wilde used green ink, and Rupert Brooke. Jim Morrison. Only Neil wasn't Oscar Wilde, much less Jim Morrison. He was Neil. Geraldine offered qualified support to John. The argument went in circles. It was almost as if they preferred it that way.

I got home after eleven and tossed my house keys into the basket on the marble shelf by the door. Ed's mobile was beside it. Normally he took it to bed in case of an emergency, even when he was off duty. I picked it up to take upstairs. Idly, I pressed the space bar and was greeted by the 'unlock' rectangle. I typed in his password but it didn't open. Fat fingers? My fingers are paintbrush slim. I typed it in again. It still didn't open. I focused, tapping in the letters with exaggerated care. Ed had used the same password for as long as he had needed a password. Phone, bank, laptop, tennis club, iTunes, Amazon, First Great Western, you name it, pension, they were all the same, the name of some saurian band that trod the boards in the 1970s, 99 or 999 added where necessary. I hit 'enter'. No dice. Weird. If anyone had asked me I would have said Ed didn't even know how to change a password. He must have had Arthur's help. I headed upstairs, my mind ticking oddly. Something didn't feel quite right but I couldn't put my finger on it.

I didn't stop at our bedroom but crept into Nell's instead. A full moon created a silvery sheen in her room. She had twisted the pillow into a neck-brace but was sleeping peacefully, breathing evenly. Nell had blonde hair, petrol-blue eyes, a haughty nose that pierced the air like a keel, porcelain skin and a wide friendly mouth. She had inherited my bone structure; Arthur had my sense of infinite possibility. Nell was precious and beautiful and I hadn't seen enough of her recently, though I always thought that whenever I stopped to think about her. I straightened and flattened the pillow and kissed her lightly on the temple. She shifted on the bed and flung an arm across her face, a wrist as delicate as glass. It reminded me how fragile the life we construct for ourselves really is. I kissed her again but by the time she stirred I was gone, pushing open the door to Arthur's room.

He looked up immediately, hair ochre-tinted in the glow from the shadeless bulb on the landing. I stroked his cheek with a finger. It was so soft an advertising company would bottle it.

'Can't sleep?'

His little head nodded on the pillow.

'Any reason?'

His head moved side to side. His mouth was open and the tips of his teeth were showing.

'You're not frightened of anything?'

Side to side.

'OK. Well, you just snuggle down and think nice thoughts.'

Up and down.

'Mummy?'

'Mmm?'

'Why is Daddy sad?'

'He's not sad. When was he sad?'

'Tonight.'

'What do you mean he was sad?'

'He was just . . . '

'Sad?'

Up and down. Their heads look so small when they don't understand. It makes you remember they're still children.

'Did he say he was sad?'

'No.'

'So why do you think he was sad?'

'He was crying.'

'He was crying?'

'Little tears.'

'Little tears?'

I was becoming an echo. But he seemed so un-Arthurish, as if he was turning outwards rather than inwards and was blinded by what he found.

'He turned away. He didn't want me to see him cry.'

'I see.'

Only I didn't see. Ed never cried. Occasionally he got beaten up by some particularly appalling pregnancy or birth story, but it had to be outside the realm of twenty years' obstetrics experience, the sort of thing that couldn't be described in words or pictures, and even then he never *cried*. Perhaps his Saturday-night hangover had caught up with him. I smiled reassuringly but I couldn't help feeling uneasy. Ed never kept anything from me. We always told each other everything. To try to put any negative thoughts out of my mind I added:

'Well, don't you worry your little head. I'm sure it was nothing or just things he had to deal

45

with at work. When you spend your life with pregnant mothers and babies you see a lot of unpleasant stuff, and that can be really stressful. It can build up inside you, maybe without you even realizing, and sometimes it all gets too much and you need to release some emotion. I'm sure that's what it was. So you just go back to sleep, my darling.'

'You and Daddy, you're not going to get divorced?'

Where did that come from?

'No. Why do you ask that? We're very happy together. I love your daddy and he loves me, and we both love you two.'

'You don't love your work more than you love Daddy?'

'No!'

'More than you love us?'

'Don't be silly.'

'Promise?'

'Cross my heart.'

He gave a little nod, I hope of belief, nodded and turned away. There was something preter-naturally defenceless in the curve of his back and the sharp angle of his shoulders poking out of the duvet. I watched him for a little while. Why had he asked that? He didn't move. Eventually his shoulders hunched and he curled into himself, legs out, as if he was a question mark.

4

On Friday night I was lying in my bath, steaming in peace, tweaking the taps with my toes to keep a hot tide flowing, skin glazed and glistening with oil, a single star in my own firmament. It's a giant, claw-footed bath, which is how a bath should be, the showerhead lying heavy and bronze on its cradle.

I reached down to pick up *The Times*, which lay on the wicker table on top of water-stained back issues of the *New Yorker*, and started leafing through the pages. On page six a large headline trilled 'SOCIETY GIRL DIES'. It's not the sort of story I usually read — 'there's no such thing as society', as the old matadora said — but the word 'Bristol' caught my eye. You don't have to be a hearse-chaser to take an interest in a newsworthy death a mile or so from home.

I read the article, written in the breathless prose of the provincial stringer, in a single gulp. A thirty-two-year-old mature art student at UWE had been found dead in her flat. There was some background. She had studied History of Art at Edinburgh and worked at Sotheby's before moving to Bristol to study to be an artist. There was no sign of forced entry but the police were treating it as suspicious.

The dead girl had lived in the Carriage Works. I know the Carriage Works. It's a nineteenth-century building in the Bristol Byzantine style, three storeys, each with an arcade of semicircular arches. It was abandoned for years before being converted into up-market flats for people on the fringes of the arts or the media, or accountants who play at being those types at weekends.

But it was none of this that made my heart stop. The detail that made me dip under the water and hold my breath for as long as possible as I tried to work out how it hung together before eventually coming up like a seal and flooding the floor was that the name of the girl in the colour photo accompanying the article, a picture of a girl in a low-cut dress and a royal blue ribbon choker at a Dering Street opening, and the name in lights in the article, was 'Araminta Lyall'.

Araminta Lyall. Araminta Lyall? I knew that name. Where had I heard it? I racked my brains. Pete! When we spoke on the phone on Sunday morning Pete had said the last person he had seen Ed talking to was a girl called Araminta Lyall.

'Ed!'

I stared at the face in the photo. It was pretty in the way of a Hollywood usherette. Araminta Lyall had long blonde hair and a narrow, angular, Modigliani face, medieval and sloping, sardine-silver eyes. She looked wayward but compelling.

I flung the paper back on to the chair and slid under the water again. When I surfaced Ed was sitting on the side of the bath, expressionless as an assassin, arms dangling, copper wristband turning turquoise, his right hand an inch from my head. He had just got back from South London, having driven there and back to put flowers on his parents' graves. They died within six months of each other (heart attack/broken heart). He went twice a year, on their birthdays, taking a day off if necessary, a pilgrimage of love and thanks for everything they sacrificed for him. It was his only link to his past.

'Hey! You gave me a fright.'

'You called.'

'Have you seen the paper?'

'Nope.'

I glanced towards the wicker chair. He leant forward to pick it up, turned it over and started reading.

'Is that the girl from last Saturday night? Where you stayed on Stokes Croft?'

He didn't answer but as he read the tips of his ears began to redden. I levered myself out of the bath. Without looking up Ed pulled a pair of towels off the rack and handed them to me. I wound them around my hips and shoulders and took a third, wrapping it around my head like a turban. Eventually he folded the paper, Araminta face up, and said,

'Poor girl.'

'She's been murdered.'

'It doesn't actually say she was murdered.'

'She didn't die of old age!'

'I guess.'

'And the police are treating it as suspicious. What was she like?'

Ed looked back at the paper as if the photo might hold some clue.

'I didn't really talk to her — at least, not until I was already too far gone. I talked to someone else, some guy, in the taxi going back to hers, went up to her flat to call a cab, was given a drink and that was it. I crashed out pretty much straight away.'

'You'll have to do better than that!'

'That's all I remember.'

'Well, you'll have to do better than that for the police.'

Ed frowned, his bottom lip turned down.

'The police? Why would I talk to the police? I don't know anything about her. If it wasn't for this photo I'm not sure I could even remember which one she was or what she looked like.'

'Of course you'll have to talk to the police. They're not doing their job if they don't come and see someone who spent a night with her a few days before she was murdered.'

'I didn't exactly 'spend the night' with her.'

'Whatever. They're bound to want to speak to you.'

Ed stared at me as if weighing the truth of my words.

'But that's ridiculous. Why would they? I mean, I hardly knew her.'

'You went to her flat. Shouldn't you ring them and tell them?'

'What? You want me to ring the police to ask for an interview to tell them I met her once but didn't know anything about her? They're going to think I'm some sort of nut.'

I knew what he said was true. And yet . . . and yet. Someone had died. Surely he had to do whatever he could? Almost before the thought had formed in my head I heard myself asking:

'By the way, what were you doing on Stokes Croft on Wednesday evening?'

'Wednesday night?' Ed looked genuinely surprised. 'I wasn't.'

'Sure?'

He frowned for a moment before his face lightened.

'Oh yes, I went to St Andrew's on Wednesday night. I crossed Stokes Croft, if that's what you mean. I had to visit an ex-patient who's had a difficult time to lend some moral support. I walked. Through Kingsdown and up through Montpelier. That was the night I said I was going to be late. Why?'

He seemed so calm and his response so logical I wondered why I had asked.

'Just Neil from book club mentioned he saw you.'

'Oh . . . OK.'

He looked slightly perplexed. He clearly couldn't see why I'd raised it, and suddenly nor could I.

'And why did you change your mobile password?'

'Why did I change my password?' He rocked back theatrically, smiling. 'Is this an inquisition? Because they asked us to at work. They're trying to drag us dinosaurs into the twenty-first century. Is something worrying you, my darling?'

'No . . . well, yes. Maybe, I mean, I don't know, just . . . things have been a bit weird lately.'

'What do you mean 'weird'?'

'Well, sort of a lot of one-offs.'

'Such as?'

'So, like you getting drunk and stopping out overnight. And Lucy Rennell telling me Marnie Latham said she was still in touch with me and then the very next day getting those flowers with Marnie's initials on them, and that woman from the medical charity who didn't know about surgeons being mister. I don't know . . . it just feels like a lot of slightly odd things have happened at once.'

'You think the charity woman might have been Marnie Latham?'

I thought for a moment. It hadn't occurred to me.

'No. I don't. At least, not unless her voice has changed.'

'Which it could have done.'

'It's possible, suppose, but it was very different.'

'OK, well the others: so I got drunk. It doesn't usually happen, but it did. Even now I'm not quite sure why I did. I think it must have been the combination of a lot of things. Work. Exhaustion. The unexpected liberation of a party with no medics, no one I knew, no one of my blood group. The fact you weren't there but these people I'd never met before had heard of me through Pete and you through your work. I've never had that before, which is hardly surprising given the sorts of places I go, and I think because I was knackered I responded in a way I never normally would. As for Marnie saying you're still friends, that is a bit weird but I wouldn't worry. She's never been in touch and if she was going to be she probably would have been by now. Maybe she was just winding Lucy up? And the flowers, that is a coincidence as I'm 99.9 per cent certain they are from Mima Langton — '

'Could you check?'

'Sure. And if the charity woman wasn't Marnie, well maybe she really was telling the truth and she did work for a charity, just not a very professional one.'

'I suppose so.'

Ed grinned in a way that instantly made me feel better.

'My darling, I think you are making connections where there aren't any.' He lifted my chin with his thumb so our eyes met. 'Which is, after all, what artists like to do.' He grinned. Ed knew exactly how to banish my fears. He always made the world seem pure again. 'Maybe you should slow down a bit. You've been burning a lot of midnight oil lately. Spend some more time with the children. Make sure they don't forget who you are!'

I didn't rise. I knew Ed thought I neglected the children when I was in the force-field of art. Then again, so did he when duty called. The difference was somehow he could always slip back in with a hug and a joke as if he'd never been away, whereas Nell seemed to make it harder for me — even if it was only when I arrived home that she even noticed I'd been gone. Now he'd doused my fears, I wanted to move the conversation on.

'And what about you? Arthur said you cried when you said goodnight the other day. Is everything OK with you?'

'Yeah, I'm fine. I was just exhausted. It's been pretty tough at work. We're a bit short at the moment. Alison's been ill, Pete's been doing his exams, Karen's on a course. Philippa's still on holiday. We haven't got enough bodies right now, so the rest of us are covering more than we should. On Wednesday a first-time mother had a placental abruption. We couldn't save the baby. We had to operate. Poor thing. She was born to be a mum, that's all she ever wanted, and now she never will be. And the husband, he was so upset, almost more than she was, completely inconsolable. When I told him he howled like a damaged animal. You could have heard it in Swansea. At times like that mine is the worst job in the world. I guess when I saw Arthur in bed it all came flooding back and I did start to cry, just thinking about how lucky we've been and how fragile life is. I thought I'd hidden it from him. Obviously not.'

I looked into Ed's eyes. They were glistening. The things they had seen.

'Old flappy ears doesn't miss much.'

Ed kissed me on my cheek. I said,

'Then there's Araminta Lyall. What do you think? Burglary gone wrong? Crime of passion?'

'Drug overdose more likely. She seemed to run with a pretty racy crowd.'

'Then why are they calling it suspicious?'

'Search me.'

He rolled the paper into a truncheon and scratched his nose.

★ ★ ★

Ed had a brief chat with the police one afternoon after his clinic but they didn't give him any more details about what had happened or even whether they were still treating Araminta's death as murder. I read everything I could about the case, online and off. I had never realized how the Internet throbs 24/7 on subjects that make the national news. Trolls, conspiracy theorists, single-issue maniacs, swivel-eyed obsessives, anyone with dodgy spelling and an iron-cast opinion, all have a new home. Daytime TV has lost its constituency. Quite soon I knew more about Araminta Lyall than her mother did. Her death dominated the tabloids, the broadsheets showed a prurient interest and when the police announced they were treating it as murder she even turned up on *News at Ten*. As for the *Bristol Evening Post*, it had never had it so good.

The reason was not hard to divine. Araminta was young, female, pretty, rich, well connected and very talented. Her tutors talked her up. Dealers in London talked her up. She had already sold a piece in New York. Though I wasn't a sculptress, had no urge to be bleeding-edge and appreciated that a well-publicized death was a fail-safe enhancer of the value of any art, I couldn't help a twinge of envy; not for her talent, which was shallower than the eulogies suggested, or her work, sub-Alexander Calder mobiles, but because she had come out of the blocks so quickly. Portraiture, by comparison, is a slow burn. Obviously she was helped by the milieu in which she moved. Her last boyfriend had been a yacht-racing Brazilian businessman more than twice her age and, it was hinted, she had once had an affair with a married TV presenter, a household name. Her father was chairman of a FTSE company. Her mother was an ex-model and a 'deb' who had 'come out' (isn't that just the best colloquial change of meaning?) with the usual crop of horse-faced girls in the 1970s. Araminta's life was exemplary of a certain type of upper-middle-class English life, set apart by the unmistakable twang of talent and her early death. As if all that wasn't enough, the police found traces of cocaine in her flat. It was all too good to be true. The papers sucked it up and spat it out. And because there was no news, no lead, no arrest, the back-story was the front story, feeding on itself in an eternal loop.

★　★　★

'You say sfumayto, I say sfumarto.'

The following Friday it was half-term and I took Arthur to London as a treat for winning a cartoon competition at school, or not annoying his sister for a whole minute, or both. The plan was to look at ten paintings in the National Gallery, one from each century, then have a hamburger and go to Hamleys. The hams were the real prize.

The Virgin of the Rocks was his favourite painting, admittedly after I had pointed out the virtuosity of the master's technique, the distance between Leonardo and his contemporaries. Arthur is competitive, drawn to winners. He also liked the Turners, the collision of the old warship and new industrial age in *The Fighting Temeraire*, the tale of the artist being lashed to a mast in order to paint his storms at sea. Children love stories. They love the suspense, the narrative arc. That's why we read to them at night. I filled Arthur with hokum as we meandered through the galleries, taking in unscheduled detours via Holbein and Joseph Wright of Derby. I pointed out connections, explaining how each artist conducted a dialogue with the past. In front of a Titian he said,

'Mummy, what is art?'

I took a deep breath — where to begin? — but before I could start talking of artifice and transformation he gave a cheese-slicer grin and said,

'It's short for Arthur!'

We ended at Cézanne's *Hillside in Provence*, the artist flattening the landscape, blocking out space, opening the door to Cubism. We were both tired so we headed into Soho, Arthur's eyes swivelling at the painted mannequins, and checked into an upmarket burger joint with a pink neon sign sandwiched between a red-lacquered bassoon shop and an Itsu. I had chosen it because it was opposite the site of Qube, the gallery where I'd had my first-ever solo exhibition.

At Arthur's request we sat on stools at the zinc bar. The man next to us wore a bootlace tie and ten-gallon hat, which made him look like he'd blown in from Dodge City.

'Mummy, why don't you pronounce 'union' like 'onion' and 'onion' like 'on-yon'?'

Wyatt Earp caught my eye. I returned his smile and let my mind drift back in time. Qube had become a coffee shop, but it didn't matter because my memories of that first exhibition were crystal clear. It had been a minor triumph, partly because it was the only show by a new young artist who — radically — painted in oil. Everyone else was sailing under the flag of fashion, which meant drawing a dotted line through the word 'ART' or producing an hour-long video of a Japanese woman repeating the word 'yes' (or maybe 'no'). There may be nothing as powerful as an idea whose time has come, but the same is true of its opposite.

The reason my memories are crystal clear is because at tea time on the day of the private view I'd rung my older brother Matt to see if he was coming as he hadn't replied. My sister Bridgey, the middle of the three of us, had predictably replied by return with regrets. I could imagine the invitation propped up on the mantelpiece of her spinsterish hive on Hampstead Hill, every surface stacked with books and magazines, scented candles. Matt was living in Oxford. He'd returned under some vague pretext he was going to finish his degree eight years after he dropped out. I rang Bridgey to see if she knew anything. She was flustered by my call, fumbling around for her own excuse and only relaxed when she realized I was calling about Matt. She hadn't spoken to him for a year. When I finally got through to him he said he didn't know the private view was happening, even though I'd sent an invitation and left about thirty messages on his answerphone.

It wasn't his answer that bugged me but his voice, which sounded as if there was a kidnapper pointing a gun at his head. I suddenly understood that what I'd taken for evasiveness was helplessness, or hopelessness, the sound of a man falling apart.

So I rang Anthea — such a 70s name — who owned the gallery and said I had to go to Oxford immediately and therefore would miss the private view. She went nuts, saying, 'What fucking difference will one day make?' But I had to do whatever I could. No one else would. So I didn't show up at my own first night, which is not a great career move, and I've had to live with a reputation for being difficult ever since. But I've no regrets. If my art is not about humanity then it's not about anything at all.

I found Matt in a mildew-stained, one-room basement in Jericho below a pagan shop having a January sale of crystal balls, which were piled high in the window like tapioca. His hair was long and greasy and his T-shirt hung off him like a paper bag. I'd never seen anyone so lonely or exhausted. I almost burst into tears on his doorstep.

We went for a coffee. I forced him. On the way to the café, Matt just looked around as if it was strange to be above ground. It was awful. I bought him a cappuccino and a ham roll with mayo and English mustard, which he hadn't asked for but which he looked as though he needed and had always been his favourite on Dartmoor picnics when we were children. He didn't touch the coffee or eat the roll.

We talked a little, his monosyllables punctuating Pinteresque pauses. I suggested he come away for a few days and stay with me in London, but he shook his head. I offered to stay in Oxford. He declined. When I mentioned Highlands he winced perceptibly and looked stricken. He was purple-eyed, breathing through his nose, hard to hear above the hiss of the coffee machine.

'Thank you for coming, Bunny. You shouldn't have.'

'I had to.'

'There's nothing for you here.'

'You're here.'

'You must go now.'

'Not without you.'

'You can't stay.'

'You must come too.'

'Your exhibition . . . '

'It doesn't matter. It's only a few paintings.'

We sat in silence. In the end he left. There was nothing to stay for. I watched him go, stooped in his long coat, heading out into the street like Captain Oates and with about as much chance of success. He was as thin as a leaf, a feather in a stream, and had been almost hollow in my farewell embrace. It had been years since we sat in the field behind the house and he read me the poems he loved.

Anthea never forgave me, even though the exhibition sales exceeded both our expectations, and I never forgave her. Not after I found out she'd told the Londoner's Diary gigolo I hadn't been at my own private view because I was helping my 'sick' brother. You didn't need a degree in pharmacology to work out what could be making him sick. She was unrepentant. 'If you're not going to sell yourself, then I'm going to have to do it for you. People love the tortured artist, the fucked-up family. Smell the coffee, darling: no hook, no story, no' — she made a gesture as if she was setting a dove free from cupped hands — '*air*. This is business.'

I glanced at Arthur. He'd eaten his burger and was licking his fingers, engrossed in his magazine. Batman was being acrobatic with a long chain in an abandoned building on a moonlit night. Wyatt Earp was paying his bill and getting ready to saddle up.

I reached for the paper. I didn't want to think about Matt any more. People reach an age where they have to live their own lives. Too often beautiful boys make unhappy men. I flicked through the news pages. There was an article about Araminta Lyall with the 'Dering Street' picture in colour: royal blue choker, pencil skirt, siren smile. I read the article, which sprinkled generic reportage with rent-a-quotes from unnamed friends and tutors. 'Minta was a brilliant artist with a bright future in front of her.' She was 'always the last to leave parties', 'seriously intelligent, intelligently serious', 'happiest really just playing with wire and coloured plastic'. On it went, her friends conjuring images of a magical girl who probably wouldn't have recognized herself in print.

And then it hit me. Right between the eyes in a word so large I wondered how I had missed it before.

How could I have been so blind? I glanced at Arthur to see if he had registered any physical manifestation of my shock. Of course not. He was totally absorbed in his comic and caramel milkshake. I looked away and counted to three. Then I looked at the paper again, even though I knew nothing would have changed. I'd already read the word, it was right there on the page in front of me, one word that changed my life and explained everything I didn't understand about the last couple of weeks, the word that I could never unread.

Minta.

'Minta was a brilliant artist.'

Minta. Minta Lyall. She was known to her friends as Minta Lyall, not Araminta Lyall. Minta Lyall was ML. ML was not Marnie Latham or Mima Langton. Marnie Latham was off in the north, telling anyone who would listen she was still my friend, and Mima Langton never existed. She was always Jemima Langton and always would be.

The flowers were from Minta Lyall.

ML xxx

5

I couldn't believe Ed would double-deal. It's just not his style. Plus, I know he loves me and he adores Nell and Arthur far too much to risk losing them, and they adore him. He's wedded — welded — to the family unit and he knows, because I once told him, that if he ever left me for another woman he could wave goodbye to the children. It might not be the best thing for them and probably wouldn't be for me, but I couldn't bear the injustice of another woman bringing them up, even if it was only every other weekend. Whether I had to move to London or Los Angeles or Lahore to ensure he never saw them, I would. I really would.

I had called Jemima Langton to thank her for the flowers and she apologetically confessed that they hadn't sent any. So they were almost certainly from (Ara)minta Lyall, meaning something must have happened between her and Ed. That made it more likely she was the mysterious charity girl on the phone who didn't know the things a medical charity worker would have done. Why would she have rung? For Ed? Not at nine o'clock in the morning. Know the competition. Every mistress wants to check out the wife, like a python measuring itself against whatever it plans to eat. It would also explain why Ed had changed his mobile password for the first time ever, why Neil had seen him on Stokes Croft and why — I'm suddenly remembering — he went down to the basement to make a phone call he could easily have made in the kitchen.

Jesus. How could I have been so blind?

Because I trusted him.

Yet the evidence, if circumstantial, suggested there were questions to answer. I had gone to the study and combed through the drawers in his desk. There was nothing incriminating or even suspicious, simply piles of bills and tax returns that would have bored the most ardent PI. Ed had never been secretive. It was one of the reasons I loved him. I checked his laptop. The password hadn't been changed. Nothing. I looked at the ribbon of blue silk lying on the desk. I had found it in his suit pocket.

Outside, a tomcat glided along the stone wall in the garden. It was sure-footed, ginger and furry, self-confident, prowling far from home.

* * *

How do you ask your faithful husband of fifteen years whether he has slept with another woman, even more so when that woman has subsequently died? Simply asking the question exposes the loss of trust. Do you come straight out with it, a blurted question loaded with tears and ultimatums? Or do you approach it obliquely, crabwise, like a yachtsman navigating heavy seas? The latter is the obvious strategy, but it's not your call. In the cauldron of the moment, raw instinct is bound to take over.

Ed arrived back at eight fifty. The children had

gone upstairs, Nell to settle down to two hours' hard texting on her bed, Arthur to kill various aliens who had invaded our television at his request. For once I didn't care. I was sitting alone at the kitchen table, a Caravaggio monograph the size and weight of a medieval tombstone positioned squarely in front of me. It was open at the painting of *The Incredulity of Thomas*, the sceptic's finger pushed into Christ's wound where the soldier's spear had broken his skin. Caravaggio was a rackety genius who redefined the possibility of art.

Only I wasn't thinking about the possibility of art as I sat there, but I was thinking about scepticism and trust. I was thinking there must be a simple explanation that would put my mind at ease. There had to be, because I wasn't sure what I would do if there wasn't. Whenever I had doubts about anything — usually my work, sometimes my mother — Ed always lifted me. From our earliest days together he had been able to stop me worrying or taking things (usually myself) too seriously, generally by poking fun at my fears until I realized it was me that was the problem, not someone else, and if I understood that I could solve it (or me).

He kissed me on the top of the head, a kiss saying rather more about hunger than love, and took off his jacket, brushing a speck of imaginary lint off a sleeve as he hung it over a chair. His shirt was cornflower blue, the sleeves rolled neatly above the elbow, lumberjack forearms, delicate hands, slender fingers — the obstetrician's toolkit. Many men who left the house at

7.30 a.m. and didn't get back until almost 9 p.m. would have fixed themselves a drink, but Ed never did. He didn't offer me one either, though sometimes he does. I invariably decline. The only thing sadder than a man drinking alone is a woman drinking alone.

He cocked his head to noise from the garden.

'The Amerys. They're having a barbecue.'

He nodded without interest. He hadn't had to listen to the squawks of laughter and clinking of bottles as they set it up, while looking at Caravaggio and waiting and wondering.

'What's for supper, my darling? I'm starving.'

'How was your day?'

'N'bad. You?'

'Yuh, OK.'

'Good.'

'I ran into Jemima Langton today.'

'She OK?'

'Yes. I thanked her for the flowers.'

'OK.'

'Only funny thing was, she said she hadn't sent any.'

'OK.'

'So they must've been from someone else?'

'Guess so.'

'I wonder who they were from? ML and three kisses.'

'Beats me.'

He was completely impassive. In hospital-world, flowers were flowers, a generic statement of solidarity or sympathy, a commoditized currency of thanks. And yet, unless I was imagining it, there seemed some quality of rebuff in his shrug, a sort

66

of inwardness, as if he was wrapping himself around something small and private. I pressed on.

'Because they must have been from someone.'

'That figures.'

'You must have seen someone whose initials were ML recently?'

He frowned and looked down at his shoes, pretending to rack his brain, still droll, tired from work, not taking it seriously. Maybe it was in my imagination and I was being ridiculous? I dared to hope.

'I don't know. I see lots of people and I deliver lots of babies, quite a lot of whose mums or dads or maybe even grandparents might have the initials ML.'

'So have you operated on anyone with those initials recently? Or whose husband or parents may have had those initials?'

'Alice, what's all this about? We were sent some flowers by someone with the initials ML. Big deal. It happens all the time.'

He was trying, not entirely successfully, to keep the irritation out of his voice. When Ed was hungry he needed to eat.

'But who?' He frowned, this time for real. 'And who knew you well enough that only their initials were needed?'

'What is this? The third degree? Someone sent some flowers. It could have been anyone. It could have been wine or chocolates but it was flowers. I don't understand what you're getting at. Sometimes people put their names or a nickname or their initials. Sometimes — most of the time — they don't send anything. I don't see the big deal. Can we talk about . . . I don't know . . . Are the children in bed yet?'

There was innocence in his response. I saw a crack of sun through the cloud but I knew I had to press on, to be sure. I had to know.

'And who liked you enough to put three kisses?'

He shook his head and shrugged. As he did so, I slipped my fingers into the back of the Caravaggio and slid out the blue silk ribbon. It had a velvet clasp. Ed stared at the ribbon, shaking his head, sticking out his bottom lip. He wasn't acting.

'What's that?'

I stared at the ribbon as if doing so would jog his memory.

'I found it in the pocket of your grey suit.'

He shrugged again and wiped a strand of hair back from his forehead.

'Which you wore to Pete's party.'

'Look, Alice, I don't know what that is or where it came from. I've never seen it before in my life, I promise. Please can we have some supper now? I'm starving.'

There was a fatal quaver in his voice. This wasn't the operating theatre, where his will was unchallenged and his word law. In that moment he had confirmed what I had known but refused to accept since I found the royal blue ribbon choker in the pocket of his jacket: he was guilty as charged. My stomach lurched up and down like the shuttle on a fairground 'test your strength' machine and, fighting a momentous sense of collapse, I turned over a page of the Caravaggio, took out the cutting, pushed it across the table, twisting it round so Ed could see. It was a colour photo of Araminta Lyall, the photo that had been in all the papers, cut out of a supplement. It showed her — Minta Lyall, ML xxx — at the gallery party, wearing the cluster of pearls and the royal blue silk ribbon choker that lay on the table between us. Ed glanced at it barely long enough to register what it was. He clenched his teeth, his head went down and the power passed between us.

Only it wasn't a power I wanted or could use. The knowledge struck me physically, like a winding blow to the stomach. I gulped for air like a muzzled animal drowning in a colourless liquid. There was orange in the wings of my eyes.

When it was obvious Ed either had nothing to say or, if he did, he didn't know how to say it, I dragged myself together just enough to say,

'Do you want to tell me about it?'

He didn't look at me. The atmosphere was surreal. Ed's whole being was built on strength and achievement, the strength that had lifted him out of his background and set him down centre stage. I realized it was his will — that, his cast-iron morality and the fact I knew he never looked at other women, he simply wasn't the type — that had made me blind to the clues for so long. Even sitting there, I couldn't believe it was true, that he wouldn't laugh and look me in the eye and give some simple explanation that would funnel my fears away. But Ed's gaze was fixed on the acorn-leaf motif on the pink glossy child-friendly kitchen table cover and he was fighting to choose the right words. I waited. When he did look up he was ashen-faced and he stared out of the window a long time, avoiding my eye. Eventually he said,

'I don't remember anything.'

I looked at the dresser. I wasn't sure I could bear to listen.

'I swear.'

'Please, Ed, don't humiliate me more than you have to. More than you already have.'

'Alice, you have to believe me. One moment I'm in her flat so drunk I can barely stand, the next I wake up in a bed and that girl — '

'Araminta.'

'Is next to me.'

'And so you had sex with her?'

'No! I was completely horrified. It was the morning. I was in a stranger's flat in bed with someone I didn't know. Someone I didn't even fancy. I was horrified. Appalled. Terrified.'

His voice was earnest and pleading, desperate to be believed. There was no self-pity in the mix.

'That's not very gallant.'

'Please, Alice. I'm trying to explain.'

I felt anger transforming into grief, an imperfect world, a small hard thing building in me.

'So explain: you didn't have sex with her?'

Ed stared at the table. Finally he lifted his head and looked directly at me.

'Not then.'

'When?'

'I don't know. In the night.'

I felt contempt rising.

'You don't know? That's ridiculous! What do you mean you don't know? You must know. Either you did or you didn't.'

He looked as if he was about to respond but he stopped, like a barren woman with a sadness too large to articulate. I said nothing. I didn't want feelings. I needed facts.

'She said we did. Only I can't remember it — but then I can't really remember anything about the night.'

'But you must remember *that?*'

'I don't. I promise. I haven't been that drunk for . . . I don't know . . . ever. Even after Finals or at my own stag night. I mean, the whole night is pretty much a blank from the moment I got to Montpelier.'

'Why would she say you had sex with her if you didn't?'

Ed rubbed his forehead unhappily. It didn't make me feel sorry for him, or any less betrayed.

'I don't know. Only . . . '

'Yes?'

'Well, Pete told me she always went for older men, particularly married men. Maybe that's why?'

'Oh my God! You told Pete?'

'No! Of course not. He said it when I told him a few of us had ended up back at her flat.'

'How many really ended up back at her flat?'

'I can't remember' — he shot me a nervous glance — 'five or six, seven maybe? Anyway, Pete said she was damaged goods and I should watch out. Not that he had to tell me by then. Obviously I didn't say anything . . . '

71

'You saw her again?'

'Yes.'

'And slept with her again?'

'No.' He sounded worn out. This was the exhaustion of someone fundamentally honest who had been required to live a lie. 'But she turned up at St Anthony's on the Monday. I told Karen I was too busy to see her. It was a nightmare.' He glanced at me hopefully. 'I hated the deception. What I had done to us.'

'Spare me.'

'Honestly, darling, if I could just go back — '

'You and me both.'

He looked at me bleakly. Was I going to kick him out? Well, was I? The gazillion-dollar question. Even I didn't know the answer. I hadn't had time to work it out, to balance the deed against either continuing or bursting a fifteen-year bubble. I hadn't had time to understand it in the context of our lives and, more importantly, to think about what was best for Nell and Arthur. I hadn't had time to prepare myself for the pain that was growing inside me or to create a strategy to cope.

'So what happened next?'

'She wouldn't leave me alone.'

'She was the woman who rang pretending to be from some charity?'

He nodded glumly.

'She told me she had hung around here, followed you and the kids in the village.'

'Oh my God!' I thought of Arthur walking back from school, kicking stones and buying sweets, impervious to anything and everyone. 'That's really creepy.'

'Exactly. That's what I was up against. And she texted me the whole time, here and at work, saying how much she loved me, how we would be so good together. I had, I don't know, maybe a hundred texts from her in four days, ranging from expressions of undying love to venomous accusations that I was avoiding her — often in the same text. She was a complete crackpot. When I said there had been a major misunderstanding, she sent a load of abusive messages.'

'So you changed the password on your mobile.'

'I had to.' He leant forward in his chair and put his hands on the table. They were pale and hairless. He had nothing to hide any more. 'Believe me, it was a nightmare.'

'*Fatal Attraction.*'

He looked desperate, consumed by guilt. No wonder he hadn't been sleeping. But it was no longer about him. It was about me, about all of us, about how we survived his elemental breach of trust. I didn't know how to do that. I couldn't tell how I felt. This was the hinge of my life, but I couldn't bring myself to look across to the far side. There was a honk of laughter from the Amerys' barbecue.

'So you went to see her.'

'Just to tell her to leave me alone. To tell her I didn't love her and never would.'

'And how did she take that? Lust but no love?'

'That was pretty much what she said. That I had obligations. That I couldn't just sleep with her one night and walk away as if nothing had happened.'

'How unreasonable.'

He licked dry lips. 'She said it would never have happened if I wasn't unhappy at home. Claimed it was only the symptom of underlying problems between you and me, maybe even ones I didn't realize were there.'

I laughed bitterly.

'So it was my fault?'

'I told her I was perfectly happy at home.'

'How gratifying.'

'You have to believe me, darling.'

He reached across the table but I withdrew my hand. I still couldn't take it in that Ed, straight-as-a-die Ed, had cheated on me. I had seen it so often — Charlie Snape, Paul Whorle, Rory Nester, the man who went on a course to find himself but found Amber instead — but there had always been structural reasons why it happened, symptom and cause.

Why had it happened to us? Ed had his failings, of course he did, they were the flipside of the qualities that made him great, but we were happy and straying was not — should not — have been amongst them. This was about trust and betrayal, about people being true to who they are. That is what I fight for in every portrait I have ever painted: to understand and to know, not to condemn.

'Go on.' I wanted to sound strong but my voice was wobbling.

'So I went to see her. I had to. Otherwise she was going to make sure you found out.'

'And we couldn't have that.'

'I did think about telling you myself.'

'But decided not to?'

'It wasn't just for my sake. Remember what you said about Rory? That he was a bastard for telling Michaela about Flashing Amber because he put the burden of the choice over whether to leave or stay on her. Leave and she screwed up the children; stay and she looked like a doormat. So I decided, rightly or wrongly, to live with it myself. But when she started coming on with flowers and texts and so on I had to see her and put an end to it.'

'Put an end to it?'

'You know what I mean. So I went there and told her it had been a terrible mistake and I was sorry but I loved you and only you and I loved my children and there was no future in me and her as a couple and we would only cause each other and a heap of other people a whole lot of unhappiness if we saw each other again.'

'How did she take it?'

'Not well, to be honest.'

'Did you see her again after you told her?'

'Nope.'

'That's convenient.'

He shrugged. But I sensed some latent quality of evasion in his shrug. I had painted Ed too often. His skin was colourless and dry. It was as if he was willing his version into reality. But Ed is not a good liar. I felt fear snaking down my back like cold sweat.

'OK, so let's get this straight: she's all over you, bugging you a million times a day, phoning, texting, sending flowers, turning up at work, ringing me here, following the kids around and so on, until you say, 'Look, I'm sorry, dear, but

this just isn't going to work because I'm married'
— and straight away she says, this fucked-up
woman who always wants a married man, she
says, 'Oh forgive me, I didn't realize! I am sorry!
I didn't realize when I googled you and your wife
and hung around and watched your children
come and go and spied on your life and rang
your wife that you were happily married! My
mistake! Of course I'll leave you alone.' Is that
how it happened?'

Ed looked down at the table.

'She was very angry. Said she'd been used — '

'This thirty-two-year-old woman said she'd
been used? That she hadn't been able to make
her own decisions?'

'Exactly.'

'But nevertheless said she would leave you in
peace?'

'I didn't give her any choice. It wasn't going to
happen.'

A vein began to throb on Ed's forehead.

'When did you tell her it was over?'

'The night I went round. Not that 'it' had ever
started.'

'Which day was that?'

Ed screwed up his face and glanced at the
cornice.

'Um . . . the Tuesday, I think.'

'You think?'

'Or maybe it was the Wednesday.'

'What time on the Wednesday?'

'What time?' He checked an irritable intonation. 'Why does that matter?'

Because I was ravenous. I needed to know

everything. Only if I understood absolutely everything was there a chance I could process the facts in such a way that I might *somehow* be able to cope. Ed owed me that. He owed our marriage that. He owed our children that. I stayed silent. He ground his teeth, his jaw moving minutely.

'Afternoon.'

'So Neil did see you.'

Ed nodded.

'How late?'

'Around teatime?'

'Where did you meet?'

'Her flat.'

'Her flat? Around teatime on Wednesday?' A dark form, hitherto submerged, began to take shape in the depths. 'You know what that means?'

Ed stared at me. His tongue was working but his lips were desert-dry. Beads of sweat glittered along his hairline.

'I didn't kill her, if that's what you're thinking.'

Stop right there.

Can you imagine what it's like to hear your husband, the celebrated obstetrician, pillar of the community, say, totally seriously, to a question you didn't even ask, 'I didn't kill her'?

'I'm sure you didn't. But it does mean you were probably the last person to see her alive. Did you tell the police that?'

In spite of the kaleidoscopic turmoil inside me, my voice sounded weirdly calm.

He shook his head. I tipped my chair backwards as I tell the children not to do, balancing on the tips of my toes, trying to take it all in.

'Why not?'

'I was frightened.'

'Frightened? Ed — for fuck's sake, a girl's died! There's a murderer out there.'

'I know. But I'm frightened they'll think I did it.'

He gritted his teeth and looked at the floor, closing in on himself the way he does under pressure. He glanced at his watch as if he might find the answer there. It was my wedding present to him.

'But you might have seen the murderer. You have to tell them. You may have seen something that's not important to you but which may give them the clue they need to find the killer.'

He frowned and gave a small thoughtful nod, as if he was considering that possibility for the first time. For a moment I thought he was, but it suddenly struck me that couldn't possibly be true. He must have thought of little else since her death was announced. He must have known exactly what time he arrived at and left her flat. Not 'around teatime'. And I suddenly realized that if he was lying to me about the time and with that dishonest little nod then — oh my God — no! — I pushed my chair backwards, as if I was subconsciously trying to get away.

'Oh my God, Ed! You . . . Did you . . . ?'

His mouth was churning, his Adam's apple bobbing furiously.

'No! Alice! I can't believe you could even — '

He swiped the beads of perspiration from his forehead.

'Ed?'

'No!'

But I knew. It was in his face, the tilt of his jaw, his frightened eyes, in the pinkness of his skin as he squeezed the arm of his chair. It was in his guilty glance ceiling-wards. It was in the tiny squeak of his chair on the wooden floor as it moved involuntarily back.

'Oh my God! Ed!'

He stared at me for a moment, but as I felt a tiny spasm of fear, his shoulders slumped, the arc of his certainty collapsed and his iron self-control drained away. The silence was biblical.

'It was an accident, I promise, I swear it was.'

His voice was cracking like an actor. I was shaking, all my uncertainty tumbling into terror. My voice wouldn't work. I tried to speak but nothing came out and then, in a rush,

'You — you killed her?'

He nodded, his face contorted by fear, and when he spoke his voice was pleading.

'I didn't mean to. I swear. She fell.'

'She fell?' Words were building, clamouring, tumbling over the horror as they tripped out of my mouth. 'Why did she fall?'

'She fell because she was attacking me and she slipped. When I said there was no prospect of us having a relationship she went completely mad and started swearing and punching and hitting me. I pushed her away, not even hard — one hand, just in self-defence — but she slipped and hit her head on the marble mantelpiece and a spike on the fender. I could see straight away it was serious. Blood was coming out of her ear. I did absolutely everything I could — mouth-to-mouth, heart, aorta, everything — but I knew there was nothing I could do from the moment she hit the spike. I swear that's the truth. Cross my heart. I was fucking desperate. I tried everything, absolutely everything. It was so . . . I can't tell you . . . You know I would never hit a woman, don't you?'

I did know that. It's not in his nature. Ed gives gifts to women, the best they will ever receive. I stared at him across the silence, my mind's eye in Stokes Croft: angry words, a shriek and a shove, a defensive push, a lamp knocked to the floor. Her body prostrate by the fender, blonde hair clogging her mouth, the bruise swelling, black blood behind the ear, his hands pumping her heart, desperately grabbing a tea towel, a cushion, sobbing at the unfairness of it, anything soft to stem the flow, that rich dark familiar colour fanning out around her head.

'So what are you going to do?'

Ed covered his face with his hands for a moment, before pulling them down as if fighting extreme exhaustion.

'What am I going to do?' He paused, control returning alongside the need for a rational response. 'I'm going to do nothing.' I stayed quiet. My husband the celebrated obstetrician was now my husband the killer. The sheer horror of it made me feel physically sick. When darkness descends it obliterates everything. If there hadn't been an open window and the neighbours having a cheery barbecue, I would have screamed. He gathered himself and spoke louder, as if he was trying to convince himself as much as me. 'I'm going to do nothing.'

'*Nothing?*'

'I've decided not to tell the police. After it happened, I was going to go straight there. But although I knew it was an accident, I also knew they might not see it like that. Then I realized I owed it to you to tell you everything, to try to explain what had happened, before I went to them. It would have been completely unfair — I mean, wrong for you to hear from anyone else. It was the least I could do.' He gave a sour laugh, brimming with self-disgust. 'The very least. Also I wanted to apologize to you for everything, for it happening, for fucking us up, our lives, the children, everything. You know, I still can't believe it happened . . .'

He tailed off. The tears were running down his cheeks. There was no self-pity and nothing left to confess. Only I wasn't ready to stop listening.

'So?'

'So . . . I came home but you were at book club. And Arthur told me he'd been in trouble at school. Apparently he'd pushed Alfie Warburton into the pond. It was almost certainly no more than that little horror deserved. As Arthur told it, Alfie attacked Arthur and when he pushed him away Alfie fell into the pond and Arthur was the one who was punished because Alfie had got wet, which he felt was unfair as he'd only pushed him away in self-defence.'

'And it rang a bell.'

'It rang a bell. He also told me he'd been to Richie Railton's party at the climbing wall, which for some reason I didn't quite get was extra fun because Richie's dad had climbed with them. He made me promise that not only could he have his next birthday party there but that I would definitely climb with him and his friends too. And you know what? Looking at that trusting little man, I knew I couldn't let him down. Maybe, even more, I shouldn't let him down, that it was his future at stake as much as mine. And that's when I decided to wing it.'

'Which is why he said you cried when you said goodnight?'

Ed nodded. A single tear on his cheek caught the light. I pictured him with the children when they were little, three in a bed, completely exhausted but insisting on reading stories about princesses and woodcutters, dark forests, brave children, cats that talked. They couldn't have asked for more love or time from a father and they loved him more than any father I had ever known. In fact, it had occurred to me once that if they ever had to lose one parent . . . My hand instinctively reached out but stopped short of him. I had to see it through.

'So I went downstairs and thought about what I'd done and what I should do and the odds and everything, and I decided I would go for it. Even though it was an accident, I would probably be charged with murder rather than manslaughter. After all, it's only my word about what really happened in the flat that night and, well, I guess after Saturday night and all the texts and so on I had a motive — or at least they could claim I did. It's not easy to prove a negative.' He leant back in his chair as if gathering strength. 'That was why I cried that night when I was saying goodnight to Arthur. Because I was so scared and ashamed of what I had done to you all, and everything I had risked. I know what I've done — what I'm doing — is wrong but it was an accident, I promise; it wasn't my fault. And yet it could ruin your and the children's lives, and you and they have done nothing to deserve that.' He was rocking trance-like on his chair. Ed had never believed in God, only in individual goodness on this earth. 'I've thought about it long and hard. Please, Alice, you've got to believe me. I know it sounds self-serving, but I decided the future of my family is more important than the accidental death of some nutcase I never even knew who tried to ruin my life and my family's lives and who no one can do anything to help now anyway.'

I was shaking my head. I couldn't believe what I was hearing. But even as I tried to process the enormity of what he was saying, Ed was continuing:

'I've chosen my family and my children's future over some legal or moral concept of justice. I can repay the debt I owe to Araminta and society far better by carrying on working at St Anthony's than I ever could in jail.'

I didn't reply. What could I say? What I wanted to do was to scream so loud they could hear my pain in Hawaii. But I didn't. I couldn't even do that. Silence rose like smoke. In the end, I said again, 'So what are you going to do?'

He fixed on me, his cheeks as grey as a Van Goyen seascape, and whispered,

'I've chosen.'

'What does that mean?'

Ed put his hands back on the table. I watched his energy leak out of them into the wood. His face was sapped of colour. What must it have been like to carry this secret alone? What would it do to you to be waiting for the dawn rap on the door, the humiliation, the transformation, the end of everything?

'It means I've chosen. It's your choice now.'

*   *   *

I was at school with Marnie Latham. It was one of those God-less girls' boarding schools that relieved parents of large amounts of money in return for a couple of O levels and an address book stuffed with the names of 'suitable' boys. Marnie was a scholarship girl from Manchester who joined in the lower sixth, her fees paid in full by a bursary. She was clever, hard-working, high-achieving, a sensitive sculptor, non-sporty and unpopular because she didn't smoke or take drugs. She was never so bored on a Sunday afternoon that she thought 'Mushroom Roulette', a game in which everyone ate a random wild mushroom from Becker's Woods and waited to see who was hospitalized, was a good idea. She had long dark hair, lightning-blue eyes, trout-lips, spoke with a northern accent, laughed like applause and swore with the venom of a Marseillaise whore. She didn't have a pony or live in a large house nestled in a sylvan Hampshire valley. She lived with her typing-pool mum and her mum's boyfriends, who stacked up like dishes.

84

Her dad, tattooist by day, knock-off merchant by night, had skedaddled to the Costa when she was five. She kept a photo of him in her wallet: a lazy-eyed man in a brown leather jacket with a stretchy waist and dagger-collared cheesecloth shirt. After five years of Eton-boyfriend talk and hair-flicking, she blew into my life like a gun-slinger, just as Ed did a few years later. I sloughed off my friends like a snake shedding skin. I'd never really been one of them anyway. I hated the pettiness and bitchiness, the one-upmanship over clothes, gigs, holidays, boyfriends, jewellery, drugs, houses.

Marnie was different. She had never developed the hard protective shell essential for anyone sent away to board before the age of ten. Marnie dreamt. She was *real*.

For two and a half terms we did everything together. I knew my old 'friends' were making fun of me behind my back, but I didn't care. I was liberated. I had someone to talk to about the big things in life — art, literature, *ideas* — and her views led me into a land I never knew existed. She was as hungry as a cougar for the world.

One afternoon I cut my knee playing rounders and came back from games early and who should I find in the dormitory kneeling down by Annabel Trim's open bedside drawer holding a ten-pound note?

Although I wanted to believe it wasn't what it seemed, the evidence was overwhelming — Marnie's flushed face turning, the gaping drawer, the note in her hand. To her credit, when she realized I'd seen everything she didn't try to deceive me. She just stood up slowly and stared at me, as if willing me to let it pass by sheer force of personality. She was my best friend. She was different and to my mind greater than the rest of us, who were only there through an accident of birth, following our father's sister or our mother, preceding our daughters. But theft is theft. And in that moment I wondered whether I understood her at all. Where were those lofty ideals now? Where was the sense of eternal quest we had spoken about so often? Was that all it amounted to: stealing money from someone's locker? Had it just been talk? Underneath was she really no better than the Costa-based father who peered out beadily from the photo in her wallet?

'Alice, it's not what you think. Really. I — '

Before she could continue or I could say anything the door was flung open and five girls burst in. They screeched to a halt when they saw us, instantly sensing the tension in the air. Jenny Raygard spoke first.

'What's going on? Alice?'

I looked at Marnie. She stared back at me, her neck flushed. The fact Jenny had asked me, not her, spoke volumes. My choice was clear. My best friend — someone I loved — or some abstract notion of justice? My throat was tinder-dry. I looked from Marnie to the five girls and back again. Marnie seemed to be holding her breath. I swallowed hard. I had to jump one way or the other.

'Marnie's been stealing money out of the lockers.'

They all turned noisily on Marnie. It was the

sound of the shires: guns firing, whisky flasks opening, hounds catching foxes. Marnie shot me a viperous look. There was nothing for it. Hooting at the confirmation of their prejudices, the vigilantes hauled her away to the lantern-jawed headmistress. As the commotion disappeared down the polished wooden stairs I was left sitting on the bed, busted by the end of a friendship that seemed the end of everything.

She left the same day, my best friend, a scholarship girl I had cut off forever from opportunity and her route to a better life. She was a girl who had a hunger and determination you'd rarely find in an old rectory and, despite what had happened, a fierce integrity only I would ever fully know.

After a sleepless night I called her at home to beg for forgiveness. While the phone was ringing I thought about the line in *Gatsby*, which we'd just studied, about Tom and Daisy wrecking people's lives and retreating 'back into their money or their vast carelessness, or whatever it was that kept them together'. Her mum answered. She sounded warm and friendly but when she told Marnie who was calling my ex-best friend wouldn't come to the phone.

Two days later I received a letter postmarked Stretford and addressed in Marnie's loopy scrawl. I tore it open. There was a sheet of cheap A4 paper with a single sentence: '*If I had to choose between betraying my country and betraying my friend, I hope I should have the guts to betray my country.*' *E. M. Forster.* There was a single X. It wasn't a kiss but a cross to bear.

6

When, as someone who has always obeyed the law — the odd university joint or no bike lights aside — you step outside it, you enter the unknown, a place with thinner air, taller shadows, weaker sun. Life doesn't just 'go on' as the cliché has it. The clocks are reset, relationships recalibrated.

Once I have engaged, whether it's with a portrait or a marriage, or a portrait of a marriage, I have engaged, and I will see it through. So my job from the beginning was to nail our story to the floor.

The first thing to do was to work out what the police might know and what they clearly couldn't know, because if they did they would have knocked on the door already. I had to take control. I could tell from the desperate never-let-me-go hug Ed gave me when I said — after much exploration of the likely outcome if he went to the police, and not without some misgiving — I would support him that he was emotionally exhausted. It was hardly a surprise. He must have taken a psychological beating since he slept with that woman. Since he *killed* that woman. Now his secret was out, now he had someone to lean on, there was nothing left in his tank. Over to Lady Macbeth, which was not a role I had ever wanted or expected to play.

I made a pot of strong coffee. When it was ready we returned to the table with big mugs and hot milk, ready for a long night. Ed's head lolled on his shoulders. There had never been a time when he was not in control of his life. I sipped my coffee, saying nothing, covering the angles, letting the bitter taste sharpen my mind. Ed waited. He had a fawn-like desire to please, to take instructions about how to escape his fate. I hadn't had this much power since the moment before I said 'yes' to his marriage proposal on the slippery wooden steps at Tintagel, the sea slapping the rocks below.

To start, he told me everything. What her flat was like, the colour of her dress, the name of the book she was reading. Ed's memory was forensic. Next, we focused on the game-over clues: CCTV and her mobile. I couldn't bring myself to call her Araminta, much less 'Minta', or even Ms Lyall. Her name left a taste in my mouth like burnt spinach. She was 'that woman', someone I had never met but who had changed my life. So: CCTV? Clearly the Carriage Works didn't have CCTV. If it did, the police would have been here already. Her mobile? All those calls and texts she'd sent waiting to be read? Ed leant forward. He was a man who dealt in cause and effect, which art could never offer.

'Actually, that is maybe one stroke of luck. I took her mobile when I left the flat.'

'You took it? I thought you were planning to give yourself up?'

'I was. It was a mistake.'

I raised an eyebrow.

'It's true. I'd left mine at work again. So I picked up hers to ring the police. It didn't really

89

seem to matter which phone I used by then, I was giving myself up anyway. Then when I decided to come home to tell you first I must have just slipped it into my pocket out of habit.'

'How convenient.'

He looked at me sharply, trying to discern the shape of my sarcasm. I stared blankly across the table. It wasn't up to me to make this easier for him.

'So where is it now?'

'In the river. Without its sim card. Which is also in the river.'

'Don't the phone companies have records?'

'Pay as you go.'

'And if they do?'

'The police would be here by now. She must have had a second phone.'

So we set to it, proper criminals casing every minute and movement and possibility of the hours between the Sunday morning Ed left that woman's flat after Pete's party sleepover and the Wednesday night he arrived home after she died. Every gesture was accounted for, every blink. Our alibi was forged in steel.

Ed asked,

'What about the flowers?'

'She delivered them herself. No one will know what she did with them.'

'The messages at work?'

'You fixed her plumbing before you left on the Sunday morning. She rang to thank you.'

And so it went on through a long night.

I asked,

'What about Karen?'

'Told her I was leaving early to go and see my solicitor.'

'What about your solicitor?'

'I forgot to book it.'

'What about Neil?'

'Neil?'

'From my book club. Who said he saw you on Stokes Croft early on Wednesday evening. You were on your way to that woman, weren't you?'

Ed swallowed.

'No reason he would put two and two together. I could have been going anywhere.'

'Visiting a recent mum?'

'Exactly. That's what I was doing.'

'No. That can be checked.'

'Good point. Then it wasn't me.'

'It wasn't you.'

'Because . . . I was on Sion Hill with you.'

'OK. Though not Sion Hill. Middle of Clifton, nice evening, quite a lot of people around. Someone might have seen me on my own. We can say we were somewhere else, somewhere we weren't, then no one is going to remember seeing us, or not. Brandon Hill? It's pretty big. They can ask as many questions as they want about Brandon Hill and no one can confirm or deny anything. And they won't be asking any questions about Sion Hill.'

'Good idea. And we can just say Neil was mistaken. I mean, he barely knows me.'

'Exactly. It wasn't you he saw.'

'It wasn't me.'

How I wished those words were true.

Lying on my back, hands behind my head, staring at a grey ceiling touched by a yellow sodium sliver from the streetlights sneaking through a crack in the curtains, I thought about what had happened and tried to fit it into the context of my life. It was hard to miss the irony. I had said 'yes' to Edward Sheahan on the steps at Tintagel for many positive reasons — I loved him, trusted him, admired him, respected him, believed in him and fancied him like hell — but just as many negative ones. My mother thought he wasn't good enough, though she parsed it as not being 'right for me'; my university friends thought he was not interesting enough; my arty friends thought he was too bourgeois. I didn't marry Ed to prove anyone wrong but I did marry him to prove me right. I also said 'yes' because, looking back, when I met him I needed someone resolute and unyielding to hold on to. If it hadn't been for Ed, I was probably heading for the Moonies or Catholicism, or some other weird sect promising the earth. Never marry a man you meet at a Cure gig or who wears sunglasses on the top of his head.

The reason I wasn't certain about how I fitted in at the time when I met Ed was that I realized if I wanted to take my art seriously I had to give up all the ties to my past. I couldn't allow myself to be stretched between high society and low bohemia. I had to succeed in an unfashionable genre without formal training or art school connections. So, like Beckett moving to Paris and writing in French, I sloughed off my past. I sacked my then-boyfriend the day after he proposed, which was horrible and cruel at the time but definitely the best for both of us. In fact, it was his proposal that made me realize I'd prefer to die by lethal injection than live north of Oban, somewhere that was practically in the tundra.

When Ed came into my world, art was the only thing I had to lean on. My family were no use. We might as well not have been related for all the time we spent with each other. Mother had a very strict definition of 'leaving home'; Bridgey's capacity to deal with human emotion was confined to Victorian novels; and things would have needed to go very wrong for anyone to consider Matt a safety net. I had learnt to survive on my own. Marnie — briefly — aside, I'd never been that tight with other girls.

My point is that around the time I met Ed I wasn't fully settled in my art or my life. The attraction of Ed was he knew nothing about art and didn't pretend to. But he knew what he wanted. I loved that clarity when my own future felt so opaque. He didn't do nostalgia. And I'd had a lifetime's worth of nostalgia at Highlands with its sepia-tinted photos of public school rackets teams filled with boys who went into the City or who didn't come back from the wars. From the moment I met him at John Morgan's party, toying with a can of Pepsi, wearing a red T-shirt with 'Halcyon Days' stencilled in small gold letters above the heart, he exuded supreme confidence in his understanding of the way things were and the way they were supposed to be.

But the roles had reversed. It was my turn. I felt strong, excited to be supporting him, and more than a little frightened. My fear was for Ed and the future, and any effect on the children, rather than anything that might happen to me. Whatever he'd done — I believed him when he said that woman's death was an accident — I'd said I would support him and when I give my word, that is it. I was going to stand by my man like a buxom, battle-scarred bottle-blonde from Birmingham, Alabama. Which was more important? The lives of four people, all of whom had the capacity to contribute to society? Or a dead madwoman who had tried to destroy our family and for whom nothing could be done? Which was more important? The freedom of a man who was party to a fatal accident — not murder, definitely not murder, not even manslaughter if the truth be told — and who would more than repay any debt by saving countless babies in future, or some abstract concept of justice? Substance or theory? Pragmatism or idealism? The living or the dead? We live in an imperfect world. Justice can be served in many ways.

★　★　★

The following morning summer began. The clouds finally parted and the sun blazed away like a cornered outlaw. Breakfast was near-silent. I caught Ed glancing at me out of the corner of his eye as if he was frightened I was going to change my mind.

For the sake of the children, I made out it was

94

a normal day by getting angry with Arthur for not doing his prep and shouting at Nell to hurry up or she'd have to walk. It was a normal day: he hadn't done his prep, she didn't hurry and she didn't have to walk.

Back home after the school run it was anything but normal. My concentration was shot to bits. Usually when that happened I battled on through — nothing will happen if you're not at the easel — but not that day, when all I could see were cinematic images of Ed in her bed, blood on her chin, those strong white teeth. There were moments when I was almost physically sick. Of course I couldn't feel my way into colours. There were too many I had to avoid and every shape took on a parallel form, a ghoulish apparition.

Eventually I gave in to the inevitable. I wanted to go for a walk to feel a restorative sun on my face but I couldn't trust myself to cope with meeting anyone I knew. So I went into the study and surfed the net, catching up on the latest about the manhunt. I tried to keep it generic, newspaper sites, the BBC, nothing to suggest I had anything more than a reasonable and passing interest in the death of a local woman. Yet I couldn't resist veering off on to gallery sites, group exhibitions and UWE shows, that woman's old girls' school association, Sotheby's, Edinburgh University alumni. In the end even those weren't interesting enough, but through Pete and Miranda I found her Facebook page and devoured the details of the life she led. I compared it to my own, and I wondered, I was always wondering, why of all the girls in the world that he had never noticed, she was the one who turned Ed's head.

I was reading an old online review of her Edinburgh degree show when the doorbell rang. I clicked off the page and headed down through the house, glancing at my still life of an old kettle that was hanging on the stairs. It had been a pivotal painting in my creative 'journey', if that doesn't sound too up-itself, the first time I combined foreground figuration and background abstraction, a shift in style as radical for me as putting his canvas on the floor and dripping paint on to it had been for Pollock. Art, like life, is about the journey as much as the destination. Without the blood and sweat and fears you won't make it to wherever you are trying to go. There will be no deception, no artifice. No art.

I knew who it would be at the door: a delivery man. It always was. The only men who ring our doorbell during the day thrust electronic pencils and signing-machines at me or have packages from some online retailer of sunny colours and Cornish dreams tucked under their arm. Or they are delivering flowers or cases of wine to Ed to give thanks for life. They are our modern door-to-door salesmen, only the sale has already been made.

But what if it was the police? The thought stopped me dead in the hall. It was too late to pretend there was no one at home because I had bounded heavily down the stairs specifically to let whoever was outside know someone was in so they didn't go away. I walked slowly towards the front door with a sickening sensation in my stomach, not just because I was frightened about who was on the other side but because I was suddenly aware that from now on I would always be frightened about who was on the other side. I would never again be able to hear the doorbell, see a policeman walking towards me or have my name called out in the street without thinking we had reached the end. My days of unthinkingly opening the door were over. My days of not caring what people were saying were over. I gave myself an extra moment to settle my nerves, to take on board the life sentence I had just been handed, to line up our story and to prepare an innocent greeting. Slowly I opened the heavy door.

It was Jerry. Thank God! Jerry was a sunburnt and straggly-haired delivery man. He wore knee-length shorts and a neatly ironed shirt. Jerry delivered flowers to Ed. He and I have got to know each other over the years. We snigger at the cards attached to the flowers: *With love, from Keith and Sharon and Apollo; From Michael, Caroline, Django and Gandalf.* 'Which one's the dog?' he asks.

Jerry was bending over, preparing to leave the flowers on the step when I opened the door. There was a bald spot on the top of his head. He straightened, smiling — Ed had helped to deliver Jerry and Gillian's baby, Annie — and held out the flowers, a burst of lilies in a brown paper cone, damp at the bottom, tied with string. They were linen-white, the brutal sun lighting the petals and purifying the green-drenched stalks.

'For you, Mrs Sheahan.'

For me? This was unusual. The last time I had been sent flowers was when I had Arthur. Nell had given me some once, for Mother's Day, but those were from the garden. I took the bouquet and envelope and slid out the card. It was embossed with the fleur-de-lys. Jerry was looking away, either to show a professional discretion or because he had looked at the card already. *My Darling, I can never thank you enough. I want to be with you forever. Ed xxxx.* I tried to look happy, but I was churning inside.

'Oh! They're from Ed. What a nice surprise!'

'Dr Sheahan?' Jerry had always called Ed 'Dr' Sheahan even though almost every letter he ever received was addressed to 'Mr'. 'An anniversary?'

I strangled an involuntary laugh.

'Birthday?' Jerry's children were still in high chairs, every birthday a major event. I shook my head. 'Whatever,' he added, 'they're lovely.' He knew who paid his Christmas tip. I looked down at the card. There were an unprecedented four kisses, not the usual three. I looked at Jerry. He looked at me. He was wondering what had happened for Ed to send me flowers.

★ ★ ★

Ed looked up from the *Financial Times*, which for some unfathomable reason he always buys on Thursdays after his game of men's doubles. Why Thursday? Why the *FT*? (Why doubles?) Because . . . I don't know. Why shouldn't he only buy it on Thursdays? He was sitting in the wicker

98

armchair in the bathroom, waiting for the bath to fill. There was a towel around his neck, a glass of Diet Coke balanced on the armrest, white-socked feet planted squarely on the white wooden floorboards. He was still wearing his tennis gear, the casual tick of Nike on his pressed shirt and shorts. Ed has the broad shoulders and sturdy calves of an Agincourt bowman, and similar subtlety. Plan A: hit the ball as hard as you can; Plan B: hit it harder. When he stands close to me I can feel his height and strength. It's a benevolent power but there are unreachable fathoms. His life is not tethered to its past. I asked,

'Anything?'

He turned a page, his arms high, opening and closing like butterfly wings.

'Not really the paper for it.'

'No news is good news.'

'Yup.'

'People talking about it at work?'

'Nope.'

'People talking about you at work?'

'Why would they talk about me?'

'About you behaving oddly?'

He frowned. Ed doesn't do lateral. His mind proceeds in a straight line from symptom to diagnosis. I learnt that early on in our relationship when I gave him the *Selected Poems of Wallace Stevens*. He read my favourite poem, 'The Idea of Order at Key West', very slowly, saying nothing, eyebrows knitted and mouth pursed, before eventually looking up and saying coolly and unashamedly: 'I don't understand a word of it.' I loved him for his refusal to bullshit. His lack of pretension was such a contrast to the students I met with their art school sophistry and annotated copies (green ink, of course) of E. E. Cummings or *Fleurs du Mal*.

Ed shifted on the wicker chair. His head was back, his face looking up like a satellite dish.

'Is anyone saying: 'Why is Mr Sheahan sending his wife flowers for the first time in fifteen years?''

'I think you rather over-estimate the interest in my private life.'

'Well, did you order them or did you ask Karen?'

'I did. Though I did ask her what — '

'Exactly. So Karen knows you sent me flowers. So whoever Karen has her coffee breaks with knows you sent me flowers. Which means the girls on reception know you sent me flowers. Which probably means everyone at St Anthony's knows you sent me flowers.'

'You seem to think no one at the hospital does anything but gossip.'

I arched an eyebrow ironically.

'And then there's Jerry.'

'Who's Jerry?' His tone suggested I'd entered the theatre of the absurd.

'The delivery man.'

'Jerry.' He said the name slowly as if he'd never heard it before and was keen to try it on his tongue.

'Jerry who regularly delivers flowers to you but never to me.'

'OK. I sent you flowers. I'm sorry. I won't do

100

it again. I did it because I thought you would like them. I wanted to say thank you. I wanted to make you happy. I'm sorry I tried.'

I dropped to my haunches beside him. My voice came out as a conspiratorial hiss.

'You don't get it, do you?'

'What don't I get?' He stressed the final word.

'You don't get that everything's changed. Irrevocably. There's a manhunt going on out there and they are looking for you. Your name's in the frame because you were with that woman at her flat a few nights before she died. You don't get that although the police haven't come here yet they may arrive at any time. They may already be asking someone the right questions, noting the answers, joining the dots. Who knows when there's going to be a knock on that door?'

'I don't see what that has got to do with flowers.'

'What it has got to do with flowers, my darling, is that if the police join the dots they are going to ask lots of questions of everybody you have spent time with since that woman died. And one of those will be Karen. And when they ask her if you have behaved in any way differently over the last three weeks she might — just might — suddenly remember the flowers and say, well yes, there was one thing, a man who she had never known to send flowers to his wife suddenly did, and the police might — just might — wonder what you or your wife did to make you send her flowers for the first time in living memory, birthdays and anniversaries included. And what will you say if they wonder that out loud in a bare room with no windows and a single bulb? What will you say if you know they are asking me the same question at the same time in another room with no windows and a single bulb? And there's no conferring. But we have to say the same thing or the game's up.'

Ed looked suitably contrite. The sword above his head was considerably larger than the one above mine.

'I'm sorry, darling, I really am.'

And suddenly, I felt sorry for him. Ed was not a man who attracted pity, he commanded respect. Yet at that moment he looked so defenceless, a single man on the run with the nation's police and press ranged against him. He shifted in his chair, a dagger of sunlight slashing his face.

'That's what you'll say, but you can never say it enough — not to me, not to that woman, not to her parents, not to the judge or jury, not to Nell and Arthur. But that's not my point. My point is nothing must change in our lives. If you never sent me flowers before, don't start sending them now. If you never washed the car on a Sunday afternoon, don't start washing it now. The only way we can survive if the police come knocking is if nothing — nothing at all — has changed in our lives. That way, when we sit in separate rooms with bare bulbs and two-way glass and are asked questions we don't know the answers to, we can give our answers confidently, because we know how we each think and behave and, so far as we can, we've nailed our lies and our alibis together. Yes?'

He nodded meekly.

'Because I've put my head in the noose for you. I will go to jail too for protecting a husband who slept with another woman and then killed her. And where will that leave the kids?'

'I didn't kill her.'

'That will be for the court to decide. The facts themselves are indisputable.' I tried not to let bitterness seep into my voice. 'You fucked her. She threatened your family and marriage. You were the only person there when she died. We only have your word it was an accident.'

'Stop it! You don't think — ' He turned away, jaw working, Y-shaped vein throbbing on his forehead.

'No, I don't, but that's because I know you. I'm not the jury, though. Look at the facts. A woman who could have ruined your marriage or reputation died violently. You were the only person present when she died. Those are the only facts. Everything else is your word.'

He looked at me, unblinking, grinding his teeth.

''He said, she said, he did, she did.' Just like Arthur and Alfie Warburton. Yes, I do believe you, but I won't be on the jury and the only *fact* we have is that woman ended up dead and Alfie wound up in the pond. Arthur was the one punished because for all the 'he said, I said' there was only one fact.'

I was almost hyperventilating. Ed nodded. I could see he wanted to help me calm down, but he knew and I knew there was nothing he could say or do.

7

The following Saturday we went to Julian and Ella Noone's for dinner. They lived in a large castellated house in Failand, a couple of miles outside the city over the Clifton Suspension Bridge. Julian was a successful fund manager who could read a balance sheet, a business situation and a handshake. Ella could spot a brand at ninety yards. We'd become sort of friends after Ed delivered their second son, Oscar, a birth with brutal complications, and they insisted on taking us out for a swanky dinner. Ed, who had no interest in money, didn't have much in common with Julian, who did. I could talk kids and schools and London shops with Ella, but only as long as it didn't happen too often or last too long. I liked Julian, though, and — I think — he liked me. He was intelligent and interested in a lot of things, art amongst them, and through business he had learnt how to hide his motives, which kept things interesting. That was why I would have liked to paint him, and the reason he would never ask.

As we approached the Suspension Bridge, testament to man's capacity to conceive, believe and achieve the impossible, Ed said,

'Oh, by the way, Pete asked if I was going to Araminta's memorial service.'

I was touching up my eyelashes with a mascara wand.

'Memorial service?'

'Apparently there's one next Wednesday. Chelsea Old Church. He wondered if I wanted to go with him.'

'You said no, of course.'

He flicked the car down a gear as we approached the bridge. A Samaritans sign fixed to the stone tower encouraged potential suicides to call.

'Actually, I said yes.'

'Yes?'

'Yes. I thought it might have looked odd if I'd said no.'

'Odd? It would have looked totally normal. It looks far odder to go to the memorial service of a girl who you met once at a party when you were four sheets gone. Why would anyone do that?'

There was a pause while he fished out a coin for the barrier. Who said men couldn't multitask? He dropped it into the wire-mesh paw. The barrier-arm lifted and we drove across the bridge. Way beneath us the river was brown between the mudflats. Two tiny figures on the cricket ground beyond: a father bowling to his son. The view from the bridge always made me feel vulnerable, conscious of the height and longevity of the million-year-old gorge, the magnificence of Brunel's achievement, the despair of the jumpers.

'If he thought it was odd he presumably wouldn't have asked me.'

'It doesn't matter what he thinks. What about everyone else? What about the police, for God's sake?' I felt a squeeze of fear. He had missed the point again. 'You don't think they won't be casing the guest list for the kooky killer who turns up to gloat over everyone trying to catch him? Jesus, Ed, that's the oldest hook in the book.'

He glanced towards the traffic lights by the entrance to Ashton Court.

'If I go with Pete it will look completely normal. If anyone asks — which they won't — I will simply say I only knew her briefly but obviously I'm very sorry about what happened and have come to pay my respects, not only to her but to support Pete, my closest colleague, who's lost one of his oldest friends. Why is that odd?'

'One of your junior colleague's girlfriend's oldest friends. How close is that? How often have you even met Miranda?'

The lights turned amber and he crunched the gears with a steel yelp. We passed a golf club and some school playing fields. It is a long lonely road, barely a mile from the city centre yet trees bend over the tarmac like a wicked wood in a fairy story.

'It's a helluva lot less odd than telling Pete I can't be bothered to have anything to do with a girl whose flat I stayed in less than a week before she died.'

Ed didn't like arguments.

'When you were so drunk you can't even remember sleeping with her. Look, surely you can see you shouldn't go to the memorial service? Partly because you will draw police

106

attention to yourself, but mainly because, however it happened, you were there when she died. You were involved. It just doesn't seem right.'

Silence. More lights. Crossroads. Ed looked grumpy. We turned right.

'I don't think I really had a choice.'

'You always have a choice.'

More silence. When he finally spoke there was steel in his voice. It was the first time I had heard it since *the* night.

'OK then, I have a choice. And I choose to go. I choose to go because it seems the right thing to do and *because* I killed her. It was an accident, I know that, but I choose to go because I think I should pay my respects to someone I watched die and who is part of my life forever as a result.'

'Well, I don't think you should go. If you are thinking about our future you have to forget the past.'

Ed changed down unnecessarily, the gears crunching. It was for my benefit.

'So I don't have a choice any more? There's a debt I can never repay so I have to do whatever you say for the rest of my life. Is that how it is from now on?

He twitched at the temples. It made his hairline seem higher than it was. I looked out of the window at the dark trees, a strand of bungalows.

'Go on then, you go, do what you like. But if the police pick you up on the way out and you don't see Nell or Arthur until they're in their thirties, so be it.'

He didn't answer. He could hear the frustration in my voice. Instead, after a moment or two, from nowhere, I sensed him smile. Then he stifled a chuckle. I didn't look at him, refusing to be seduced, but that only made him laugh again, louder. It was exactly like it had been when we started going out and he would defuse my outbursts by laughing, and because everyone had always taken me seriously until then, it worked, and I loved him for it, even if I hated it at the time. This time I paid no attention. I just stared ahead, even though his laughter was a sound I hadn't heard for so many days, a sound so uninhibited and unexpected it could have blown in from anywhere. I sat stony-faced. Ed was alternately looking at me and the road, his whole body beginning to rock, head bouncing off the headrest, becoming ever more incapacitated by my refusal to bend. In the end I couldn't help it. I grinned. Ed heaved uncontrollably. My smile widened. He tried to speak but it was lost in hysterics. I started to laugh, I had to. He hooted and buckled in his seat. He howled. I laughed. He was laughing fit to burst, tears beginning to roll down his cheeks. Finally I let myself go.

But the timbre had changed. I suddenly realized he wasn't laughing any more. He was crying and the tears washing down his face were real. I couldn't help myself, I began to cry too, unstoppably, for the way our world had changed and for that dead girl and her parents, because I knew how I would feel if it was Arthur or Nell, and we had to pull in at the side of the road because my mascara was smudging and I wanted to turn around and go home, and Ed's tears meant he couldn't see to drive, and neither of us could see the way ahead.

★ ★ ★

Julian Noone had pale eyes that circled like search-lights. Many a potential investor, company FD and, if the rumours were true, pretty maiden had been trapped in their beam. As he swooped in to kiss me they seemed to be on maximum power. I had the uncomfortable feeling he had clocked my red eyes and reapplied mascara and suspected a row in the car. He was wearing an expensive shirt, burnt sienna, with a ludicrous cutaway collar and four buttons at neck and cuff, which made him look like a celebrity chef. Greying chest hair was visible at his throat. Ella's blonde hair cascaded over her shoulders and her teeth shone. She was wearing a brilliant turquoise shirt with its sleeves furled, 'Joseph' written across her breasts in sequins, and Escada sport jeans so tight she must have shaved her legs to get into them. I caught Ed glancing downwards to her décolle-tage as he leant forward to kiss her hello. He minutely raised an eyebrow.

While Ed struggled to find common interest with Ella, Julian fixed on me, pouring us both large glasses of a pricey Chassagne-Montrachet. Ed had lime and soda, Ella a crackling G&T. Having asked how my art was, and made an insider's observation about the difference between headline and actual revenues at the big auction houses, Julian moved smoothly through the gears, using art fakes as an intro to financial markets. For those who play with it, money is like water: it always finds a way in.

'You see,' he said, topping up my glass even though it was half-full, 'the stock market is no different to any other. When any market gets a sniff something's wrong it's like a dog looking for a bone. It keeps sniffing around and no matter how often a dealer or a company says everything's kosher it won't let it alone. It's a confidence thing, like a sixth sense, an intuition that can't be satisfied. The market will always get there in the end.' He leant back in his chair and said smugly, 'As the man said, bankruptcy happens slowly, then quickly.'

I nodded and looked pretty. When we sat down in the middle of their vast dining room Julian refilled our glasses with a joie de vivre that suggested he was not planning to invest in some overseas market after dinner. I held up my hand, but he poured the wine anyway. I was already feeling light-headed and knew I shouldn't drink more, but Julian was so charming and enthusiastic it was like trying to fend off a puppy. I wasn't even sure I wanted to. His brand of positivity had been in short supply of late. So while Ed splashed in Ella's shallows, Julian probed the nexus of art and money (he owned an early Caulfield and a late Kossoff, a drawing of Spitalfields, not one of his best) and roamed the byways of 'high f'nance' as he pronounced it. Eventually we swung round and talked as a group, moving through the dinner party staples

— holidays, schools, politics, the death of Araminta Lyall (Ed mentioned he'd met her at a party but offered so little colour the conversation moved swiftly on), marriage and divorce. Julian's brother had just separated. With Ed turning back to Ella to explain how NHS under-funding manifested itself daily in a practical way (though not without surreptitiously catching my eye and touching his water glass with a forefinger), Julian re-ran the argument that kicked off his brother's marriage's death waltz. They were running late in the car on the way to watch their son play hockey at a school they couldn't find. Why were they late? 'He said, she said.' That's how it started. Symptom not cause. On the day it was the Winchester one-way system, but it could have been anything. Julian uncorked a Margaux that Hemingway would have written a florid sentence for, and said,

'Apparently 69 per cent of all break-ups are kicked off by a row in the car.'

I didn't need any more wine, but I did need a night off. I could feel Ed looking at me as I let Julian fill my glass. I didn't catch his eye.

'Where on earth did you get that ridiculous statistic?' I teased.

He feigned hurt.

'You don't believe me?'

'I just want to know where you got that absurd stat.'

'Lies, damn lies, eh?'

I forked my last potato. I was feeling slightly giddy, but warm and in control. It almost felt as if life had returned to normal.

'No.'

''No' meaning . . . ?'

It wasn't hard to see how in different circumstances — dinner in Knightsbridge, a meeting in Mayfair — people did what he wanted.

'Just, we had one on the way here and I was wondering whether we were going to join the 69 per cent.'

'A break-up argument?' he ventured eagerly.

'A 31 per-center.'

As soon as I said it, I knew I had made a mistake. The wine was talking. Julian leaned forward, interest flaring, and I remembered his searchlight-stare when we arrived and he took in my red eyes and reapplied mascara. For a moment I wondered whether he had steered the conversation round to divorce and his brother's argument in Winchester on purpose — and as I thought it, I knew he had. I felt a bolt of fear, but before I could move the conversation on he said,

'Really? What about?'

I screeched into reverse.

'Oh, nothing really.'

'Come-come, my dear, you can't leave a man dangling.'

A smile as dangerous as the Doom Bar. I took a sip of wine to buy time to think, but all it did was make me realize how much I had already drunk. My toes felt pinched in my heels.

'It was nothing.'

'It never is.'

'Just the usual.'

'But you know the way here well enough. Come on, there's no need to be so secretive.

112

We're all friends.' I handed my plate to the girl-next-door they'd employed to cook for the evening. 'We've all been there.'

I momentarily considered lying, but I knew I had to stick as closely to the truth as possible if I was going to line the barricades.

'Oh, just about a funeral. Nothing much.'

'Nothing much to whoever died. Who was he? She?'

'Someone Ed knew. He thought he should go, I thought he shouldn't.'

'Why not?'

The girl reappeared with a wheel of camembert and a hillside of grapes. I felt my neck beginning to prickle. This was the first time I had had to think on my feet about that woman. I clenched my fists under the table.

'What is this, Julian, twenty questions?'

I gave an overly relaxed laugh. He didn't answer. The candles felt bright on my forehead and my cheeks were hot.

'Okaaaay . . . because he hadn't seen them for years, not since we left London. So it seemed a bit, I don't know, prurient to suddenly get in touch now. It's not as if a funeral is the obvious place for catch-up.'

'But Ed said old friends are always old friends and you have to support them.'

'Exactly.'

Had I blurted out agreement too eagerly? Julian leant back in his chair thoughtfully, wiggling his fingers like a dentist warming up. I glanced at Ed. I could tell he was listening intently even if he seemed to be giving Ella his full concentration as she waxed about the Provençal villa they had just bought.

'And that was it?'

'Yes. Silly, I know. That's marriage, I guess.'

'Doesn't sound much.'

I relaxed and reached for my wine. I had got away with it.

'I guess we're the 31 per cent.'

'But compared to the Winchester bypass, maybe death is a big thing.'

'Anything can be a big thing. It's what you make of it.'

'Never trust a rowing couple.'

'Who said that?'

'I just did.'

He looked at me shrewdly, lips glistening in the candlelight. I felt like a finance director caught fiddling the books. How easy it was to let the conversation move the wrong way, how deceptively easy to lie. The problem, I knew, was the more lies we told, the greater the risk of discovery. Lies compound like debt until you can no longer pay the interest. And, it struck me as I turned away to see Ella cut a sliver of camembert so thin it was almost transparent, that was only part of the problem. The real problem was how was I going to live with an infinite lie when my work was forged in the cauldron of truth?

Soon after, I accidentally knocked over my glass and amongst the chaos and salted tablecloth and apologies that followed, Ed was almost indecently quick to his feet, saying it had been a lovely evening but was that the time I think we really ought to go.

The moment our car turned on to the road, the Noone electric gates gliding silently shut behind us, hiding the spotlights in the grass that lit up as we drove down the drive, creating a magical Eden, Ed gave a theatrical sigh. I had slumped into my seat. My head felt thick. Our headlights picked out the midnight-blue canopy of the trees as Ed said,

'Darling, how did you let the conversation go there?'

'I'm sorry. I didn't know what to do. It just happened.'

'It's like you told me with the flowers. We have to concentrate. We can never let the guard down.'

'I know. I'm really sorry. It just appeared out of nowhere.'

'I guess we've got to make sure things don't appear out of nowhere, particularly with someone like Julian. He hasn't made that much money without being able to sniff out a weakness.'

I was annoyed by his words. It was obvious he didn't like Julian or approve of his job, so he was implicitly recasting his shrewdness in the most unfavourable light. I had drunk too much and the car felt oppressive.

'What? You go and kill someone and somehow the fallout is down to me?'

'You know that's not what I'm saying.' His voice was steady.

'What are you saying then?'

'I'm just saying that if we're going to get away with this, we can never talk about it or anything to do with it ever again. Not at home. Not in the car. Not on top of the Mendips. Not when there's nobody within a hundred miles. Not ever. It didn't happen.'

He didn't want a fight. He wanted equilibrium. But I was angry and frustrated and I didn't. I wanted to register that because of him I was going to have to live the rest of my life under the smothering blanket of his secret.

'I see, you screw up and I have to do everything exactly the way you want.'

His manner was calm. He kept on looking at the road.

'Darling, you know I can't be permanently in your debt. It won't work. We'll never be able to stay together.'

Tight with drink and angry as I was, I knew he was right. No marriage can survive inequality in the long term. Whatever passed between us, however unfair it seemed, I had to bite back the bitterness. The moral high ground was the road to the gallows. The only way through this was to work as partners-in-crime. He was making the same point I had made in the car on the way to the Noones': the only way we could have a future was to forget the past.

Afterwards we drove in silence, stopping only to pay the toll on the bridge. As he fished in his pocket for change he leant towards me, looking for a connection, a softness or gesture, but I couldn't give it to him, not then. I sat rigid in my seat and stared straight ahead at the barrier and I felt the tears forming, because in my mind's eye I could see the outline of his head on that woman's pillow — sanity is the capacity to edit — and I knew I was trapped.

8

The following Wednesday, on the day of that woman's memorial service, I was awake-not-awake, in a warm dreamy state I wanted to last forever, when I was woken by Arthur's urgent hand.

'Mummy, there's two men who want to see you at the door.'

A spasm of fear. I stretched out an arm for the digital clock and knocked the *Selected Poems of Philip Larkin* on to the floor. It landed face down. Phil would have expected no more. Seven twenty-seven: too early for friendly visitors. My shoulders felt stiff.

I'd half-woken when Ed left at five thirty. He had work to do before he headed to London with Pete for that woman's memorial service. I hadn't got back to sleep, drifting in and out of consciousness, dark shadows in my peripheral vision. A horn honked somewhere beyond the open window and a car changed down as it ground up the hill. I propped myself up on an elbow.

'Two men?'

'In jackets.'

'Jackets?'

'And ties.'

'What do they want?'

'They want to talk to you and Daddy.'

'OK, tell them I'll be down in two minutes.

Take them into the kitchen.'

Arthur nodded and disappeared. I pulled on a check shirt with a frayed collar, paint-spattered jeans and a pair of cherry Converse. No socks. I didn't want anyone to think this wasn't a typical day in the life of the stay-at-home painter. I checked the mirror: my skin looked dry, my hair a mess. It would take more than the Manhattan skyline of lotions and potions on the chest of drawers to make myself look attractive. I lined up my opening, straightened my story. They would have to take me as I was.

They always say plain-clothes policemen are still obviously policemen and I can now confirm that to be true. The taller had a beard flecked with grey, owl-rimmed glasses, a soft, feminine mouth that reminded me of the mother of a boyfriend I'd once had and a grape-coloured birthmark on his neck. He looked tired, worn down by the gap between what people did and what they said they'd done. He wore a plain suit and his tie was polyester, maroon with diagonal gold stripes. It conjured memories of sporty drinks parties at Cambridge, when all those young blades the world owed a living to strutted around in light-blue blazers with red lion logos, maroon and gold ties and too-short-at-the-ankle-too-tight-at-the-thigh grey slacks they'd been given for some sports tour or other.

'Mrs Edward Sheahan?'

'Yes?'

The muscles around my mouth felt as if they were flickering like strobes. I prayed nothing was visible externally. These men were trained.

'I'm Detective Inspector Pullen. This is Detective Constable James. I apologize for getting you up so early, but may we have a word?'

'What is it? What's happened? Is someone hurt?'

I nodded at DC James but he didn't acknowledge me. He was younger, smaller, a thuggish man with a centre parting and a boxer's neck, shifting uncomfortably in his suit. His top button was undone and his tie loose. DI Pullen glanced at Arthur and raised an eyebrow. He was sprawled across the sofa reading a book, a cartoon of literary concentration, the son any mum would wish for. I wasn't fooled.

'Go and get dressed, darling, you've got to go in half an hour. And have a shower. And wash your hair. It looks like candyfloss.'

Arthur kept 'reading'.

'Please.'

He looked up.

'Now.'

Arthur dragged himself off the sofa as if he was made of lead and disappeared upstairs. DI Pullen smiled and his whole demeanour changed. I made a mental note not to be deceived.

When Arthur had gone I offered them coffee. They both declined. Pullen indicated the armchair. I could feel DC James looking me up and down as I crossed the kitchen. Men are so transparent. They stare at your cleavage or legs or ass and when you catch their eye they pretend they've got some amazing interest in a British Gas billboard behind you, or a shop selling lightbulbs across the road. I sat down and crossed my legs. Pullen pushed his owlish glasses back on to the bridge of his nose and, in a voice that implied 'at last', said,

'Is your husband at home?'

'I'm afraid not.'

'Where is he?'

'Look, can you tell me what this is all about?'

Anyone who was innocent would focus on the police's presumption — just bowling in and asking intrusive questions without explaining why they were there. DC James was studying the kitchen as if trying to memorize everything for a TV quiz with prizes.

'We'll get to that in a minute. Before, could you please just tell me where he is?'

'He's at work.'

Pullen glanced at his watch.

'He's going to a memorial service later, so he went in early to finish off some work.'

Pullen nodded at James, who promptly disappeared into the hall.

'A memorial service?'

'In London.'

'Can I ask whose?'

'A lady called Araminta Lyall.' I felt a metallic taste in my mouth. 'You know . . . '

'We know Araminta Lyall. Will he have left the hospital yet?'

'I don't know. He's going with a colleague.' I was about to add 'who knew her very well' but stopped myself. Ed insisted we should only ever give the minimum information. 'I'm not sure what time the service is.' A nice touch, not too interested.

'OK, thank you. Now, the reason we are here

is about your husband and Araminta Lyall.'

My face automatically creased into a frown. I even surprised myself. Nature taking over. It is one thing to 'know' the truth, it is another to be formally confronted by it. While it had been mine and Ed's 'secret' that woman's death had almost seemed hypothetical. Suddenly the real world was encroaching.

'Sorry?' I managed.

'Mrs Sheahan, how well did your husband know Ms Lyall?'

I summoned maximum indignation.

'Hold on a sec. Can we go back a step? What do you mean, how well did my husband know Araminta Lyall? He didn't know her at all.'

'Mrs Sheahan, we are investigating the murder of Araminta Lyall. We have reason to believe your husband may have been involved with Ms Lyall.'

'That's ridiculous!'

I shook my head vigorously, hoping I didn't sound like my mother at her most haughty and trying not to give the impression I was some sort of little wifey who had no idea what her dirty stop-out of a husband got up to at night.

'And yet he is at her memorial service?'

Pullen had seen every type of bluster. It was a brisk reminder he was better at interviews than I was. I should have done Footlights when I had the chance. All I could hope was that this was a fishing expedition.

'As far as I know he met her once, at a party given by his colleague Peter Spurling the week before she died.'

'He only met her once, at a party, and yet he's gone to her memorial service?' Pullen gave a dry laugh. 'He must go to quite a few.'

I dipped my head to acknowledge his thrust but knew I had to press on.

'Somehow, because my husband doesn't normally drink, he got completely plastered at the party and ended up back at her flat with a whole lot of others. That's why he's gone today. That and to offer support to Pete, who's his protégé and who has lost a friend.'

'If your husband doesn't drink, why did he get . . . plastered?'

'Because he was exhausted. He'd just finished a forty-hour shift.'

Pullen took a narrow notepad and plastic biro from his breast pocket and jotted a few words on it. He looked back at me. I felt prickly heat at the back of my neck.

'He said he had one to try to get going because he was so tired. He didn't want to go to the party but he had to because it was Pete and he was celebrating passing his finals. And because he never drinks, one made him light-headed, and because there was no one else from the hospital there and Pete kept holding him up as the great obstetrician and telling everyone how fantastic he was, he was flattered, anyone would have been, and so he had another. He said every time he tried to leave, Pete introduced him to more people. So he got his second wind.'

'Has he had a problem with alcohol historically?'

'No. He hardly ever drinks, never has, mainly

because he works so hard.'

'And when he does drink — on the rare occasions — does he . . . is he . . . ?'

'Inspector, I've been married to him for fifteen years and I can categorically say I have never seen him tipsy, let alone drunk. And there has never been any change of character if that's what you mean. My guess is he thought he was twenty years younger and twenty degrees cooler than he is. You know how men are.'

I left the words hanging in the air. Pullen drummed his fingers on the island. When he was thinking he rolled his tongue around his mouth.

'Didn't you try to stop him?'

'I wasn't there. I was painting a portrait in Suffolk.'

'On a Saturday night?'

'It overran. Was supposed to finish on Friday but went through to Saturday teatime, which meant I was never going to be back in time for the party.'

'Pink ticket?'

'He was there on his own, if that's what you mean.'

Pullen looked sharply at me. James appeared in the doorway.

'On their way, sir.'

James disappeared back into the hall.

'And presumably he became involved with Ms Lyall or he wouldn't have gone back to her flat?'

'Or he may have been chatting to one of the others who went. He didn't go into a huge amount of detail. He did say he tried to get the taxi that had taken them to Montpelier to bring him home when it dropped everyone at her place, but the driver didn't speak English and drove off while my husband was saying goodbye to everyone.'

'So he went into her flat?'

'To call a cab.'

'Mobile?'

'He'd left it at work.'

'And he stayed?'

'I think he was pretty embarrassed to be there.'

'At Ms Lyall's?'

'Getting drunk at a much younger colleague's party. Going back to a flat with people fifteen years younger than he was who he'd never met before. Crashing out. Waking up in some younger woman's flat in an armchair. Which bit of that is how a senior obstetrician should behave?'

'Everyone has to let their hair down.'

'Probably best not to do it in front of your juniors.'

Pullen rolled his tongue.

'I thought you said there was no one else from St Anthony's at the party?'

He stared at me, glassy-eyed. DI Pullen unnerved me. Sentences linked. Patterns loomed where before there were none. I felt a web being weaved and I was suddenly conscious he probably knew a lot more than he let on. On my side, everything definitely needed to hang together. The children's whole lives were at stake. I leant back in my chair and pulled an ankle on to a knee.

'Just the host.'

'Ah, of course, the host. Mr Spurling.'

'A hundred to one against he would have drunk at all if there had been any more of his juniors there.'

Pullen paused, as if to contemplate his own tiny mistake. I tried not to stare at his birthmark.

'So, going back — or forward — do you know what happened when he got to Ms Lyall's? Did they talk?'

'I don't know. I don't think so. By the sound of it he crashed out pretty much straight away.'

'And he didn't talk about her at all.'

I shook my head.

'Even when she died and it was in all the papers?'

'Well, yes, of course then he did. And I asked lots of questions. But the problem was that he didn't have much to say. He could remember talking to her briefly at the party, right at the end, which was why he'd gone back to Stokes Croft, but he couldn't remember much about what she was like, or what they talked about, and his memory of the time at her flat was minuscule.'

'So he said.'

'I have no reason not to believe him. My husband is scrupulously honest. It's one of the reasons I married him.'

'What about on the Sunday morning?'

'Said he got up and left. I don't think they shared coffee and croissants, if that's what you mean, or exchanged life stories, but maybe they did. I guess you'd have to ask him.'

'We will be asking him, but I'm asking you.' Pullen's face was granite.

'Well, I can only assume he was embarrassed and wanted out ASAP.'

'But you didn't ask?'

'I didn't ask.'

'Even after she died?'

'After she died I asked what she was like, not how they spent their time together. He'd already said he barely knew her.'

'And what did he say she was like?'

'He didn't say much. Said she was obviously intelligent, and that an art dealer at the party told him she was an amazing artist. That was about all he remembered.'

'Would you say your husband is attracted to 'amazing' artists?'

'He was attracted to me, not my art, if that's what you mean. I'd barely started in those days.'

Pullen flicked back a page on his pad to read a note he had taken earlier. I prayed I hadn't contradicted myself.

'And from the Sunday morning when he left her flat to the Wednesday she died he had no further contact with Araminta Lyall?'

'No.'

'As far as you know.'

'As far as I know.'

'So he could have done?'

'Of course he could have done. But I don't see why he would've.'

'Unless he didn't just 'crash out'? Unless something happened that meant he had to go back?'

I shot him a quizzical look. It was essential to maintain the façade of bewilderment. If you don't act like a victim they think you are a perpetrator.

'Detective, could you explain why you think Ed might have been involved in her death?'

'Have you talked to many people about how your husband spent the night at Araminta Lyall's flat just a few days before she was killed?'

I sighed. It said: this is very inconvenient. I have children to get to school and although I may not look like I'm dressed for work, I have work to do. Pullen took no notice. We had discussed the case in a general way at the Noones', but Ed hadn't opened up about his night at her flat.

'No.'

Pullen put his pen in his mouth and twirled it. His eyes were heavy-lidded, sleepy but as dangerous as a snake.

'You are a very discreet pair.'

I gave a courtroom smile but didn't answer.

'Almost unique, I'd say.' He tapped his pen against his chin.

'Thank you.' I could do laconic too.

'Perhaps you haven't seen anyone since the police announced they were treating it as murder?'

'We get about.'

'But no one's thought to mention the reason Bristol is on the front pages?'

'I appreciate it's different in your line of work, Detective, but I was brought up not to trample over other people's misfortune.'

I sounded like my mother, which was half what I intended. No one was better at closing a conversation through sheer breeding. She could stop clocks with a glance. Pullen nodded contemplatively.

'Has your husband ever had affairs?'

'No.'

'Not as far as you are aware?'

'Are you telling me that he has?'

'I'm not sure I can tell you anything, Mrs Sheahan.'

The words came out in his loping drawl but contained slow poison. I decided to fish. It must be better that he was doing the talking.

'Meaning?'

'Meaning you are very sure of yourself, and your husband.'

'Are you married, Inspector?'

'Uh-huh.'

'Long time?

'Twenty-six years.'

'You know your wife?'

Pullen frowned. The pen came out of his mouth and went back in. I leant back in my chair. I had nailed it.

'Then perhaps you can tell me why Araminta Lyall came round here and left your husband a bouquet of flowers on the Monday before she died.'

Silence.

I tried to show no emotion but my mind was boiling like a swollen river. The obvious question, but also the road to dusty death, was: 'How the hell do you know that?' I should have been upfront about the flowers, but it was so unlikely they would have found out about them. Or was it? They must have been through her credit card records. But how would they know she had brought them here? It wasn't the time to worry about the how, simply the explanation. This wasn't Watergate. No one would be hanged for the cover-up.

'That, oh those, yes, that was because Ed helped to sort out her plumbing or something.'

Pullen flicked back in his notebook, scanning the pages.

'Even though he . . . ' He read his notes out verbatim. ' "Said he got up and left. I don't think they shared coffee and croissants, if that's what you mean, or exchanged life stories, but maybe they did.' Yet he still had time to 'sort out her plumbing or something'?'

I held his eye when he looked up. It was essential I showed no weakness.

'I don't think it was very much, just turning a tap or a switch.'

'Enough to make her bring round flowers?'

'Eye of the beholder?'

'But which you didn't think it was worth mentioning when I asked you whether he had any further contact with Ms Lyall?'

'I'm sorry. I thought you meant 'contact' as in seeing her, or speaking to her. The flowers were delivered while he was at work and I was picking up the children from school.'

Pullen turned away from the island and walked over to the window. He had the lithe movement of a former athlete. There was silence while he looked at the garden. If he was waiting for me to add anything he was going to wait a long time. Everyone knows you let silence build. Don't leap in. He looked out far longer than could be justified by our postage stamp of a garden with its single cypress and ornamental pond, a neglected, now-stagnant pool riddled with waterborne disease. Eventually he turned and said,

'Do you think the fact the flowers were hand-delivered rather than sent is relevant?'

'I've no idea.'

'Because normally it's a lot easier just to send flowers.'

'Maybe she was passing?'

'People usually hand-deliver flowers because they want to see the recipient.'

I shrugged. I could hardly be responsible for the thought processes of a woman I had never met, a woman who was, by the sound of it, capable of some very wobbly thinking indeed. Pullen picked up a wooden salt cellar from the marble worktop, weighed it in his hand.

'Mrs Sheahan, can you think of any other reason why you might hand-deliver flowers rather than send them, when you are standing in a flower shop on one side of Bristol and the person you want to thank lives on the other?'

He replaced the cellar and inspected his hands for traces of salt. His message was clear. He didn't have to watch my face as I answered because there was no answer.

'Wasn't she at UWE? If she drove there we're pretty much on the way.'

'And she wanted to see the recipient?'

'Or save the delivery charge?'

The door opened. James gave a thumbs-up. I glanced at the clock. The children needed to leave for school in twenty minutes and there was no sign of Nell. Pullen turned back to me. When he spoke his voice had a businesslike tone.

'Mrs Sheahan, I am going to ask you to accompany us to the station to answer some questions.'

'What?' My surprise was totally genuine.

'Because we have reason to believe you and/or your husband may have been involved in the murder of Araminta Lyall.'

9

I realized immediately Pullen had known how this was going to end from the beginning. He'd just been playing me for time while they caught up with Ed. I was always going to be taken in. Nothing I said would have made any difference. I was the mule at the bottom of the MI6 pyramid, Pullen the all-seeing handler at the top. To stop myself crying, or giving myself away, I focused on the practical.

'But what about the children? How are they going to get to school?'

Pullen's voice was equally practical, almost paternal. He was only doing his job.

'Can someone give them a lift?'

'Um . . . I don't know.'

My mother had brought us up not to ask for favours. I could call Bea Washington, but I didn't want to. Her long nose would be twitching on overdrive.

'Otherwise we can.'

That settled it. I wasn't having Nell and Arthur arriving at school in a police car, unmarked or otherwise, even if Arthur would love it.

The next twenty minutes passed in a dream. Pullen went out to the car but DC James stood silently in the corner as I explained to the children when they came down there had been a misunderstanding and I had to go with the

133

policemen to clear it up. They ate their breakfast in silence. Arthur was close to tears. Nell kept turning around and looking at James as if she was thinking, 'Why is this stocky little man in our house?' I just sat there, unable to speak. I tried to think about what I was going to say, but thoughts and events came crashing in from all sides and I couldn't think in a straight line — which was what Ed was referring to whenever he joked about the problems of being married to an artist.

Bea appeared in cubist-patterned leggings with go-faster fluorescent stripes, a mango hoodie and giant Nikes built for bouncing. Bea is part of the school-run-have-coffee-play-tennis-back-to-yours-for-a-gossip-and-a-salad-and-a-glass-of-wine-and-oh-go-on-then-I'm-not-driving-OMG!-it's-time-to-pick-up-the-kids brigade. I'm not. But she's friendly and will do anything. She even offered to pick the children up and bring them home after school 'if that would help'. I said that was very kind but I hoped it wouldn't be necessary. Then I gave Nell and Arthur huge squeezy hugs and waved them away quickly in case I burst into tears. I'm pretty strong but everyone has their limits and I was deep into unknown territory. Anything could happen. Anything was happening. Speculation about why the police were at the Sheahans' and why the Sheahans were at the police station would start in earnest the moment Bea touched down in gym or coffee shop.

Pullen drove to the station, two hands on the wheel, and James sat half turned in the passenger seat, as if he was about to start a conversation or

134

thought I was going to make a run for it when we stopped at a traffic light. There were two Costa cups squeezed into the front seat cup-holder, a ghostly outline of coffee discolouring plastic lids. I was in the back, my jeans squeaking every time I shifted on the plastic seat. I didn't listen to their chat. It was male stuff, cop stuff. Saturday-night heroes. I was thinking about the children, how they would be taking it, and also about Ed. Somewhere across town he was in the back of a similar vehicle, or had already arrived at his destination — a word, I noted as I watched the Bristol ferry criss-crossing the harbour like a cat's cradle, that was uncomfortably close to destiny.

I looked out of the window at my adopted home. It was strange to be looking at Bristol from the back of a police car, as if the narrative of my life had been bent out of shape. Bristol is a city of stories. They are written in the names — Corn Street, Wine Street, Lewins Mead, Union Street, Horse Fair, Anchor Road, Narrow Quay. It's an ancient port, starting point and endgame.

The police station was in a drive-through part of town, an area I only knew from having been to a gig there with an out-of-town friend mad for a singer-songwriter who could draw a crowd of sixty. There were dingy clubs and pubs, no-brand fast-food emporia and 24/7 grocers with metal grilles and halal options. An army surplus store for men kicked out of the army or too weird to be allowed in in the first place had paint peeling from its fascia.

When we arrived at the station I was guided into a lino-floored reception, unobtrusively flanked by Pullen and James like a real-life criminal. In the foyer an old fan turned slowly on a windowsill as if we were in some mosquito-infested outpost or remote saloon. A blank-eyed man and woman sweltered in shapeless track-suits and baseball tops with American place names (Brooklyn, Chicago), lounging on the plastic chairs as if in a queue at a fried chicken take-out in the Deep South. Pullen pressed a buzzer and a duty sergeant unlocked the door at the end of the Formica counter. We walked deep into the bowels of the station. I deliberately hadn't asked about Ed. I didn't want to show any concern beyond giving off a sense they were making a terrible mistake. Besides, as I was led down a cold brick passage painted institutional cream and into a cold brick interview room also painted institutional cream, I wasn't feeling that sorry for him. He'd got me into a place I never expected to be.

Pullen gestured towards a chair on the far side of a metal table with rounded corners and smooth sides. The table and chairs were bolted to the floor. I looked over my shoulder. James nodded forward. I didn't acknowledge him but went into the room.

'If you wait here someone will be along in a moment. Can I get you anything? Cup of tea?'

'Thank you. And a glass of water, please.'

He nodded and left. The door clicked ominously loudly in the silence. I had heard a click like that once before.

15 December 1986. We were having supper in the dining room at Highlands rather than the kitchen because it was nearly Christmas. Our father was in London that night. No change there. He was always in London. We didn't really miss him, partly because we were so used to his absence and partly because even when he was with us he seemed to be absent in spirit if present in body. He was gentle and loving, softer than Mother, but he always seemed to be at an angle to the family, incapable of playing his designated role. We were having dinner when the phone rang in the hall, cutting the silence that had descended after Matt had turned the conversation towards Boy George's cross-dressing specifically to wind up Mother.

She was on the phone for a long time. When she returned she stared at each of us in turn, as if fixing in her mind what we looked like in the moment before our childhoods changed forever.

'I'm afraid there's been an accident. A car crash. Your father's died.' She looked down for a moment and swallowed. 'I'm sorry.'

Although the words were unambiguous, for a few moments I couldn't process them. It must be some sort of joke. It was nearly Christmas! I felt a sudden searing emptiness, a pain I couldn't locate. We couldn't have Christmas without our father. He might not have been the most attentive of fathers — that was a masterpiece of understatement — but he was still our father and he brought a sort of pained hope to Highlands that didn't exist when he wasn't there. I looked at Matt and Bridgey. They were older. They would show me how to understand. Matt smiled weirdly. There were bubbles of saliva in the corners of his mouth. Bridgey was staring at the table, showing us the top of her head, her glasses misting.

Seven years later, I played hockey for my school in Oxford. Matt, who was deep in his troubles at Christ Church, came to watch and afterwards took me to the Ashmolean and for tea at the Randolph, where he sniffed about 'Scottish baronial' and 'grisly Victoriana'. The ceiling in the dining room seemed twice the height of a bell tower. We'd never spoken about our father before, not on the night he died nor any time afterwards. Having gingered around the subject, he said in a voice scarred by unreleased emotion,

'You know, Bunny, I couldn't believe it, even then, even knowing her. I couldn't believe she could just walk into that room and say, 'I'm afraid your father's died', as if he was the cat or some mad uncle we'd never met. And then she said, 'I'm sorry.' *Sorry?* What sort of response is that? How is that going to help small children? How can she apologize when she wasn't even there?'

He blew a bitter smoke-ring upwards and lit another cigarette with the butt of the previous. Outside the window the rain glittered in the lamplight against the slow-moving traffic and shadowy Ionic columns of the Ashmolean. His hair was tangled. There were grey rings around his eyes. A kale-coloured scarf was tossed mock-jauntily over his shoulders, an ironic student gesture, giving an entirely false impression of how he was feeling. It didn't seem a good sign that he remembered her exact words, or that he was still working away at his loss. God knows I'm no apologist for Mother but it can't have been easy to work out how to react in the few seconds between putting the phone down and having to tell us, and she'd just lost her husband. If the circumstances don't offer an excuse, then her governess-heavy and loveless childhood probably does. Don't shoot the messenger.

Matt stirred his coffee morosely and laid his coffee-wet spoon on the tablecloth rather than his saucer. It made a small sepia stain.

'And then she sent us to bed! No big hug. No togetherness. No detail. Nothing for us to *live* with.'

'She did come into our rooms later,' I ventured, conscious I'd been young enough to be protected from comprehension. I was awake, trying to fix my father into my memory so he would be there for ever, when Mother came in and sat on the edge of my bed. I inched over to the wall to give her more room. What I really wanted was for her to be a real mummy like everyone else's and to get into my bed and sleep there, all night, her body wrapped around mine, comforting me. I knew it wouldn't happen, and I'm not certain I would have known what to do if it had. But you always hope. She didn't, of course. She sat on a corner of my eiderdown and fiddled with my sheets, mumbling about how the bed hadn't been made properly and when was I going to learn how to do hospital corners and, finally, just when I thought she wasn't going to say anything at all about him and I'd almost fallen to sleep, she whispered in a cracked voice,

'Your father was a good man, a kind man, and he loved you all very much. You must never forget that.' She paused, waiting for me to speak but I couldn't because I didn't know what to say. I had a curious feeling she was persuading herself rather than me. I nodded on the pillow. She bent towards me as if about to kiss me, paused, and just patted my shoulder. Then she left, closing the door with a loud click behind her, leaving me prisoner of my memories and fears. That was the click I was reminded of thirty years later as I sat with my memories and fears in the Trinity Road police station, in the room with painted brick walls and industrial piping, a room that, with only a modest leap of imagination and a few more tables, could have been a too-hip-to-handle allotment-to-table restaurant in Shoreditch or Southville.

'She never came into my room.' Matt's face was pale in the artificial light of the dining room, his cigarette-fingers yellowy brown. 'I asked her why she hadn't come in to see me a couple of years ago when Bridgey told me she'd gone in to see her and you.'

'What did she say?'

'That as I was now the head of the household she thought I'd want time and space to get my thoughts together. So she moved my bedroom away from you two and into the graveyard slot at the end of her corridor. As if that would make me an adult!' He looked up desperately. I didn't know it at the time but Matt was only days away from dropping out and beginning the peripatetic and forlorn existence that would wind up in a net-making business in Whitby. 'I was thirteen, for Chrissakes! She gave me nothing to live with. She owed me that at least.'

★ ★ ★

I was on my own in the interview room for twenty minutes before Pullen returned, long enough to count every brick on those retro-industrial walls. I didn't, of course, that sort of thing is for lifers, or people with no interior life. Instead, after remembering the day in Oxford, I covered every moment and movement from the Saturday night Ed went to Pete's party to the Wednesday night of my book club, when he returned from that woman's apartment with, however accidentally or metaphorically, blood on his hands. If we screwed this up, it wouldn't be down to me.

But then, when I'd combed all the events backwards and forwards and sideways like a baldy desperately trying to tease a few sparse hairs across his crown and Pullen still hadn't reappeared, I found myself exploring a different possibility. Maybe that's why they leave you as long as they do, to allow you time to consider all the options. Because suddenly I found myself wondering if we wouldn't be better off if I just came out with it. Why didn't I just explain the

141

whole thing was a terrible accident and we — Ed — hadn't owned up on account of a completely understandable fear no one would believe him? It could only be a couple of years for manslaughter, tops, possibly suspended after a *Les Misérables*-sized chorus queued up to vouch for his good character and insist their lives and cots would have been immeasurably emptier without him. Surely that was better than living forever — FOREVER — in this suffocating atmosphere of lies and fear?

But I couldn't do it. I couldn't go through with it unilaterally. If I sang, that would be it. Our marriage would be over. Whether he got ten months or ten years, Ed would never forgive me. He would never come back. When Ed was set on a course, that was it, nothing could shift him.

There was another reason why I couldn't do it, a bigger and better reason. I couldn't turn him in because I believed him. I trusted him. Whatever did or didn't happen in that flat that night or any other night, I *knew* he didn't murder that woman. Murder requires intent, the mens rea, and there was no way Ed would ever intend to kill someone. No matter how mad or bad the situation, he would never have killed her to save himself. It just wasn't credible. Nothing Pullen or anyone else could say could make me change my mind. And if I believed him, if I believed in him, I had to go through with this. Ed was a man who saved lives. He was a man who gave life, he didn't take it. And they weren't charging him with adultery.

The door opened. DI Pullen was holding a

styro-foam cup of milky tea in one hand and a paper cone filled with water in the other. He didn't apologize for leaving me so long, even after I gave a theatrical glance at my watch. It was important to let him know the innocent don't like having their time wasted. I gave the cone an ironic look — whoever thought that was a sensible design? — and drank it in a single swoop. Another man, not James, had followed Pullen in. He had small black eyes and curly hair over his collar and a moustache which ran under his long thin nose like a water rat. I thought moustaches, like squash players, had run out of road at the end of the 1970s. 'Never trust a man with a moustache,' my mother had said by way of explanation when she sacked the gardener, Oakham, for sleeping with Kelly, the second wife of old Peter, who'd run the village shop and pulled pints part-time in the Leg of Mutton and Cauliflower in the village since my mother was in short skirts.

Pullen perfunctorily introduced the moustache — 'This is Philips' — no rank offered. He wore a grey suit with the widest lapels since Abba won the Eurovision, trousers flaring east-west, and a tight waistcoat, top and bottom buttons undone. A kipper tie with a vast Windsor knot was flying half-mast. Philips nodded but made no attempt to shake my half-proffered hand, which hung momentarily in mid-air, limp and uncertain. The incongruity of his suit and low-slung way he stared at me made me uneasy. This was a man who wouldn't trust his own shadow. Pullen grunted.

'Vending machine.'

'Stay, you get real tea,' Philips added without a flicker of humour.

Pullen sat down opposite me. Philips leant against the wall. I reminded myself these men were capable of putting Ed away for a very long time for a crime he didn't commit. It was essential I focused on that.

Pullen felt in his pocket and pulled out an old-style tape recorder. Was that budget cuts or was he telling me he was an old-style gumshoe, a detective who would nose his way to the truth through thinking about clues, motives, coincidences, without any help from new-fangled technology? He laboriously adjusted the microphone so it was pointing towards me and clicked the recorder to 'record'. He started by repeating the questions he'd asked me at home. Why did I think Ms Lyall had sent Ed flowers?

'I can only assume because my husband had helped her by fixing her plumbing on the morning after he'd stayed at her flat and she was kind enough to thank him with flowers. She didn't need to, he certainly didn't expect it given whatever he did was pretty minor, but it seems she did. I've told you that.'

'Mr Philips would like to hear.'

'I've just told him.'

I didn't mean it to come out quite like that, so arrogant and adversarial, but it was their decision to bring me in.

'If he did so little to deserve the flowers, is it not possible she was thanking him for something else?'

144

I held out my hands. 'You tell me.'

Pullen shuffled his notes and read one of the pages. Philips showed no interest and asked no questions.

'And I'd like you to explain to Mr Philips why you and your husband didn't share the best bit of gossip you'll ever have with any of your friends.'

'We don't do gossip.'

He waited but I didn't offer anything more. The less you said . . . At last Philips spoke.

'Mrs Sheahan, can I take you back to the night Araminta Lyall died?'

He had a Birmingham accent. Maybe he'd been parachuted in to handle a high-profile case that was going nowhere? Those lapels would work well as a parachute.

'Sure.'

'You went to your book club.'

What? How did he know that?

'Um, yes, that's right.'

I tried not to sound flustered.

'And your husband planned a visit to his solicitor.'

Oh my God! They weren't fooling around. My stomach tightened. Had he already spoken to Karen? Or had Ed told him that? Or was he simply showing me that they knew more than I realized. For just a moment I couldn't even remember whether I was supposed to know he had told that lie at work. Fortunately our story flooded back like revision in an exam.

'That's right.'

'But he didn't go.'

145

'No.'

'Where did he go?'

'Brandon Hill.'

'Does he often go there during work hours?'

'No.'

'Why that day?'

'He'd booked an early afternoon at the hospital but forgotten to book the solicitor's appointment. So rather than not take the time off, because he works so hard an early afternoon is a rare bird, he thought he'd go and sit in the sunshine on Brandon Hill for a while, just to chill out.'

Philips listened with the air of a man who knows the answer before he receives it.

'He was alone?'

'No. I joined him there.'

'At what time?'

'Five thirty, maybe six. After I had picked up my son from a birthday party in St Werburghs. You can check.'

'We will. And stayed until . . . '

'I guess about sevenish. Then we went home to give the children tea before I walked to book club.'

'Which way did you go home?'

'Jacobs Wells Road, Constitution Hill, Goldney . . . '

Philips mumbled unintelligibly.

'Sorry?'

He walked over to the table with a wide, bandy-legged sort of slouch, balled his fists and put his knuckles on the table, his face close to mine.

'I said, 'That's lucky.''

He smelt of cheap aftershave and tobacco and his Chi-Lites suit was made of lab-fabric. His closeness annoyed me. It was intimidation.

'How so?'

'No CCTV.'

'I'm not with you.'

'No proof you were there.'

'I'd say that was unlucky.'

'For us?'

'For us.'

He stared at me for a moment, close-up, shark-eyed. Then he pulled away and said,

'How did he let you know he was there?' He looked up at a pipe. 'Phone you from work?'

I was about to nod when Ed's words about calls being logged and checkable came back to me. Leading question.

'No. He remembered at breakfast he'd forgotten to book the solicitor. As it was shaping up to be a lovely day we decided then and there to forget the solicitor and take the time for ourselves. You don't get that much when you have children.'

'And who did you see on Brandon Hill?'

'No one in particular.'

'Anyone you knew?'

'No.'

'Sure?'

I was about to reply 'Yes' when something made me pause. Had we seen anyone we knew? Obviously not, given we hadn't been there. But why had he asked the question? Had Ed said we had? Why would he? He wouldn't. Then why was

147

Philips looking at me like that? Because he was bluffing. Maybe Ed had said we had without realizing I was here and thought he could square it with me tonight? My tongue felt dry and furry. There was no choice. I had to go with the obvious.

'I'm sure.'

He ran a stubby finger around his mouth. As the nano-seconds mounted, I realized I'd got it right. To stop myself high-fiving Pullen, I added,

'There were lots of people around because it was a sunny evening, but no one we knew.'

'Which bench did you sit on?'

My elation inverted instantaneously. Philips could ask questions for as long as I could answer them, and then some. I felt a prickly heat on my neck. Where were the benches anyway on Brandon Hill? Which one would Ed have said? Why-oh-why hadn't I stuck to Sion Hill? That was the only truth I had. I tried to disguise my mounting panic.

'We sat on the grass.'

'Even though your husband was in a suit?'

In the early days in Bristol, when we lived in Ambra Vale, I sometimes brought the children to meet him after work on Brandon Hill. I'd always bring a rug.

'I'd brought a rug.'

'Did you have a picnic?'

Pause. What would he say? Surely he'd know I'd eat at book club. And six thirty was too early anyway.

'No.'

'Ice cream?'

Christ! He'd be asking which way the flake was pointing in a second. Tiny tears pricked my eyes.

'No.'

'Was the ice cream van there?'

'Not so as I noticed.'

'I thought artists noticed everything. Aren't they supposed to have better powers of observation than the rest of us?'

'I find I notice ice cream vans more when I'm with my children.'

Philips ignored the diversion.

'What did you talk about?'

'This and that. The usual. I don't think we talked that much. Just lay there and enjoyed the sun.'

'What's 'the usual'?'

'Oh, children, school, where we might go on holiday, admin. Stuff.'

'Very romantic.'

'We try.'

'Was someone cutting the grass?'

'Didn't see anyone.'

'Hear a mower? A busy bee? They can be quite loud.'

'Not so as I remember.'

'You don't seem to remember much, if I might say so, Mrs Sheahan.'

'Look, until an hour ago it was a normal day, totally indistinguishable from all the others. Nothing happened. I've been to Brandon Hill hundreds of times. I couldn't tell you what I had for breakfast on any of those other days either.'

'You could try.'

I gave Philips an assertive look. It said: I'm a busy and innocent woman and I want to get this over and done with as quickly as possible, so I can go home and you can get on with what you are supposed to be doing, which is catching criminals, not hassling innocent(ish) people with smart-arse comments.

'What were you wearing?'

'Not sure. Jeans. Espadrilles maybe. A shirt.'

'A shirt? Hold the front page!'

'I mean not a dress.'

'Which shirt?'

'Jesus! I don't know.'

'Please try to remember, Mrs Sheahan.'

'I'm sorry. I am trying. I'm just not very good at this.'

'That's what everyone says until they really try.'

I turned away and glared at the wall. See, I am REALLY TRYING. I'd worn a thin-cord shirt to the book club.

'A khaki shirt? Corduroy?'

Philips sniffed unpleasantly and took a mini digital tape recorder from his pocket. It was a long way from Pullen's. He stopped and started it a few times before finding the spot he was after. He clicked it on: an unknown voice.

'And what was your wife wearing?'

'An old green tracksuit top with black stripes on the arms. Jeans. She'd come straight from her studio.'

'You sure?'

'Yes.' There was no doubt in Ed's voice.

He clicked it off and looked at me. I was

thinking how impressively assured Ed sounded. I would have believed him.

'So what? I said I couldn't remember. Can you remember what you were wearing on a particular day three weeks ago?'

'Yes.'

'That suit?'

Philips nodded. I smiled. I would remember if I was wearing that. He took a pack of Marlboro from his breast pocket and tapped the bottom with his fore-finger. A cigarette fell out. I looked from Pullen to the 'No Smoking' sticker on the door. He shrugged. Philips produced a plastic lighter, nudged his styrofoam cup into position to use as an ashtray, lit the cigarette, took a satisfied pull and blew a bully's smoke ring. I shook my head contemptuously. It was exactly how Matt said the Oxford police had behaved when they first pulled him in for drugs. It only made me more determined. Philips flicked ash into his empty cup.

'Mrs Sheahan, has your husband ever had an affair?'

'No.'

'You seem very sure.'

'I am.'

'How?'

'I know him.'

'I knew my wife until she left me.'

'An easy line.'

'That she left me?'

'That you knew her.'

It was essential to show no fear.

'How did you and Mr Sheahan meet?'

151

'At a party.'

'He get drunk that night?'

'On Pepsi?'

'He didn't need to, of course.'

I looked at Pullen. 'Is waterboarding allowed?'

No answer. Philips raised an eyebrow at Pullen as if to say he could be tempted.

'So he doesn't have affairs, as far as you know, but he does have a history of following women he meets at parties.'

'A woman. Once.'

'Once. One fact. And one supposition based on previous behaviour.'

'A supposition.'

'At present.'

'Mr Philips, my husband is one of the most remarkable men I have ever met. He doesn't deal in bullshit or snobbery or politics. He doesn't want to chase a girl home from a party, whether I'm there or not, whether he's drunk or drinking Pepsi. He never has. It's not his style. I know him and I know that.'

'Present company excepted.'

'Present company excepted. Only he didn't have a family then.'

'He didn't have a family then.' The words lingered in the air like smoke. 'Or a good name he might want to protect.'

I thought of his parents' house, his tiny bedroom, the horsehair mattress, sheets as thick as curtains. A room filled with work and ambition.

'He's not interested in baubles.'

Philips smiled for the first time, mean and professional.

'End of, Mrs Sheahan. You are free to go.'

He turned around and without another word swept out of the room. I looked at Pullen for confirmation. He shrugged, jerked his head towards the open door and grunted, 'For now.'

10

It was because I was looking in my handbag for money to pay the cab driver that I didn't spot the small crowd milling around on the pavement outside our iron gate. Having got out the far side and been faffing around with my purse and trying to find the right coins for a tip, I only saw the hounds from hell when the creaking taxi-van swung around and swept off down the hill. Someone shouted,

'Over there!'

Before I could take in what was happening, the swarm had crossed the street and I was surrounded, camera lenses and microphones shoved in front of me, a furry boom riding high, an elbow in my ribs, voices rising, climbing over each other, the modern press-gang. There were probably only four or five of them, but my surprise and their aggression made it seem like more.

'Did you kill her?'

'Did your husband murder Araminta Lyall?'

'Mrs Sheahan, what are they charging you with?'

'Alice — will your husband get bail?'

I was shaking my head, eyes fixed on the tarmac, thinking there must be a law against this sort of thing and pushing to get across the road to the sanctuary of the garden and the house. Flashbulbs popped. Questions rattled. A microphone hit my shoulder. A grunted apology, another breathless question. Yet I had a weird feeling of being in control, because even as they swarmed around me, hemming me in and jostling, I wasn't physically impeded. I struggled on towards the gate as if it was a dream.

'Is your husband still being questioned?'

'Do you have to go back?'

'Are you on bail?'

I turned and gave the questioner a contemptuous look. A flashbulb exploded in my face.

'Alice — this way.'

A female voice, warm and welcoming. I looked up for the first time. A lady in her early twenties with dyed-blonde hair, a soft round face and an upturned nose was holding a notebook, her pen poised. For some reason she seemed old-fashioned, out of place amidst the hard-edged microphones and dead-eyed cameras. She was smaller than me, looking up, a friendly face in the pack. I rolled my eyes as if to say 'What on earth are you and I doing here?' She rolled hers back sympathetically, shook her head and said,

'Why did you do it?'

I stopped. The swarm stopped. The assumption of guilt caused a momentary silence, as if some ancient omertà had been broken and even the press-dogs of war shied away from anything so explicit. Even though I knew I shouldn't respond, just press on, her question crystallized all the feelings of betrayal and terror that I had carried around from the moment I realized ML xxx was Araminta Lyall. I couldn't help myself. I stopped and said,

'What did you say?'

The round face continued smiling equably and said calmly,

'Why did you do it?'

Suddenly it seemed as if everything had been leading to this moment — the discovery, the uncertainty, the fear, the shock, the secret, the lie, the confession, the tension, the unfairness, the inescapability, the infinity of the situation in which I found myself — and the dam burst. I broke the first rule of being hounded by the press: I allowed them to unsettle me. I screamed,

'How fucking dare you? You've never met me or my husband and yet you stand there and make arrogant assumptions and false accusations about us just to sell your crappy paper. I hate you. You're despicable. You're all just scum, ruining people's lives!'

There was silence. Was it my imagination or did the crowd silently part, like the Red Sea for Moses, embarrassed by its very existence? I pushed on past them, my head down. No one followed. It was only when I had closed the front door behind me and leant against the cool silent wall in the hallway that I realized there might have been another reason the scrum had stepped aside to let me through: everyone had got their story.

★ ★ ★

Ed clicked the television off as the screen switched back from our street to the anchor-woman on the local six o'clock news, a large picture of the Ashton Court Balloon Festival

156

filling the wall behind her.

'Possibly that wasn't a good idea,' he said with a ghost of a smile. He had arrived back half an hour after me, barely a hair out of place, the hounds long gone to file their stories. The telephone burst into life. 'Don't answer it. I think we may have done enough damage for one day.'

★   ★   ★

After we had explained the concept of 'mistaken identity' to Nell and Arthur, who wanted to know so many gory details it was possible he hoped we were murderers, I phoned my mother. She was surprisingly cool about it, primarily because she'd loathed the press since Dad died. She wouldn't even let the local newspaper take photos when we hosted the village fete at Highlands each year. It must have been the only fete in the country that didn't have a picture of a child beside a giant marrow or a policeman eating an ice cream or a baby or a dog being adorable.

Ed gave an extraordinary performance. Whereas I was a nervous wreck, unwilling to go near the windows because I was convinced paparazzi lenses were trained on us and bugs were in every bookcase and vase, he seemed entirely unfazed, though he turned on a tap to be safe, even as he laughed at my paranoia. We'd dovetailed on the flowers, Ed saying he'd fixed that woman's loo — 'house pipes are basically the same as human pipes' — and had been surprised to hear she had left flowers as it had only taken him a minute or so. 'A very straightforward procedure', he'd called it.

He did admit he was shocked, though he hoped he hadn't shown it, that the police had found out about them and admitted he couldn't work it out. The difference between what I said I was wearing and what he said I was wearing on Brandon Hill he'd simply laughed off — 'Alice is an artist. She lives in her head.' He then told me where we were on Brandon Hill and that he would always answer 'didn't notice' to any question he could.

'Was there an ice cream van? Didn't notice.'

'Was there someone mowing the grass? Didn't notice.'

'Were there people on the swings? Didn't notice.'

'You don't notice much, Mr Sheahan.'

'No. I was having a rare moment of peace and quiet with my wife. I wanted to feel the sun on my face. When I wasn't staring at the sky, my eyes were closed.'

'They're after the oyster,' he said, offering an out-of-character metaphor, 'give them the grit.'

He crossed the room to where I sat unhappily at the island and touched my cheek with the back of a finger.

'Would you like me to speak to the press on your behalf, my darling? I could make some sort of statement? It was completely outrageous the way they treated you.'

I shook my head, there was no point fanning the flames, and snuggled into the crook of his neck. At that moment he seemed so strong and brave and protective that I loved him completely.

There is something out-of-body about watching yourself on TV, particularly when you're surrounded by the press as if you were David Beckham or the Yorkshire Ripper. I watched *News at Ten* with guilty fascination, simultaneously knowing what was about to happen yet unable to believe it actually would. The moment arrived: the round-faced young girl, the outrageous slur, the sudden silence, an expensive accent, bleeped expletives. Infamy. I had almost reached the pavement. There'd only been five more yards to the gate.

I switched it off the moment 'my' item finished. I hadn't got the stomach for any other news. I felt cold and exposed, like a roll of film. This was how it would be to the power of ten if Ed was charged. I would be dragged out from the darkness behind the easel to become the sitter, the lab-rat under the microscope. But who would be painting my portrait? No one who was trying to understand me. There wouldn't be any truth in it. When is a portrait not a portrait? When it's a picture painted by someone who isn't trying to understand. When it's a picture painted by someone who doesn't know you.

I glided over to the island where Nell's laptop was charging and sparked it up. While it creaked into life, I opened a bottle of Pouilly Fuissé Ed had been given by some grateful new parent and poured myself a tumbler. The wine was delicious. It sluiced through my insides as I typed 'alice sheahan' into Google and a fanfare of references lurched into life. Might as well start at the bottom. I clicked on to the *Daily Mail* website.

They hadn't let their readers down. Under the heading 'Society Painter in Murder Investigation' there was a large picture of me haranguing round-face and an opening paragraph shoehorning everything the paper and its readers held dear into a single sentence: 'Alice Sheahan, the Cambridge-educated society portraitist, was involved in an extraordinary outburst today after helping the police with their inquiries into the death of the heiress Araminta Lyall, daughter of business tycoon Sir Rudolph Lyall, who was found murdered in her flat on Stokes Croft in the Montpelier district of Bristol last month.' Immediately below this ridiculous sentence was a video opportunity to watch me exploding. My cursor hovered momentarily above the 'start' triangle before scrolling past. There's only so much fame you can take.

The 'story' had nothing to say but said it at length. It namechecked my Great-Uncle Oliver, who had been i/c paperclips in some pre-war government, the Querry family firm (long since sold), Tenterden Naseby, the city broker started by my grandfather, Ed's professional rosettes, meaningless quotes about us from unnamed 'friends', a map of Bristol with arrows pointing to Clifton and Stokes Croft, an OS ruler emphasizing the mile or so between them, photos of Ed and me, his from the St Anthony's website, mine from God knows where, the tired old picture of that woman at the Dering Street party, and the Carriage Works apartment block, described gleefully as 'the murder scene'. It concluded that this could be a Lord Lucan-sized story of murder amongst the privileged classes that could add greatly to the gaiety of the nation and profits of newspapers while destroying the lives of participants and bystanders in some style.

I scrolled down to the blogged responses below the article. Fatal. First refuge of the time-rich and perspective-poor. In the old days they just shouted at the telly. Now they have a platform for their bile. @Drizzlybriton reckoned I was 'a stuck-up bitch who is definitely guilty'. Obviously they're entitled to their view, though why anyone would want to share an uninformed opinion on someone they've never met with lots of people they will never meet is beyond me. Maybe Nell would know. 'What is it with the rich', wondered #modernman, 'means they think they can do whatever they want?' I flicked through them quickly to see how many comments there were — twelve, plus a couple deleted, presumably too rude to publish on a 'family' website. Only one took my side, berating the press invasion even as he or she hitched a ride on it. Eleven to one. Convicted.

A tear formed. That's not how it was. How would these people like to be pushed and shoved and turned into public property just because their husband had combined bad luck and bad judgement to an unprecedented degree? I clicked on to another site. I didn't want to but it was weirdly compelling. For the first time I understood why people who were being bullied on social networks felt compelled to read on. Who were these people? How unhappy must they be that they had to sound off about everything from my looks to my presumed guilt to, in one instance, what he (or she?) would do to me, a punishment the law courts were not empowered to give and which suggested he/she had wound up on the wrong website.

By the time I'd finished, tears were careering down my cheeks, of a size and saltiness I hadn't tasted since my father died. They weren't tears of self-pity, though I could justify it if they were; they were bigger tears for a new world in which I found myself, one I was no longer sure I under-stood, which seemed too complex, too violent and interconnected, one without boundaries, one in which everything I had been taught or encour-aged to hold as true counted for nothing. Everyone had a voice now, and how ugly and vicious they sounded when they all shouted together.

I shut down the computer and climbed the stairs to our bedroom. Ed was asleep, breathing smoothly. The bedside lamp was still on, a copy of last week's *The Week* on the duvet as if he had fallen asleep mid-sentence. I got into bed. I hadn't the energy to clean my teeth. I needed to put my arms around an offline human being. I needed to reclaim myself and the only way to do that was to try to reclaim our love, to try to return to a green and innocent world, the way it was before this had happened. I touched Ed. I ran a finger in slow rhythmic circles down his back, his bottom, his thigh, his knee. He slept, he stirred, he mumbled. I continued, my finger describing looping patterns on his stomach, homing in, my hand gliding imperceptibly along his flesh as he grunted in a lazy male way and slowly awoke and turned towards me, pleasure cracking his face as I wondered whether even perfect intimacy could soothe the pain and loneliness I was feeling inside.

★ ★ ★

'Ed?'
  'Mmm.'
  'You awake?'
  'No.'
  'I can't sleep.'
  'Mmm.'
  'I've been awake since one.'
  'Love you . . . '
  'I'm frightened.'
  'Uh-huh.'
  'They're getting close.'
  'OK.'
  'Everyone is on to us — the websites, the police, probably even Julian.'
  'Don't worry. They haven't got anything.'
  'But what if they have?'
  'They haven't. They were fishing.'
  'That's not what the trolls think.'
  'The trolls don't think.'
  'I can't think about anything else.'
  'If they had anything they wouldn't have let us go.'
  'If they didn't have anything they wouldn't have taken us in.'
  'Pretend it didn't happen.'

163

'But it did.'

'We've just got to stay calm.'

'This sort of thing doesn't happen to people like us.'

'It won't.'

'But . . . ?'

'We'll get there.'

'What if it's too late?'

'If what's too late?'

'If there's no there there.'

'What do you mean?'

'Ed, I'm frightened I won't ever be able to paint again.'

'Why shouldn't you be able to?'

'Because I've become the subject.'

★ ★ ★

At breakfast, Ed was his usual businesslike self. He ate muesli with Greek yoghurt, a piece of dry toast with Marmite and swallowed a mug of tea and a beaker of orange juice he machine-squeezed himself. He asked about my plans for the day, if Arthur was in a cricket match and hoped Nell had done her Science prep. There was nothing in his demeanour to suggest that less than twenty-four hours earlier two men had knocked on his office door shortly before he was due to head off to London for a memorial service and the taller had said: 'Mr Sheahan, please could we have a word.' There had been no question mark, no choice, just the gun-barrel flash of a police badge cupped in a palm catching the overhead light.

In his only concession to the scrum the day before, he left via the back gate, walking down the overgrown path behind the crescent to the river. He needn't have bothered: news moves faster than a fox and the hounds were already hunting elsewhere.

After he'd gone, I looked at Nell and Arthur silently eating their Cheerios, Arthur reading the back of the packet, Nell memorizing French verbs. It was impossible to know how yesterday would affect them or even how much they would know. They had still been at school when I was press-ganged and we had made sure they hadn't seen the news. That wasn't hard. Their interest in current affairs is silicon-chip thin. The danger lay in what other children had seen, or what their parents had told them. I was reasonably confident their friends' interest in the news was as vigorous as Nell's and Arthur's, but what about the Internet? No one could control that Hydra and, whatever I might hope or believe, it was inconceivable someone somewhere — an older sibling, a random surfer — would not chance upon my name or a link. I shuddered. Please God, don't let either of them see the comments beneath the clips.

And suddenly I realized I couldn't face the outside world, not yet, and I certainly couldn't face the crucible of gossip and innuendo that is the school playground, which meant there was no alternative but to ask Bea to take the children to school again. Bea who, being Bea, would definitely have seen the news, the links, the videos, the comments and who also, being Bea, would let me know she had through the silent generosity of her help. Plan Bea. She was always there when there was no alternative. I reached for the phone. It was answered immediately, as if she had been waiting for the call. Her voice sprang into action, the anticipation of meeting the star of News at Ten offering greater pleasure than a brand-new pair of Air-Nikes. When she came to pick up Nell and Arthur she patted them on the head as they passed her at the gate, almost as if she was counting them out — any other dead bodies in there? — gave a cartoon grimace of support and hissed, 'They're no better than animals, those people.' I nodded and murmured, 'Thank you', but I was thinking that if I wanted orchestral sympathy or to be looked at like a specimen in a jar I could have dropped them at school myself.

★ ★ ★

I don't know how long I sat in my studio. I couldn't work, or read, or do anything at all except stare at the wall and the resting canvases stacked against it and wonder how or if I would ever recover the objectivity required for portraiture. All the tricks I used for concentration whenever things were tough proved hopeless. I was the one blinded by the light. If you cannot see, you cannot paint. But if I couldn't paint I couldn't live. There was no way to square the circle.

I could see how much had changed. There had been occasions — not many, but more than once

— when I had to be called by the school because I was so engrossed in a painting I had forgotten to pick up the children. Having received the call from the trying-not-to-sound-irritated duty master, who no doubt assumed I was shopping or lunching, maybe playing tennis or had stayed too long in the gym, I sheepishly had to collect them from the man himself, feeling like a naughty schoolgirl. Nell's and Arthur's expressions asking, 'Why can't you be on time like everyone else's mum?' or, more likely, 'Why can't you be like everyone else's mum?' or even, on a really late one, 'Why can't we have someone else's mum?'

In the end the silence and inactivity and smell of defeat in the studio were broken by my mobile. Even though it was on the metal trolley beside me it took me a few moments to register it was ringing. I clicked it on and grunted. An unknown voice, as haughty as a national institution actress playing a salty-tongued matriarch, said 'Alice Sheahan?'

The voice belonged to Chrissie Wright, PA to someone who, for reasons Chrissie didn't wish to elaborate, preferred to remain anonymous but would like me to paint their portrait in early July. It was, I hoped, what I needed to get me going again. After an impressive amount of cross-referencing and diarizing and conference-call-style clarification we agreed a date.

Chrissie's refusal to divulge the sitter's name didn't bother me. Pre-portrait secrecy didn't happen often but it wasn't entirely unknown. It was usually employed by men who were rather less famous than they thought, sunset actors, fading politicians, CEOs who wanted to impress. Women were different. They instinctively under-stood the emotional negotiation in a portrait so they actively wanted to meet you. They wanted to befriend you. Ironically, on the rare occasions some self-important minor celebrity had refused to reveal his identity it had proved a bonus as it gave me an angle to take into the first meeting, one that wasn't necessarily to his advantage.

The bigger problem was my inability to meet the sitter at all before we started. Chrissie's boss was in the US for a week, back home 'but completely hectic' for a short period, and off again on a quickfire tour of the skittle-cities of the Gulf. My suggestion that we meet, however briefly, wherever, was brushed aside. Yet the pre-portrait meeting is essential. It's amazing how much you learn, even if only over a cup of coffee. Simply where the sitter chooses to meet reveals so much. Do they want to come to my studio, meet on neutral ground, or on their home turf? If the latter, which is normally the case, given it allows them to feel in control of a project that is essentially out of their control — not a situation they are used to or comfortable in — do they want to meet formally in their office or less formally at home? Do they stand while you sit? How do they treat their kids or the cleaner? People assume the sitter will be wary, showing their best side like a teenager on Facebook. Yet aspects of their character will shine through, often *because* they are on guard. That wasn't going to apply here. I just had to hope that staying at the sitter's home during the sitting, as Chrissie had suggested, would allow me time to take what I needed for the portrait. If not, it could affect the psychological realism of the finished work. I wasn't sure what I would do if that did happen, because even if no one else noticed, I would, and I was my own sternest critic. I had to be. It was my reputation, not the sitter's, on the line.

So I ran a finger down the cement-coloured spine of a concrete-block-sized tome on Oscar Niemeyer, glanced at the postcard of the Sagrada Família Ed had sent me from a gynaecological conference in Barcelona (how long did it take you to choose that image, Mr S?) and said,

'You do appreciate that not meeting the sitter beforehand can have an effect on the final portrait in terms of my understanding and representation of the subject?'

I expected Chrissie to reply along the lines of she was very sorry but it simply couldn't be helped, she was sure I'd be able to pull it off, but the weird thing was she appeared not to care whether the portrait would be affected or not.

11

'I thought you didn't believe in full-on abstracts. I thought you said there always had to be some figurative element.'

Ed stood in my studio looking at a small all-black canvas sitting on the easel. He was in his suit, erect and professional, silhouetted against the open window. The air was hot, as thick as paint. He rarely came up to my studio, any more than I went to St Anthony's. We respected each other's workspace and I think, just then, he realized I needed my own space more than ever. I was perched uncomfortably at one end of the chaise longue.

'I don't believe in them.'

'An escape?'

He moved across to the paint-spattered table and leant against it, having wiped a finger across the edge to check the paint was dry. He was wearing an ochre-lined sharply tailored narrow-lapelled herringbone suit and a cerulean shirt, open at the neck. He moved smoothly, the regular tennis player, retriever of lost causes. Ed hadn't put on any weight in the last few weeks, or lost any. When he shot his cuffs, gold monogrammed cufflinks glinted at his wrists. I gave them to him when we got engaged. Momentarily, I glimpsed the man from years before, the handsome young doctor in a rented morning coat and golden cufflinks turning from the altar towards his veiled bride as she glanced nervously at the man walking up the aisle beside her, at her brother's pale brow, his drenched grey collar, and I feared my love for him had changed. My desire to paint had changed. Yet standing in my studio, Ed looked as if nothing had happened to disturb the rhythm of his life from his wedding day forward. I guess if you spend your days working with life and death you learn how to move on, to shut down anything that might distract from the task at hand. Even so, Ed's capacity to compartmentalize was awe-inspiring. I said,

'There's no escape.'

A streak of remorse flashed across his face. He wasn't as strong as he gave off. The appearance of strength was for my benefit. He took two large steps across the room and sat down beside me on the chaise longue, twitching his suit at the knee to ensure he didn't crease it. He put his hand in my hair and started to stroke my head, up and down, running the back of his fingers around the nape of my neck. They were cold and I was conscious of their strength despite his gentle touch. He didn't speak for a long time, just ran his fingers contemplatively around the side of my throat. I waited. There had been times before the children when we'd made love in my studio, my fingers teasing Ed out of his suit, his unpeeling my jeans, popping the buttons on my dungarees, sliding my belt out like a train, but this mood was different. Having taken the decision not to give himself up it was too late to go back on it. Manslaughter was no longer an option. This was what living with it would be like.

'Darling, I am really sorry about this and believe me I understand what you are going through. But everything will be all right just as long as we keep our cool. I promise. They're shooting at shadows. If they had anything on us at all, they wouldn't have let us go so easily.'

'Easily? Honestly, I don't know how you manage to stay calm. I'm being eaten up inside. I'm frightened to go out. I can't work. This whole thing, what it means, not just what might happen, it's hanging over me like . . . I don't know . . . but I've got three portraits lined up and with the state I'm in I won't be able to do any of them.'

He took my hand.

'You have to try not to think about it. Because there's nothing we can do, except wait.'

'I can't just not think about it. *It* exists. It's a physical thing.'

'Think of it as a science, not an art.'

'That doesn't mean anything to me.'

'IQ not EQ. Try to think logically, not emotionally. We've got this far. If we can survive a few more weeks, the heat will die down, the police will lose heart, other crimes will be committed and one day they'll announce they're winding down this investigation. There's plenty of scope for them to decide it was an accident. She slipped, she tripped, she didn't take the drugs, she took too many drugs — boom, we're in the clear. Life will go on as it always did.'

I twisted my hand out of his, feeling his

reluctance to let go.

'Sometimes I could hit you you're so fucking rational.'

'It's the way it is.'

'No. It's the way you are. 'It' is infinite and out of our control.'

'Darling, there's nothing we can do except sit tight and ride out the storm.'

'It's also a question of what's right and what's wrong.'

Ed picked up my hand again and studied it as if he was trying to see the world as a portrait painter.

'You know, in medicine sometimes there is no right and wrong. Sometimes there's no possibility of a perfect outcome. Things happen that are beyond anyone's control. As a doctor one sometimes takes decisions and then just hopes for the best. Sometimes you get lucky, but sometimes . . . It's all about getting the best *possible* outcome, because the situation is such that perfection is not a realistic outcome. Humanity isn't perfect. Life isn't perfect. You have to learn to live with that.'

'I guess that's the difference between us. I believe in aiming for perfection, trying to grasp that underlying truth. I may never get there, but I know it's out there, that perfect colour, the perfect composition, the perfect insight that ties it all together, and I always shoot for it.'

'Which probably guarantees disappointment or failure.'

He was right, of course, as per, and in a single sentence had explained perfectly why so many

173

artists are crushed by life. But it was a depressing line, an acceptance of fate, of second best, an idea I would fight all my life to refute.

'At least my way it's a glorious failure. At least there is hope. I will always have the knowledge I shot for the sun. That's how things improve.'

Ed nodded thoughtfully. I pulled my hand away. I could tell he didn't agree but he wanted to humour me because he could sense my fragility. You couldn't fault him as a husband — in that way. Wednesday had burned me far more than it had affected him, yet I had to be strong if we were going to survive. He said gently,

'We have to live in this world.'

'Which doesn't make it any easier to take.'

'You'll go mad if you spend your life trying to make it something else.'

'I feel I'm being squeezed out of shape.'

'Darling, you have to remember we're doing this for the children. We mustn't let this appalling accident ruin their lives. I won't pretend it's easy for either of us living like this and if I could apologize enough or turn back the clock or do anything to make it up to you, I would, you know that. But I can't, and that's why you need to keep yourself occupied right now. It's the only way we're going to get through.'

I knew he was genuine. If he could have done anything to reverse time he would have, but I was suffocated by the oppressive heat in the room and our situation. I no longer felt in control of my own life and there was nothing he

174

could do to change that. I wasn't even sure if I was going to be able to go on doing what I had always wanted to do — to hear people's stories, to analyse and understand them, to paint their portraits. A lump formed in my throat. I couldn't hide it. Ed wrapped a broad arm around my shoulder and kissed me softly, affectionately, encouragingly on the cheek. I didn't move.

'Nothing lasts forever, my darling. But remember, when you feel unhappy, we're in this together, all of us. Be strong.'

The sun was sinking into Ashton Court, ducking into the trees, stretching the shadows. I glanced at his hand on my arm and shook involuntarily. My skin had goose pimples. Ed didn't say anything. He had strong hands, surgeon's hands, a life-giver's hands. A life-taker's hands.

* * *

On Saturday afternoon I took an old tartan rug on to the lawn to lie like a cat in the sun. Ed was on call and had been called, Nell had gone to meet a friend for strawberry milkshakes in the village and Arthur was high in the house building a jet engine out of moulded plastic. He didn't like the sun. I had tried to find things to do around the house, and had even gone up to my studio, but I was too listless and couldn't concentrate. The only benefit of not knowing who was sitting for my new portrait was I didn't have to do any research or even think about it, which may have been just as well. So I decided not to fight the frustration and prickliness I felt simply by being in my studio, but to go outside to sunbathe and try to relax under that great azure bowl of a sky. I picked up *Franny and Zooey*, which I had to re-read for book club, and took it into the garden with a tall lemonade, the ice crackling in the glass and sticking together like lashed barrels at sea. The grass was turning brown, victim of the recent dry weather and the cowboys who laid our lawn without digging deep enough to lay sufficient soil. They cut so many corners our slim rectangle might as well have been octagonal.

I had scarcely settled when the doorbell rang at the front of the house. I toyed with not answering — who comes to the front door mid-afternoon on a scorching Saturday? Evangelical Christians? Window cleaners touting for business? — but I knew Arthur wouldn't budge from his bedroom. In case it was Amazon (Arthur's birthday was hoving into view) I put down Salinger, pushed my sunglasses on to my forehead and dragged myself up and through the house, plunging into darkness and back into light as I opened the front door into the squinting sunshine.

Philips. No rank known.

He stood quite still in a prune chunky-collared shirt, three buttons undone, and a copper-coloured leather jacket with a stretchy waist. His chest was frothy with hair. The fat brass buckle of his leather belt shone in the sun. Standing there in too-tight jeans and cowboy boots with vertical calligraphy he looked less like an extra

176

from *Starsky & Hutch* than a midnight cowboy. He should have packed a piece in a shoulder-holster. Instead his mobile was in a dinky little pouch attached to his belt, which made him look as threatening as a tennis umpire. Nevertheless, I felt a spasm of fear and tried to switch my brain into gear.

'Mrs Sheahan, I'm sorry to bother you on a Saturday. May I come in?'

That Brummie accent. He didn't look sorry. I didn't reply. I wanted him to know that if I genuinely had any choice the door would be shut in his face. He, or one of his leaky colleagues, no doubt taking baksheesh from the press, was directly responsible for what had happened to me in the road three days before. His antennae were fizzing, I'll give him that.

'Look, I'm sorry about what happened on Wednesday. It shouldn't've. I don't know who told them.'

I let a long pause develop before, wordlessly, I stood aside. He nodded and brushed past me into the house, turning right into the kitchen as if he'd been directed. I didn't offer him anything but just watched from the doorway, my mind working overtime, while he slowly looked around the room before moving over to the island and perching on a stool. He lifted his left leg across his right knee and picked at some imaginary dirt where the spurs should have been on his boot.

'Nice place.'

I didn't answer. I had no desire to spend my Saturday making small talk with someone who'd given me the third degree earlier in the week. He nodded towards the other stool. I paused a fraction of a second, to make the point I didn't quite trust him, before moving over and pulling it out. My obvious disdain snapped him on to business.

'OK, Mrs Sheahan, I'll get straight to the point: what would you say if I said your husband was seen leaving Montpelier in the early evening on the night of the murder?'

Time stopped. Philips's eyes cut into me and I was conscious my jaw had slackened and my mouth stopped working. It might be a trick question. I had to play it straight, just stick to the story. I shrugged. The movement released my tongue.

'I'd say it's not possible. At least during the time I was with him. Then he was at home with the children. He was still here when I got back from book club.'

'And what time did you say he got to Brandon Hill?'

'Wouldn't it be better to ask him?'

'I'm asking you.'

'I dunno. Four thirty?'

'And you joined him at?'

'At five thirty, six?'

'So he could have been seen leaving Montpelier on foot at, say, five o'clock?'

'Not if he was on Brandon Hill.'

'*If* he was on Brandon Hill.'

I gave a theatrical cough to show I was trying to keep the irritation out of my voice.

'I thought we'd been through all this.'

Philips shifted on his stool. There was a glitter

of gold from his necklace.

'And after he got home, he didn't go out again?'

'No.'

'Not to get milk? A beer?'

'He doesn't drink.'

'Of course he doesn't. Milk then.'

'No.'

'But you weren't here.'

'The children would have told me.'

'That he went to buy milk?'

'That he went out.'

'What if it was after they went to bed?'

'I thought you said early evening? Nell doesn't go to bed until ten-ish, and Arthur was awake when I got home. Wasn't the girl murdered around six?'

'That's the theory. And that's when he was seen on Stokes Croft. Does that sound like a coincidence?'

'It sounds like mistaken identity.'

'Mrs Sheahan, I only have your word he was on Brandon Hill. What would you say if I said the person who says they saw him knows you well?'

'I'd say the person doesn't know us as well as they think they do if they seriously believe my husband is a murderer.'

I felt a surge of hope. He didn't have the killer Q. If he did he would have turned up formally, with warrant and handcuffs, not sidled in to ask a favour on a Saturday afternoon.

'So you don't accept any possibility of this having happened?'

'Nope. I don't suppose I'm allowed to ask who . . .'

'You can always ask.'

Philips enjoyed his power. His badge meant he could go anywhere, ask anything, confront anyone, and answer nothing. His eyes swept confidently around the room, the renegade cop in his very own feature film. He'd washed his hair. It bushed over his collar.

'Have you been to see my husband?'

'A colleague . . .' he tailed off deliberately.

'So you thought you'd come round here and see if you could trick or bully me into confessing to something that never happened?'

He stared at me. I held his stare, giving as good as I got.

'I came to ask — '

'And you've asked. And the answer hasn't changed.' I felt a Mother-like hauteur creeping into my tone. 'Is there anything else I can do for you today, officer?'

'Are either of your children here?'

'Arthur's upstairs.'

'Could I have a quick word with him?'

I made to go to get him but he raised an arm.

'Could you just call him, please?'

I stood at the bottom of the stairs and called, more than once. Eventually Arthur appeared, dishevelled, holding a magic wand, at first bewildered then delighted to be questioned by a real detective in plain clothes with a real badge. How cool was that? Not that there was anything plain about Philips's get-up. He could only have gone undercover in Studio 54. Arthur listened carefully and tried to look as grown-up as it is possible to look in cut-off jeans and a Futurama T-shirt, pipe-cleaner arms poking out of the sleeves. Philips asked his question. I prayed silently to the God I didn't believe in that he wouldn't say anything about Ed being 'unhappy' or crying on the night of the accident. I was ready with the placental abruption story, appropriately vague as to date, but that could be checked against the records. It didn't mean it couldn't have come back to bite Ed days or weeks later when he was feeling low. Arthur hesitated. 'Go on, darling.' Arthur said yes, Ed had been with them after he got home that night.

'Got home from where?'

Arthur frowned and looked at me. I nodded. Answer the man.

'Work, I suppose.'

Philips glanced at me. Satisfied now? He turned back to Arthur, unwilling to let the fish off the hook so quickly.

'You suppose?'

'Yes.'

'And he was the same as ever?'

'Yes.'

'No different to any other night?'

'Yes.'

'Not stressed or anything?'

'Well . . . '

'Go on . . . '

'Yes.'

'He did seem stressed?'

I could feel Philips glance at me but I didn't meet his eye. Instead I continued looking at

Arthur, who looked quickly from Philips to me and back again, willing him not to go further.

'Yes.'

Philips's voice softened, as if it was holding out a shiny sweet. 'How did he seem stressed?'

'I meant yes he was no different to any other night.'

I breathed out, not too obviously. I could see the air coming out of Philips's balloon. He was trying not to look as if he was enticing a schoolboy into a car.

'And he stayed in the whole time? Didn't pop out at all, not to Clifton Village to pick up some food?'

'Yes.'

'Yes to which?'

'He stayed in.'

Philips blew his cheeks out. 'OK, that's great, thanks very much. You can go now.'

Arthur looked briefly at me and I nodded. He shot back up the stairs. My chest was still heaving. I looked at Philips — what now? He stuck out his bottom lip like a petulant child and nodded ruminatively.

'That's all — for now. You can have your Saturday back.'

'Thanks.'

He got off his stool. It was the moment he would have touched his Stetson if he'd had one. He narrowed his eyes like the Marlboro Man and said,

'You know, Mrs Sheahan, something doesn't feel right here.' I shrugged but didn't say anything. 'It's just a feeling, but in my game you learn to trust your gut.' I stared at him impassively. I disliked him and his self-confidence. It made me determined to support Ed until it was over. Philips could feel whatever he wanted but unless the game changed he would never be able to prove it. 'I'll get to the bottom of this. I will. You can be sure of that.' I moved towards the door but he raised a hand. 'Don't bother. I'll see myself out.'

When he'd gone I went up to Arthur's bedroom. He was kneeling on the floor with a frown of concentration, clicking one minute piece of grey plastic into another, consulting the heavily folded instructions in forty-eight languages as he did so. Without looking up he said,

'What did the man want?'

'Oh, it was just after the other day. He just wanted to confirm a couple of things.'

'Why did he want to ask me?'

'He was just checking what we said about Daddy being here.'

Arthur looked up quickly.

'Is Daddy in trouble?'

'No.'

He frowned, suspicious. 'With the police?'

'No. It's nothing.'

'Was it the night Daddy was crying?'

'Yes.'

'I didn't tell him that.'

'No, you didn't. Which is probably right. Because everything you tell him just makes him ask more questions.'

'Why was he crying?'

'See what I mean!'

'Well?'

'He'd just had a terrible day at the hospital. A little baby died. He thought he should have saved her. Why didn't you tell the man he was crying?'

Arthur looked thoughtful. He was obviously thinking: was that how it worked? Who'd want to be a doctor if it was?

'I didn't know what day he was talking about but I wanted to be helpful so I just said yes to everything.'

★ ★ ★

'Amsterdam?'

I put my book face-down on my lap and adjusted my position against the pillow. I was lying on our bed reading the 'Zooey' section of *Franny and Zooey*, windows open, a pitiful breeze trying but failing to cool the baking air, the walls a brilliant white. Of the two novellas I'd always preferred 'Franny'. Ed stood in the doorway. His cheeks were shining the way they do when he has given me a present or hopes he has surprised me.

'Amsterdam. You and me. Next weekend. Two nights. Museum passes included. You need a break.'

I had never been to Amsterdam but I had always wanted to see Rembrandt's late self-portraits in the flesh. They were the first properly psychological self-portraits ever painted; psychological in the modern sense, by which I mean they should have been painted after the clever

184

men who populated the cafés of Vienna at the turn of the twentieth century had published their theories, not before.

'What about the chil — '

'Sorted.'

I felt as if there was water in my ears. I didn't know how to react. I wanted to go but I didn't want to go. I wanted to see Amsterdam. It seemed ridiculous I had never been to a city so close and so beautiful, and the Rijksmuseum was a glaring omission in my first-hand viewing, but I also knew I didn't want to spend two days alone and in such proximity to Ed, without my own space, no matter the artistic benefit, no matter how seductive the city. It was impossible to articulate, but I needed to see less of him just then, not more. I needed my studio at hand to escape to, even if I had been reduced to sketching my own hands over and over, front and back, pencil or charcoal, as if I was in a losing battle to find something tangible to hold on to.

'Um . . . '

'I've booked a hotel overlooking the Keizers-gracht.'

'I'm not sure . . . '

A cloud passed in front of the sun. His brow knitted together.

'What do you mean, 'not sure'?'

It might have been easier to back down, accept the situation, and move on, but that had never been Ed's style. If he saw a problem, he wanted to deal with it head on.

'I mean, I'm not sure it's right, just now, for us. I'm not sure I feel up to a holiday. I'm not sure I deserve one.'

The truth was I knew there was nowhere I could go to escape the one thing I needed to escape. Ed tried to hide his disappointment and, deep down, a shapeless fear this might be the beginning of the end.

'Darling, you don't have to deserve a holiday. It's enough to need one. Or just to want one. I really think it would do you good to get away for a couple of days.' He spoke softly. He had a better bedside manner than I'd imagined. 'Change of scene. Somewhere completely new.' I looked him in the eyes. There are eighty muscles in the eyelids and every one was working. I shook my head. I couldn't explain it in words he would want to hear. 'Fresh air. Or as fresh as it can be beside a canal. Every doctor recommends it.'

'I don't think so, darling, not just now. It doesn't feel right somehow.'

He ground his jaw. 'One night?'

I shook my head again and looked down at my book. I didn't want to have this conversation.

'What about somewhere round here then? Bath? Outside Bath? Just one night. The Pig? Royal Crescent? Money no object.' He didn't get it. Before I could answer he was sitting on the bed, pressing on, helplessly. 'Come on, my darling, I promise it will do you good. It'll do both of us good. I really think we need it.'

I tried to imagine how I would feel in some boutique hotel with its plumped pillows and feature wallpaper. I shook my head almost imperceptibly. I couldn't do it. I couldn't articulate properly why not, and yet I had always been able to articulate my feelings, but I just couldn't get the words out. It frightened me. Ed nodded. 'OK, I understand.' Then, as if he was the one who had made a decision, he leant forward and kissed me on the forehead. 'I love you, I hope you know that, and I am unbelievably grateful for your support. I appreciate how much this thing has hurt you and I can't say how sorry I really truly am. I only want you to be happy.'

His mouth puckered as he struggled to hold the line. I almost burst into tears. Although he tried to hide it, Ed's eyes were glistening. The famous clinician, the man who had seen it all, was struggling to stay afloat. I wished I could throw my arms around him and say everything was going to be all right and we should go to Amsterdam to look at some of the greatest portraits ever painted and forget everything and have some fun, but it was impossible, I couldn't offer him that. And I hated myself for it.

12

The following week, we — Ed and I that is; the children were in bed, probably awake, hopefully reading, Nell more likely messaging — were sitting on the sofa watching TV, waiting for *News at Ten*. I was trying not to be irritated by endless adverts for BBC programmes we would never watch. We paid a licence fee so we didn't have to sit through adverts. Ed's jacket was hanging on a kitchen chair, a diamond-patterned tie tossed over its shoulder like a college scarf. The night was hot-hot, the air still. It only needed the sound of crickets and we could have been on Barbados. Ed gave off a warm muzzy smell that might have been sweat but was not unpleasant. The first painting I ever completed was above the TV, a weeping willow, tight and symmetrical on a gold-paper background. The tree was on the Backs in Cambridge, visible from the room I had in my last year. I spent hours sitting on the wide stone windowsill, smoothed by generations of lounging undergraduates, and watched it sway in the breeze, dipping green fingers into the Cam. It was not bad for a first effort, good enough to fire my ambition, to ignite my hope.

The clock hit ten.

Bong — Thirteen dead in Homs bomb attack.

Bong — Rumours swirl around the solvency of a major finance house.

Bong — The Department of the Environment

188

says building houses on the Green Belt is inevitable.

Bong — Man arrested in the hunt for the killer of Araminta Lyall.

Bong — Oh my God!

I looked at Ed. He didn't look at me even though he must have felt my eyes sliding over his face like eggs in a pan. He'd turned surrender-white and was staring at the television, his jaw working. After a few seconds I said,

'Darling?'

He shook his head. The TV started on about Syria. There'd been a bomb in a marketplace. Images of bodies covered by sheets at the roadside, the injured carried away on makeshift stretchers, the anguish of survivors, wild-eyed and babbling, platitudes from politicians who send us to war. The politicians who say they listen but never learn. Collateral damage. Every action has collateral damage.

Next a man with ridiculous enunciation started talking about stock market rumours a bank was in trouble. I tried to focus on his words but my mind was still on collateral damage, only not the sort that queued up on pavements to take their savings out when they lost trust in their bank. I couldn't wait any longer.

'What do you think?'

He was staring at the screen. He wouldn't look at me.

'Ed?'

'Wait.'

I waited. I waited while an environmental man gave his depressing prognosis on the future of

189

the Green Belt, the government explained what it was doing to alleviate the problem and an opposition politician who had cut the environmental budget when he was in government popped up to say in as many words that global warming was the government's fault.

Finally, after what seemed a lifetime, the screen filled with that woman's face, the Dering Street photo, before a female reporter standing outside Paddington Green police station told us a twenty-nine-year-old art dealer named Johnny Trumble had been arrested in West London that afternoon on suspicion of the murder of Araminta Lyall.

Ed clicked the TV off, exhaled deeply and lay back on the sofa, cheeks pallid and papery. I took his hand and held it, saying nothing. We sat like that for a long time but I didn't want to speak because Ed had to make his own decision.

'What do you think?'

'I think . . . ' What did I think? My first thought was, 'Who is Johnny Trumble?'

'Never heard of him. No — wait, maybe he was at Pete's party?'

'Maybe he went back to Stokes Croft afterwards?'

Ed shrugged. Anything was possible. His memory of the after-party hadn't improved with time. He lay back on the sofa again, shoulders slack, his lips tight. He wanted me to have complete silence for as long as I needed to turn things over. But I didn't need to turn things over. I already knew what I thought. I had been brought up to tell the truth. Yet Ed didn't deserve to be arrested, put through a trial, possibly go to jail, probably be struck off — and that was if they charged him with manslaughter, which must be the least we could expect. He didn't deserve to lose everything. But we couldn't let another man swing.

'You can't let another man swing.'

'No one's swung.'

'You can't let him go through this.'

'He'll get off. He has to.'

I didn't answer. Ed would do the right thing. He just needed time to get there. Not least because he'd promised he would never give himself up and he was not a man to go back on a promise.

It wasn't going to be easy, not for any of us. I could already see Philips's look of triumph. He knew we were involved, he always had. Philips could feel it but he didn't quite know how to get there. That's why he kept circling. What happened to me in the street the other day would seem like an afternoon nap compared to where we were heading. Ed said,

'We could at least wait. See if he is charged.'

It was a statement. It should have been a question. I could understand that. His face was parched. A great man was being taken to the scaffold and I was hauling the tumbril. For a moment I thought it was unfair he was forcing me to do this but he had to conserve his energy. He had plenty of battles ahead. I shook my head. Ed said,

'He'll have a thousand alibis. Probably wasn't even in Bristol on the night it happened.'

'Mistakes happen.'

'If he hasn't got an alibi, then, of course . . . '

'It could ruin him, regardless. Time on remand. No smoke without fire.'

'I promised I would never give myself up. For the children's sake. And yours. For all of us.'

'I know. I understand. But there's no choice now.' I touched his cheek. It was unexpectedly hot. 'You can explain everything. Everyone will support you. Everyone will know you would never have done it on purpose. They'll know it was an accident, that there wouldn't have been any intent. Your character references, the good you do, the stream of satisfied patients, no one could have better character witnesses. At the absolute worst they'll go for manslaughter.'

'At the absolute best they'll go for manslaughter.' He paused. There was bitterness in his voice but also anguish and, that rare beast for Ed, incomprehension. He genuinely didn't know what to do. 'It might have been manslaughter if I'd put my hand up immediately, but after a month of running round like headless chickens, taking me in for questions and letting me go, the police will want their pound of flesh.'

He looked pleadingly at me. Gone was the power, the certainty that had driven him onwards and upwards. This was the man I married laid bare. For a moment I was wrong-footed, tempted to follow his suggestion to wait and see, but then I remembered that woman, imagined her chalked body lying by the fireplace, police 'do not cross' tape hanging as limply as last Christmas's decorations, and I shuddered. I thought about the adultery that started it all. I felt the fear of Johnny Trumble and imagined how he must be suffering, his parents too. I couldn't watch him swing. I said,

'Sanity will prevail.'

He was quiet for a moment, feeling his way to the conclusion, before sighing and saying,

'If that's what you want.'

It was the sound of defeat, as if all the air had left his body. This was the man who'd set out to be the finest obstetrician in England and, Gatsby-like, his dream must have seemed so close that he could hardly fail to grasp it. Yet slumped on the sofa in the gloaming he was already less imposing, his face as green as the light at the end of Daisy's dock. I had seen that look in men who had lost their confidence, most obviously Matt, in the stoop of the recently unemployed. Tears welled but I tried not to show them. It was going to be hard enough for Ed without me crying. The last thing he needed to worry about was how we would cope. We would cope. We would cope in the same way I coped with the death of my father, by carrying on. We would cope in the way Matt had never been able to, by carrying on. Keep on keeping on, the writer wrote. Does that suggest hardness, or lack of empathy, simple realism, or ice in the heart of the artist? It doesn't matter. I loved Ed, that's what he needed to know, but we couldn't let someone else go down for murder.

I glanced across at him. He was leaning back on the sofa, his head against the cold radiator. What was he thinking? When finally he spoke he sounded hoarse, as if someone had stolen the carry from his voice.

'Will you wait?'

I nodded, holding back the tears.

'We'll wait.'

'For three years?'

'Yes.'

'Ten?'

'It won't be ten, my darling.'

'Fifteen? What do you get for murder?'

'We'll wait.'

I spoke softly, comfortingly, but even as I did so I knew I didn't know the answer. Who could predict the future?

Ed nodded, but his look told me he understood. The tension of the past few weeks was dissolving in my stomach, being replaced by a different, emptier feeling, one no amount of 'bring it on' chutzpah could hide. Whatever route we chose, this was going to be a lonely road for all of us, Nell and Arthur especially, and particularly if I went down too for being an accessory after the fact, sheltering a criminal, cooking lunch for a murderer, whatever it was they hit you with. All I knew about prison had been gleaned from occasional glimpses on *News at Ten* and in colour supplements: creamy brick walls, safety nets hanging from metal walkways, steel doors with chunky bolts, burly warders, clanking keys, the odour of sadness and defeat, the bullying, the homemade tattoos, the apathy and ennui. Doing time, literally. Casual but extreme violence, lock-downs, claustrophobia. There would be no sympathy or joy. No colour.

What did Paul Klee say? 'Colour and I are one. I am a painter.' I suddenly felt cold even though the temperature was still somewhere up in the seventies and the air was hanging as hot and heavy as a jazz note in Preservation Hall.

With a superhuman effort Ed dragged himself up off the sofa. He proffered a hand. I took it and he lifted me up. I could feel his sinewy strength, the sense of purpose that attracted me to him all those years ago. We stared into each other's eyes. His were misty grey, the pupils like insects in fluid.

'Let's sleep on it,' he said.

I nodded and touched his cheek. I knew how I would feel in the morning.

13

What do you take to the police station when you are going to confess to manslaughter, possibly be charged with murder, and may not see your own front door again for months if not years? Old hat for the recidivist, as unfathomable for the obstetrician as a placental abruption is for the safe-cracker.

'I don't think you'll need all that.'

I tried to splice in some humour, though neither of us felt like it. Ed looked at the bed as if seeing his haul for the first time. His blond hair was wet and dark and scraped behind his ears. His cheeks were flushed from the purging heat of the shower. An aquamarine towel with a flying porpoise hung loosely around his waist. His upper body was still in good shape, sleek and powerful, testament to weekly tennis, hilly Bristol cycling, a balanced diet, demanding work. What would it look like after months or years of limited exercise, mindless food, dreary work, mental inertia?

On the floor above, Nell shouted, 'STOP IT ARTHUR, I SAID STOP IT, GET OUT OF MY ROOM' as much for our benefit as his. Ed raised an eyebrow: the things he wouldn't miss. We ignored her and surveyed the items arranged in neat piles around an overnight bag on the bed: electric razor, which I'd bought that day, cut-throats presumably being non grata wherever he was going, deodorant, toothbrush and toothpaste, a tub of my skin moisturizer, three pairs of folded pants and socks, two crisply ironed single-cuff 'City' shirts, a turquoise V-neck as if he was going to play golf, GAP jeans, a Boden fleece, Nike trainers ticked off. I wondered when he thought he'd get the chance to go running. There was the latest edition of the *Lancet*, an obstetrics textbook he'd been meaning to annotate but never had time, and John Le Carré's *A Perfect Spy*, a hefty work for the man with time on his hands, its bookmark a photo of us on the beach in Mallorca, Nell glancing down at her phone and Arthur pulling a silly face just as the pre-timed shot went off. His herringbone suit hung on the back of the door, the Royal College of Obstetricians & Gynaecologists tie hooked limply round the hanger.

I put my arms around his bare shoulder, a muscular shoulder designed to protect his family, not check out on it, pulled his head down to my level, nuzzled my cheek against his ear and said,

'Darling, we're in this together. We're all losing the thing we love most.'

Ed nodded. There was grandeur in his resignation. I understood how much the simple things of family life meant to him after his lonely upbringing and ancient parents. It was the spine running through every word as he listed all the boring things I had never had to think about: the gas meters and insurance renewals, where to find spare bulbs or the number of a plumber, how to access direct debits, what to do if the dishwasher shorted, who to call if the boiler broke, why we owned an Allen key and where we kept it. These were things I had never known. From day one he had been my keeper.

'ARTHUR, GET OUT, WILL YOU PLEASE LEAVE ME ALONE.'

'Some things I won't miss.'

'Because you won't have to. Think positive.'

He grunted. I kissed him on the ear.

'When shall I tell the children?'

'When I'm charged. When I'm away longer than I realistically would be at a conference. When my name's in the papers. When the rumours start flying. When — '

'When I think's best.'

'When you can't put it off any longer.' There were tears on his cheeks.

'They have to hear it from me first.'

'Of course.'

'They'll be sad you never said goodbye.'

'I'll say goodbye. And when they know what's happened they'll understand why I said what I'll say even if they think it's a bit weird as a pre-conference trip goodbye at the time. Anyway, it's better if you explain. It'll give them time to understand everything that's happened, to know what I did and what I didn't do before they have to see me or read about it in the paper.'

'Online more like.'

I had been reading about Johnny Trumble online. I had spent most of the day digging out everything from broadsheet reports to Trumble bios, speculative blogs and bilious trolls. I had even come across my own name muddled up in there — @brazenfish8 sharing the view that 'the painter woman with the doctor husband' was the more likely suspect. The doctor husband glanced out of the window. The early evening sun laid bare Ashton Court where the parkland swooped and swelled to the woods in the distance, deer wilting in pools of shade on the upper slopes. A pumpkin-coloured hot-air balloon with Dulux written in giant letters was drifting towards the river. There was a burst of fire and height. This sort of thing just didn't happen to people like us. I wanted to scream like a birthing mother but Ed simply inclined his head and said,

'Or online. Best you don't go there, my darling.' He grinned mirthlessly. 'I certainly won't.'

I knew he wouldn't. Our only hope was that someone as rational as Ed could deal with what he was about to be put through. Only someone as rational as Ed could coolly pack his suitcase with things he must know would be taken from him on arrest without thinking about everything he had lost, without breaking down or cursing God or roaring like a bull calf at the miserable hand fate had dealt him. It wasn't as if he had ever done a single thing in his entire life, a life of making families and supporting our family, which meant he deserved what was coming. Well, maybe one thing. He had broken a moral law. I held out an arm but he turned back to the bed and started packing his suitcase. Only Ed could face his destiny without the brief touch of human consolation.

I collapsed into the bow-legged armchair we'd

bought in a junk shop in Golborne Road in the days when you could still find bargains there and watched him pack. I felt exhausted yet the full horror was still to come. More than anything I wanted it to be over — the goodbyes, the tension, the charges, the announcement, the humiliation, the hounding, the court case, the sentence, the publicity, the looks, the whispers, the false concern, all the things from which we could never hide. I wanted to go to sleep and to wake up on the far side, wherever that was and whatever it meant. I wanted to crawl into my hole and do my work. I wanted to protect myself and my family.

★　★　★

He finally left after supper. It had been an unsurprisingly subdued affair, every word pregnant with double-meaning, every sentence drenched in loss. Ed had waited until the children had gone up to bed before he went to say goodbye. He was on the top floor for twenty minutes. I didn't ask him what he'd said. I wanted it to be between him and his children. It might be the last thing they would take with them. Neither of us spoke. We just hugged silently — hugged and hugged and hugged — pressing our bodies together so hard it was as if, right at the death, we could fulfil our marital vows and become one. Moments later he was gone, without a backward glance, the front door clicking softly behind him, his broad back disappearing into the dusk as he clutched his bag, his posture erect and defiant. The gate clanged as he went out into the road and there was silence. I imagined him pausing, sniffing cool scents in the warm air, before heading for his car. If it were done when 'tis done, then 'twere well it were done quickly.

For a few seconds I felt vacant, out of my own body, as if I was somewhere or someone else, on the upper deck of a Saga cruise or answering the phone in Italian. Had what I thought just happened really happened? When the moment passed I looked around the kitchen for a magazine. I couldn't go to bed as there was no way I would sleep, but equally there was no chance of concentrating on a book or a poem or even looking at a painting. I spotted *Bristol Magazine*, a glossy freebie, on the wooden worktop. It was exactly the sort of brain-dead fodder I needed, pictures of houses for sale and minimalist German kitchens I would never want or could probably afford, certainly not now. I went downstairs to the basement fridge and fished out a bottle of Sancerre donated by some generous new parent happy to provide more expensive wine than we would ever drink, oblivious to the circumstances in which it would be drunk. I figured we might as well go down in style and, anyway, just then I needed a drink so badly I could have been an alcoholic. Maybe I should follow Matt down Addiction Road? My route hadn't brought me much more happiness in the end. Maybe we Tenterdens weren't built for happiness? Maybe I had simply staved off the unhappiness for longer? Or maybe I had simply appeared to? I pulled out a tumbler. The phone rang. I left it. It kept ringing. I kept leaving it. With what sounded like a final peal of outrage, it stopped. I picked up the corkscrew.

The first glass didn't touch the sides. I rebooted. Yet even as I refilled my glass with the pale yellow wine I knew I didn't want it. I didn't need it. My thirst was slaked. Whatever happened to Ed, I wouldn't be going down Matt's road. I had Nell and Arthur, which he didn't, and they needed me sober, fully lit and protective as a tigress over the next few hours, days, weeks, months and, probably, years. I poured the glass and then the bottle down the sink, taking a malicious pleasure in sluicing such expensive wine.

I looked briefly at the magazine but it couldn't settle my nerves. So I reached for the TV flicker and landed on the news on some twenty-four-hour channel. The Middle East, violence flaring. A finance company's share price was collapsing. A big slug of a man who had eaten too often and too well was angry with everyone for saying he was bust when he said he wasn't. He didn't look trustworthy. I thought if I didn't believe him then Julian Noone and the market definitely wouldn't believe him and his company would go down. A good-looking young soldier had died in training on the Brecon Beacons. I clicked off the TV. There was only so much bad news you could take in a day. I went upstairs to the study and dug out a back issue of *Apollo* with a beautifully illustrated article on Georgia O'Keeffe I had meant to look at for ages, and headed up to bed. I wanted to absorb her colours. I needed her lyrical eye.

★ ★ ★

I was standing at the round mirror in our bathroom, lit by the crescent of bulbs as if I was a star of stage and screen. The light was pore-bright. It picked on every blemish and imperfection. Imagine what it must be like to be an actress.

How would I paint my face? First the physical: crystal-blue eyes, almond-shaped when I smile. A straight nose, petite, softer than my mother's. My hair was cut in a bob as it was easier for work. It was mousey, with a strain of ginger from my father's side and curled inward naturally at the neck. It needed a wash. Somehow, with everything that was going on . . . I widened my mouth. The tips of my two front teeth peeped out. They are always with me. I have been lucky with my skin, though in the bright bathroom the laughter lines seemed as deep as canyons. The take-no-prisoners glare revealed the faint impress of lines on my forehead, not yet centre stage but undeniably there, the result of childbirth and motherhood and painting self-obsessed people. This was the beginning. It was not hard to imagine what the next few weeks and months might do.

I looked into my eyes. Always start with the eyes. They tell you how strong someone is, what reserves they have, how far they could go. They reveal the structure. The rest is cladding. Mine were flecked with red and, no matter how much I tried to pretend otherwise, they looked exhausted. I couldn't hide from it. They told the whole story to anyone who knew how to read them. Nabokov once said you couldn't read a book, you could only re-read one. Maybe you can't paint a self-portrait but only re-paint one?

★　★　★

I put down the O'Keeffe and switched on the radio. It's a Roberts radio, a long-ago present from Ed for my studio that I moved to our bedroom when I realized I didn't want to listen to the crap that gets talked all day on Radio Four. All those smug types playing word games, rejoicing in their own wit and cleverness, the earnest plays, the glib analysis, spouting heads. Politicians telling lies. It's all just words, swirling around formlessly like the onset of dementia. Opium for the intelligentsia. How can you do anything when you're drowning in verbiage? Why would you do anything? Art is the opposite. It must capture a moment. It must tease out meaning, engage with nuance, reach an understanding, ascend to a truth. It must be approached obliquely, not through a barrage of me-too commentary. Art is not an opinion.

The midnight DJ on a random station introduced a singer-songwriter I had never heard before. There were a few chords of acoustic guitar before the harmonica cut in — a sure sign of a performer about to take himself seriously — and a gravelly voice grouched on about heading out west over wide open spaces in search of his love. After three minutes of hope and frustration and maybe redemption the harmonica blew back in like tumble-weed. I lay back on clean sheets and puffed pillows in the half-empty bed.

A moment later the phone rang. I hesitated for a moment before picking it up. In the micro-silence before he spoke I knew it was Ed. His voice was soft but urgent.

'Darling, have you heard the news?'

'No. What news?'

'They've let him go.'

'What?'

'It was on the news. Didn't you hear it?'

'Hear what?'

'They've let Trumble go. Araminta's man.'

I felt my stomach lurch.

'Oh darling! But where are you?'

'Don't you see?'

'See what?'

'There's no need to give myself up because they've already let him go.'

'But aren't you there already?'

'No.' His voice was triumphant. 'I'd been driving around psyching myself up, and by the time I was ready it was ten so I thought I'd listen to the local news one last time before I handed myself in. And they said they'd let him go.'

'Darling, that's — '

'Fucking fantastic! It's awesome is what it is. I'm the luckiest man alive.'

'Alive,' I echoed.

'Yes, isn't it great? And, darling . . . '

'Mmm?'

'You OK?'

'Yuh?'

'Only you sound a bit, well, not quite ecstatic.'

'No, no, I'm good. I'm good, oh darling, that's fantastic news.'

'It is. I can't believe it. You know what it means . . . ?' He didn't wait for me to reply. 'It means everything's going to be all right. Darling, I'm so happy I can't tell you. I'm on my way home.'

I lay back on the plumped pillows, the phone in my hand. I couldn't hide it from myself. I didn't feel elated. I didn't feel as happy as I knew I should. This was officially the best news we could have had as a family and yet . . . and yet . . . I tried to revive the sense of despair I had when Ed left in order to conjure up the relief and joy I should be feeling. But I couldn't clear the one question which was zinging around my mind.

Why didn't I feel fucking fantastic?

14

The following day, though to all appearances nothing had changed, I couldn't face taking the children to school. So I rang Plan Bea and busied myself with laundry at the back of the house, sending Nell and Arthur out to meet her in the road where she hovered by the gatepost, having arrived a couple of minutes early on the off-chance of a catch-up with Clifton's most infamous woman. When I was certain she had gone, I crept up to my studio and collapsed on to the chaise longue. I hadn't slept after Ed got back, triumph oozing from every pore, and I was exhausted, my limbs too heavy to move. The sun was already high in a cloudless sky and the hot air enveloped me. I wasn't sure how much more I was going to be able to take. But there was no escape. We were public property now, to be poured out and pored over and pawed. Whatever Ed had or hadn't done had cost us our privacy, the privacy that was essential for painting portraits. I had to cancel my three contracted sittings. I didn't have the strength to undertake them.

For a while I didn't even have the strength to make the calls. I lay on the chaise longue for hours with my mind in turmoil while the sun beat down and a pack of wild dogs snapped at my mind. As time passed I sensed the afternoon's pick-up hurtling towards me like a packed court-room and I knew I had to make my calls before

Ed returned home and persuaded me not to bail, but still I couldn't move. I was trying to raise the energy to start with the easiest, Eddie Sander-stead, a sweet modest man whose portrait is a sixtieth birthday present from his wife I suspect secretly he'd rather not have, when my mobile rang. I answered. There was the slightest pause before a shy voice said, 'Bunny?'

It was Matt. Matt had been to Highlands and missed his connection to Leeds and Whitby. He had an hour to kill at Temple Meads. Was there any chance I could meet for a quick coffee? He was typically apologetic about the lack of notice and quite understood if it wasn't convenient. I said I would be there in ten minutes. His voice lit up.

Driving the back way along Spike Island beside the muddy Avon, I thought only Matt, who I hadn't seen for a couple of years, could give me ten minutes' notice for a forty-minute cup of coffee in the middle of the afternoon when anyone else would have been at work.

He saw me before I saw him as he had posi-tioned himself to one side behind a large menu with a perfect view of the door. It was as if he wanted advance warning of the arrival of — I don't know what. Dealers? Creditors? Ex-girlfriends? Land-lords? Mother? He ought to feel safe in Bristol, a city in which he'd never lived or worked, in a café at a railway station, but evidently he'd learned not to take any chances. He waved, his face splitting into his hopeful grin, almost as if he thought I might also have arranged to meet some-one else. I looked around the high-ceilinged, near-empty café and felt a sudden sadness. A railway station, not even a terminus, seemed a wretched place to meet such a restless soul. Matt had always been waiting for his connection.

We hugged. He was still handsome, though the lines were deeper. Matt had shiny hair, no trace of grey, Tenterden cheekbones, a well-cast nose and a generous mouth with the full flush lips of a Rubens beauty. But slim had turned to gaunt and he looked tired. The drugs or the years, or the net-making business, were beginning to take their toll.

I bought two coffees. Conscious of the clock, we sped through — or in my case glossed over — our recent lives. Matt, of course, hadn't seen the news, and amazingly (or not) Mother hadn't mentioned it, which allowed me to give a par-boiled account of that woman. It was short on truth, which made me feel bad as I had always told Matt everything about my life even if it wasn't always reciprocated. His economy was never false-hood; evasion perhaps, that and his desperate urge for privacy. There were dark places no one was invited and I never ventured. How was Whitby? Whitby was great. How was Jo? Jo was great. How was net-making? Net-making was great.

'And . . . profitable?'

It was hard to imagine Matt as a businessman. He was too gentle. He was not equipped to deal with suppliers and distributors and the hard northern fishing folk who had seen their industry collapse and pared their spending to the bone.

The battle for control of his face told me everything. I probed. They were struggling to turn a profit. Jo's business lacked the scale of the industrial net-makers and it was hard to persuade under-pressure local fishermen to pay a premium for quality and service. That was why he was passing through Bristol. He had been to Highlands to ask Mother if he could borrow some money to provide short-term cash flow to shore up the business.

'I think I can guess the answer.'

He nodded grimly. We both knew he was not a sound bet. He wore his failure like an old coat.

Jo had started the business five years ago. She had left school with a single GCSE in English Literature, sat on a checkout stool in Asda for five years before realizing if she was going to make anything of her life she was going to have to do it herself. She was twenty-seven to Matt's forty-five, an uneducated entrepreneur to his wasted life. What was the attraction? Who could say? Maybe they'd shared a dealer. Maybe she was drawn to his gentle demeanour, his love of poetry, the promise of a different life. However they'd met (Matt had always been reticent about his emotional life, generally with good reason), I knew she worked hard and was on the level.

'It hasn't always been easy — with Jo, I mean.'

'The age difference?'

'Not only that.' Matt gave the wary, hooded look I remembered so well. 'We are different. She's very determined, focused. She's got quite a temper on her.'

'So Bridgey said.'

He took a sip of coffee as if to rebalance himself.

'That wasn't a good time.'
'She stayed with you?'
'Jo?'
'Bridgey.'
He gave a wistful laugh. 'Not even a night.'
I had heard. Bridgey had spoken at a Brontë festival in Haworth and afterwards taken the train to Whitby. She had never learned to drive. The plan had been to spend the weekend with Matt and to meet Jo. She ended up checking into a B&B at 10 p.m. on the Friday night and caught the first train back to London on Saturday morning. There had been an argument between Matt and Jo about his habit and Bridgey had been too embarrassed to stay. She is not built for confrontation.
'But things are better now?'
'Yup.'
'And you love her?'
'Jo? Yuh. She's great.'
'And she loves you?'
'For now.'
I pulled what I hoped was an optimistic face, but it was hard to be confident. Matt was a man in motion, an alien in the north, a fragile soul who had crash-landed in the world of commerce. It was hard to imagine the business question to which the answer was: 'Matthew Tenterden'.
'And you're clean?'
'Almost.'
'Jo?'
He shook his head. I didn't know whether he meant she was clean or she didn't know he wasn't. I didn't even know whether she'd ever

been a junkie. I also didn't know how far 'almost' stretched, but I couldn't ask. Matt was my big brother and his habit was a place I couldn't go. He absent-mindedly stirred what was left of his coffee with a toothpick he took from a packet in his pocket. 'She's been very good to me.'

'And how much money do you — does she — need?'

'Doesn't matter.'

'No, go on. I could lend you some. I've got three commissions on. Things are good. Money's no problem.'

I didn't add that after the three phone calls I planned to make that afternoon I would have no commissions. Matt was probably the only person in the world who at that moment could make me say, if only comparatively, 'Things are good.'

'No, Bunny, that's really sweet of you. You've always been so generous.'

'Hardly.'

'The kingfisher?'

Ah yes, the kingfisher. The kingfisher had gone down in family lore. One day at Highlands when I was eight a kingfisher had somehow got into the house and become trapped in a high-up window. Neither Matt nor Bridgey could reach it. It was so desperate that I could see by the time one of us found an adult it would have broken its beak on the thick green glass. So without thinking I hurled my tin of coloured crayons — the last present my father had ever given me — through the window, which shattered into a million glittering shards. The

hadn't seen for years as he thought of Jo.

'I haven't felt like this before.'

There was another indecipherable announcement over the tannoy.

'Look, I'd better go. Don't want to miss another train. I said I'd be back in time to cook supper.'

I nodded. He stood up, picked up his holdall and heaved it over his shoulder. I spread my arms around him and hugged him tightly, rocking sideways against his eggshell cheek, until he gently disentangled himself.

'You must come and see us.'

'We will. And you must come and see us.'

'We will. Say hi to Ed and the kids.'

'And to Jo.'

I sat down again to let him go. There was nothing more to say. At the door he turned and gave a shy little half-wave, as if we were old friends who had fallen out but now were back on terms. I waved back. Matt always did me in. As the door shut behind him I clicked on my mobile and tapped the bank icon. By the time his train pulled out heading north, Matt, though he didn't know it, was £7,400 richer, the possessor of all my savings, his bank account fattened by a transfer with the reference: 'For Jo xx'.

* * *

The moment I got back to my studio I made the calls. I had to, even though my gift to Matt meant I was broke and was going to have to rely on Ed for cash. No matter. At that moment

215

money was far less important than not having to spend four days apiece with three people I didn't know but who would all know everything about me. Money couldn't buy twelve days' space for me to try to get my head into the right place.

The first call, Eddie, was sweetness and light. He'd seen the news and said of course he understood. He didn't even ask for his advance to be returned but told me to keep it in case I felt up to undertaking the work. I wondered if his wife would have been so forgiving.

The second call was to Alex Quoyle, a straight-to-the-point property developer who preyed on old ladies with short leases in expensive London boroughs. Unlike Eddie, who was a proper gentleman, Alex refused to understand. When I asked for some space he didn't reply. Alex is the master of silence. He knows how to run a call. He lets it grow around you. Old ladies can't cope with silence, because they are lonely, or because their leasehold on life is short. I can. I can't get enough of it right now.

'Alice, the date's been set for six months.'

'I know, and I'm really sorry.'

'But what about Tabby?'

Tabby? What about Tabby? Tabby Quoyle was the one person who had no concerns over timing. It didn't matter to her which four days she took out from tennis and Pilates and pool to sit for a portrait. She hadn't been smeared all over the news and roasted on every blog from here to Japan.

'The thing is, you see, you have to be in a certain place when you start a portrait. Your mind has to be completely blank, literally a blank canvas. It's the only way you can be properly objective, get into the sitter and their mind, because you paint people inside out.'

Alex snorted, which might have related to the impossibility of finding anything in Tabby's mind, and put the phone down without another word, leaving me wondering whether the portrait had been postponed or not. I went into the bathroom and poured a glass of water which I drank in a single swallow. It was cool and clear and reminded me of the cold clean streams on Dartmoor. I took a second back into the studio. I felt lopsided, unsteady, exposed, as if — even though I was on the third floor — anyone could look in and my guilt was obvious. From deep in the room I looked out over the rooftops of Hotwells towards Ashton Court. Cool water, prickly skin, an ache at the base of my forehead. I needed to regroup, to regain some control of my life before the intangible began to eat me up. The view was comfortingly familiar: rooftops, terracotta chimney pots, the Georgian crescents of the Paragon and Polygon and, over the muddy flats of the river, the redbrick Chicago-blocks of the old bonded tobacco warehouses with their metal Z fire escapes and slave-stacked history. The sun rode high in the sky and the earth was baked. There was no shadow. No hiding place.

I picked up the phone again and dialled. A crisp voice answered, softening when I said my name. Chrissie Wright was going to be easier to manage than Alex Quoyle. I said I needed some time out.

'I'm afraid that won't be possible.'

What? The inflexibility of her tone completely took me aback. It left no room for negotiation. I could only utter an inarticulate,

'I'm sorry?'

'Yes. My boss, your sitter, talked about the prospect you might want to pull out but decided postponing was not possible. We simply couldn't find an alternative date. I'm afraid the contract stands and we wish to hold you to it. We appreciate much of what has been said or written about you and your husband is unpleasant and you have our deepest sympathy. Nevertheless, that is not our problem.'

I wasn't sure I could believe my ears. Since when had clients ever overridden the judgement of the artist? It didn't happen — and I was used to dealing with some of the most spoilt people in Britain. I tried to say that I simply wasn't up to it, emotionally or intellectually, but Chrissie was having none of it. Whatever I said rebounded like a golf ball hurled at a brick wall. When it was obvious I wasn't going to be able to wriggle out, no matter how much I pleaded, cajoled, promised or threatened, I said: 'Well, who is your boss, for God's sake? And why does he — and you — have to be so mysterious?'

'I'm afraid I can't tell you.'

'Then I can't come. That's it.'

Dammit! As soon as the words left my mouth I realized I'd made a mistake. Chrissie didn't miss her chance.

'If I tell you, you'll come?'

'Well . . . '

'Then I'll just say that you know my boss.'

'I need more than that. I need a name. Who is he?'

'Who is he?'

'Yes.'

'I think you may've jumped to the wrong conclusion. My boss is not a man.'

'Not a man?'

It was always men who liked to pretend they were far too important to divulge their names to the person with whom they were about to make a connection. Women had too much EQ.

'No. She's a woman. She's called Marianne Hever.'

She sounded as if she expected me to know the name. I racked my brain and tried not to sound wrong-footed but it didn't mean anything to me. I didn't know any Marianne Hevers. I didn't even know any Mariannes. And I would definitely remember if I did because I had the usual no-one-understands-me thing for Leonard Cohen when I was a teenager and, OK I know, Rimbaud and Kerouac, Camus, tick, tick, tick, all the clichés. I said,

'I'm sorry but you're mistaken. I don't know a Marianne Hever.'

I'd been expecting a cabinet minister at the very least.

'Actually you do.'

Her tone was light. I was annoyed with her games. It was hardening my resolve not to go to Cheshire, whatever the cost. I tried not to sound irritated.

'I can assure you I don't. I've never heard that

name before. I don't even know anyone called Marianne. Not that I can remember anyway.'

'Forgive me. I should have said. That's her married name, though as it happens she is divorced. I believe you knew her by her maiden name.' She paused, long enough to let me dangle.

'Latham.'

Oh my God!

'I think you knew her as Marnie Latham.'

15

Marnie Latham/Marianne Hever lived in a two-storey house constructed from an interlocking series of white-painted concrete blocks with ceiling-height windows. It was approached via a quarter-mile drive that gun-barrelled through parkland having dropped away unexpectedly from a suburban street on the edge of Ashton-under-Lyne.

I was tired after the long drive. There'd been an accident on the M6 and a noose of traffic looped around Birmingham, strangling my A-road progress. Yet even though I was running late I'd stopped half an hour south of 'Bow House' at a service station for a cup of coffee and a pack of chewing gum. I needed time to gather myself, because I wasn't sure I had enough of what Lucian Freud called 'morale' to undertake any commission, certainly not one carrying as much baggage as Marnie Latham. But they had left me no room to wriggle out of it. Ever since Ed returned in understandable triumph from not going to the police station, I'd barely slept. Although he hadn't picked up on it — his relief and delight was all-consuming — I was conscious that, however much I wanted it to be otherwise, every expression of his luck, every tiny look or gesture of happiness and liberation, had the reverse effect on me. I tried to rejoice in his freedom, to tell myself the children were the real beneficiaries, but I couldn't. Soon I found I was locking myself in my studio for long hours to avoid him, claiming I was preparing for the Marnie portrait when in reality I was doing nothing more than staring at my hands with the intensity Monet brought to his haystacks and water lilies. But whereas he transformed his staring into art, I had nothing to show for mine bar a few scratches on paper, bolts of burnt umber and flake white, cobalt, Titian red, colour-stabs that turned my fingers into stubby sausages. I pegged my failures to a washing line in my studio to force myself to refocus and to spur myself on. I had always been my own harshest critic — there were portraits I considered failures the sitter had loved, probably for the same reason — but this felt less like creative analysis than self-analysis.

The Johnny Trumble incident had made me realize that deep down I wanted Ed to tell the truth. I *needed* him to come clean, to be the man I married once again. The untruth had grown too large for me and now it was potentially infinite. But I couldn't live with a lie between me and my children, between myself and the world, when my entire oeuvre, my raison d'être, was based on honesty, on searching out and defining the truth of the sitter. How could I 'know' a sitter when I didn't even know which way my life was heading? I was also beginning to think about the lack of justice for that woman. She had parents too. They deserved closure. Maybe I had offered to support Ed too quickly, before we had thought through all the angles, particularly what it would actually entail to live with the lie forever. Then there was the adultery. I couldn't help wondering, however much I dismissed the idea, to what extent that was contributing to my distress. No matter Ed claimed he couldn't remember the night and didn't fancy her; adultery, breach of trust, is a fact. There's no need to prove desire. Facts can be repeated.

I stood at my easel with these questions swirling around in my head, dabbing anxiously at the canvas until I began to think maybe I would never be able to paint the way I once had. Maybe I would only be able to paint pure abstracts that drained the colour from life? Maybe I would only be able to paint children, or pets, because they have no motive in their faces, no experience of suffering or regret? My fears stacked up so high they built a prison wall. A door had clanked shut and it couldn't be opened.

I had cut off the A road and taken a random B. I had had enough of the chains of traffic and needed to regroup. My mind was turning in on itself, funnelling towards the destruction of my family. I needed clean air and shining water, soft heather, purple moorland. I needed some way of conjuring up long-buried memories that could give shape to my feelings. I needed to regain my balance. That, I realized as I ground northwards in a shining river of cars, was ultimately why I had let Chrissie bully me into carrying out this commission: because I had to get out of the house. I needed space to think, and, if I was honest, I needed space from Ed and his suppressed joy. Of course I dressed it up to myself as payback for my failure to stand up for Marnie in the dormitory all those years ago, plus a natural interest in seeing how she had turned out. Maybe there was even the spectre of — dread word — redemption.

The problem was that having accepted the commission I now had to fulfil it. Only I had no more idea how to paint Marnie in my current frame of mind than I knew how to be with Ed. So I sat in my car on the fore-court of a petrol station-cum-shop for more than an hour watching overweight people with tourniquet arms wobble out clutching vats of coffee and XL bags of Haribo sweets and tried to clear my head of all the gunk and fear and stop myself driving past Marnie and renting a house in the Lake District until it was over. But would it ever be over? And how *do* you paint a portrait of someone you betrayed — even if it was the truth that led you there? Can it be a portrait of her or does it have to be one of you both?

Marnie. Marianne. I rolled the names around. Marianne, Marnie. When had Marnie become Marianne? Why did Marnie become Marianne? What did it say about Marnie that she became Marianne? How would that feed into her portrait? A portrait is a painted answer; I only had a canvas of questions.

★ ★ ★

Marnie was not at home. Instead I was greeted by a horsey-looking woman in her late forties wearing mustard cords, a quilted sleeveless Puffa jacket and a string of pearls. She had rosy cheeks, auburn hair, a hefty signet ring with no crest and no make-up. Chrissie Wright. She welcomed me to Bow House, pronouncing 'Bow' like the bough of a tree. Marnie had always loved wordplay.

Chrissie led me through a large empty white-painted square hall lit by the light flooding through the floor-to-ceiling windows and a sun-scorched circular orange abstract. It was a gorgeous roll-in-it orange painted by someone who was to orange as Yves Klein was to blue. We passed through an invisible door in the wall, walked along a passage, white-walled, sheet windows overlooking the park, climbed a glass staircase and crossed an empty landing. At my bedroom door she turned and said,

'I'm afraid Mrs Hever's flight has been delayed and she won't be back until late. She asked me to apologize and said she'll be ready for tomorrow morning. Could you make a prompt start at eight thirty?'

What could I say? That it's impossible to paint a portrait when you haven't seen the sitter in twenty years? That I had changed from school and, judging by her house and her name, Marnie had too? I felt uneasy but it was too late to back out. I injected maximum irritation into my response.

'O-kaaay. Of course it's not ideal, but . . . '

'Dinner will be in the dining room, which is to the left of the hall. Johnson will serve at eight. That should give you time to freshen up.'

The way she ignored what I said gave me an

eerie feeling Marnie's absence, her refusal to tell me who I was painting, her inability to meet me ahead of the sitting, even though I offered numerous dates, had been predetermined. It was as if in some indiscernible way I was being set up. Marnie was on home territory. She had decided the time and place. She held the cards.

After Chrissie left, I called home. I needed their support. I needed human softness and nuance amidst the blank walls of my bedroom and those brutal blocks of concrete. Nell answered, perfunctorily, the guitar lick that was the theme to *Hollyoaks* swirling in the background. She tried to pass me to Arthur but he shouted he was 'busy', though with what remained a mystery. It wouldn't have been prep. Ed's mobile went straight to voicemail. Standing in my vast decoration-free bedroom I suffered a jag of homesickness and nerves. I had done countless portraits and been a four-day guest in numerous houses, all as atmospherically charged as their owners, but something about this one didn't feel right. It was impossible to put my finger on anything specific; there was simply an amorphous fear things had been left unsaid. I unpacked — four days' worth of paint-encrusted work-wear, four nights of smarter clothes for dinner — as slowly as possible and sent Ed a text saying I'd arrived safely and everything was great. Beneath my window a Giacometti-like sculpture of a woman contorted improbably and painfully on a plinth of iron.

★   ★   ★

Marianne Hever marched into the drawing room a minute after half past nine. I'd been there an hour, erecting my easel, sorting my paints, waiting. There was nothing to read and almost nothing to look at — a life-size wire sculpture of a grand piano in a corner, a glass coffee table, an olive and green abstract (think Ben Nicholson) that reminded me of maths prep. Two white four-seater sofas faced each other. They were almost parodic given the lack of conversation I'd had. It was pointless to mix paints or transfer any to my palette as I had no idea what clothes Marnie would be wearing or what colouring she would have. I had refused Johnson's saturnine offer of 'a full English' as I sat alone at a dining-room table that could seat twenty. My stomach was unsettled as it was.

'Dr Livingstone, I presume?'

Despite the irony, Marnie's tone was neutral. There was scarcely a trace of the drawn-out Mancunian vowels that had set her apart at a southern private school. She crossed the room briskly. The last time I had seen her she was being hauled out of the dormitory. It was hard to equate that girl with the sophisticated woman standing in front of me. Menthol cigarettes mingled with expensive perfume.

I stood up. Marnie's face looked as greedy for life as it had twenty years before. Her hair cascaded downwards from a centre parting like a theatre curtain framing a perfectly symmetrical stage set containing those radiant eyes, come-hither lips, that broad slash of a mouth. When she smiled the sun flooded in, as if we had been friends forever. It wasn't hard to see how she had built a successful business. I momentarily wondered whether we should kiss or hug, but she coolly held out her hand. Her grip was firm.

'Marnie!' The moment I said it I knew I wasn't ready to paint her and wished I hadn't come. 'How lovely to see you.'

'It's Marianne now.'

I understood. In a single sentence I realized that, unlike almost everyone else at school, she'd never wanted or needed to do the 'right thing' — where she'd come from there was no 'right thing'. She had always understood a possibility most people only grasp when it's too late: her life was hers and she could do with it whatever she wanted. And she had done.

'Marianne. How lovely to see you.'

'It's been a while.'

There was no sarcasm, only the faintly ironic lilt I remembered, a kind of distance that held a mirror to the rest of us who thought we were so worldly-wise because we had stayed at country houses and summered on Paxos, or partied in SW3. I had been Marnie's only friend and she'd been mine and, whatever she'd done wrong, I had failed her. I felt more than regret for the way I had behaved, the years I had missed. She sat down on one of the sofas and indicated the other for me.

'You are happy to talk before we start?'

'More than happy, it's essential. I knew Marnie. I've got to paint Marianne.'

'You think they'll be different?'

'I know they'll be different.'

She nodded thoughtfully as Johnson appeared with a tray. Cups and saucers and a pot of coffee. Petits fours. He was a small man, swarthy as a Spaniard, short-sleeved, frowning. A snake tattoo slithered out on to his forearm. Marianne waited until he had gone before saying,

'Well, where do you want to start?'

I had thought a lot about where I wanted to start. I wanted to start with an apology. The problem was it wasn't my prerogative to raise the subject, that ghost at the feast.

'Tell me about yourself. Everything that's happened in the last twenty years.'

I kept it as neutral as possible. She could start after school if she wanted, or the day it happened. I could go either way. In such a way does the portraitist proceed, withdrawing behind the easel, luring out the sitter like a rabbit from a hole.

Marianne started after school. She touched on her brief marriage as a nineteen-year-old to a songwriter named Rob and its failure after he slept with his key-boardist. She spoke about being a single mother, how it had forced her to take any job, initially as the only girl in an M&S warehouse, a bracing world of wolf whistles and catcalls, next as a shop girl, later still a buyer. She told me how an older man, a supplier with whom she'd had a relationship, who believed in her, lent her the money to start on her own. 'And the rest . . . ' She inclined her head mock-modestly, gesturing to the size of the room.

Gradually, as she talked about her son who had just started university, her therapeutic sculpting, and played down her success,

Marianne became Marnie, enthusiastic and loquacious, hungry to hear about Ed and Nell and Arthur, Bristol, the people I'd painted. When she'd been answering and asking questions for almost an hour, school unmentioned, and it was probably time to start, I said,

'One thing: I ran into Lucy Rennell the other day and she said she'd bumped into you in London a couple of years ago and you said we still saw each other. I was wondering, why did you say that?'

Marianne's face creased as if I'd told a joke.

'No reason.'

'No reason?'

'We shared a taxi. She was being so boring about all her do-gooding and school, saying how she saw all these people I couldn't even remember, so I said I saw you.' She shrugged. 'It was no big deal.'

'Oh, OK. I just wondered.'

'And can I ask you a question before we begin?'

'Fire away.'

'That thing that happened the other day: why did the police pick you and your husband up for the girl's murder?'

I should have known Marnie would never stick to the script. I rapidly pulled myself together and, hugging the party line, explained about Ed's exhaustion and out-of-character drunkenness at Pete's party, how he went back to Stokes Croft with Araminta and several others from London, how he'd thought better of it but there were no cabs and he'd forgotten his mobile, which meant he had to go up to the flat to call one, how he'd had another drink and crashed out and fixed her plumbing before leaving, and how the flowers had been enough to set the police hares running.

'Had she called a plumber before?'

In all the time I knew her, Marnie had never asked a stupid question. It was a timely reminder. Marianne Hever didn't owe me any loyalty. Marnie Latham certainly didn't. Chrissie Wright had rung the morning after I had been on the news. I suddenly realized that probably wasn't a coincidence.

'I've no idea.'

'Because if she had and for whatever reason he hadn't turned up then Ed would be totally in the clear. Isn't that worth checking?'

She crossed her legs, her elegant calves. I licked dry lips. This was not terrain on which I wanted to find myself. I tried to sound relaxed.

'Yes, it is. Good idea.'

'You mean you haven't done that?'

There was incredulity in her voice. I shook my head.

'But surely that was the first thing to do?'

'Maybe the police have. I haven't. I trust Ed.'

'I trusted Rob.'

★   ★   ★

By the time I had primed the canvas I understood exactly how the infectious Marnie had become the poised Marianne. I also realized I had a compositional problem. How could I paint Marianne Hever in her own home without reference to the singular spatial geometry of the house she told me she had self-designed? Yet how could any geometric construct do justice to the wit, perceptiveness, common sense, determination, vivacity, curiosity, sensitivity and intelligence of the woman I had been talking to? The brutal logic of mathematics denies the exceptionalism of the individual (how many times have I told Ed that?) and rarely had I met anyone as exceptional as Marianne. She had slept and fought and manipulated and charmed and worked and thought her way from pretty much the absolute bottom to pretty much the very top, and she'd done it with no benefit from the scholarship she'd won to a southern boarding school.

While we talked I assembled the pose. She would stand. Her energy and engagement with the world outside demanded it. Julie had sat on her throne because she was queen of all she surveyed, but it was purely ceremonial and didn't extend beyond Ray's four walls. Standing is tiring but Marianne would cope. She's a tough cookie, her history told you that. I would sit, perched on my stool, palette and paint trolley to hand, looking up literally and metaphorically, acknowledging a woman in control of her destiny. I decided to use the orange abstract in the hall as the only colour in an otherwise all-white background, unanchored, off-centre, sans fireplace. The sitter needs a point of reference, and what could be better than that circular painting? The nod to geometry was essential. Not just because of the house but because mathematics is part of who Marianne is. You didn't become as successful as she had in business without a Euclidean feel for figures and spreadsheets, all that stuff I've never understood and never wanted to understand. At the same time I would have to undermine the geometry if I was going to capture her humanity. She needed to be floating in space, cut off from her roots, yet still be the source of the painting's energy. Marianne must be enhanced, not outshone, by that sunburst of orange. That would serve as an oblique contrast, a mathematical motif, a painting within the painting.

She had chosen an expensive black business suit, 'not from one of my shops'. The skirt revealed a glimmer of thigh. Her legs are good. I never make suggestions about what my sitters should wear and refuse if they ask for advice. It is their choice and one way they reveal themselves. Tyrants invariably turn up in jeans and a T-shirt, self-delusion being an essential characteristic of the tyrannical. Marianne's suit was the first chink in her armour. It told me she wanted to be respected, maybe even needed to be respected. Maybe she needed to be respected by me? I would try to capture that hint of doubt.

I squeezed gouts of colour from tubes, alizarin crimson, ultramarine and flake white for her skin, raw umber to temper her mine-black suit, before sketching her outline in pencil. I needed a sense of the whole before starting, like Hansel dropping his pebbles. By the end of the session I was making progress.

The second day did not start well. Marianne had worked through dinner, leaving me to eat on my own again, missed breakfast and didn't reappear until ten, an hour and a half after we were supposed to start. She didn't apologize. I didn't say anything. We both knew we only had four days. If we didn't finish I could add the final touches in my studio, though given it was west-facing there were obvious implications for colour and tone. It wouldn't be the first time. More than once a problem I'd wrestled with interminably in front of the sitter had been solved as soon as I was home alone and liberated from his or her desire to shape the outcome. Those moments of sudden resolution are ones you chase, when the clouds part and the sun breaks through. Almost in spite of her, the painting gained weight and strength.

At lunchtime she excused herself again, citing business. Did she ever eat? I sat alone in her dining room and picked at chicken chasseur, scented with cumin, and broad beans from the kitchen garden. Johnson was an excellent cook but I wasn't hungry. I rarely am when I'm working. Yet I knew it was more than that. Although the portrait was progressing, I had a feeling I was not in control. It was as if Marianne was undermining me in some way. Nibbling on the chicken, I couldn't work out whether the feeling related to her or her portrait.

Half an hour after we should have restarted Chrissie bustled in wearing her heatwave outfit of red cords, Puffa jacket and pearls. She said Marianne had had to go into work. There was no apology. I was becoming irritated. I wanted to work. I wanted to spend time with Marianne. I wanted to eat with her. I wanted to immerse myself in her. I didn't have to be her friend again but I only had four days and I wanted to squeeze them dry. It was her portrait, my career. Sitting in that bright shell of a drawing room, it was hard not to feel there was movement behind the story, some purpose about which only I was unaware.

Chrissie was full of useless suggestions. Was there anything I wanted to do? Everything could be arranged. Would I like to explore the park? Go riding? Boating? Go into Manchester? A driver was available.

'I'll work on the background, thanks.'

She disappeared through an invisible door in what I had previously assumed was bare wall, leaving me in the empty room. Almost every door here was concealed in a wall. I looked around wondering if there were any others I had missed, or anything else. In the top corner of the room there was a small silver ball I hadn't noticed. Smoke alarm? CCTV? It was impossible to know. Was I being watched by Chrissie, or Johnson, or even Marianne? How did I know she had gone into Manchester? I hadn't seen or heard her car leave. For all I knew she was still in Bow House watching me. Standing there in that stark white room, every corner lit by a bullying sun, I felt as exposed as a Sunday kiss-and-tell. And suddenly I wondered if the whole project was designed to be some sort of career-destroying revenge for what had happened in the dormitory all those years ago.

Don't be ridiculous! She hadn't even mentioned the dormitory. Marianne Hever ran a multimillion-pound company. She made a thousand decisions every day. Of course some would require her to be at her desk, not standing at home having her portrait painted.

Maybe she had only worn the business suit so she could slip off to work at a moment's notice? But if that was the case, then she wasn't wearing it because she 'needed' to be respected or, specifically, 'needed' to be respected 'by me'. That would change the dynamic of the portrait. But how to reflect it? The question prompted a second: had I jumped to too many easy conclusions? My stomach gave an answer I didn't wish to acknowledge. That had never been a problem before. It couldn't only be the result of the lack of time I spent with her before the sitting because, if rare, that wasn't unique. So if I had, there could only be one reason for it.

I stared at the portrait helplessly. I had been planning to work up the left side of Marianne's face in the afternoon, but now I wasn't so sure. I stood and moved back from my stool to gain a wider perspective. It didn't feel right. I looked hard. I had to understand what I needed to do to create the balance that would enable me to start on her left side. Maybe her forehead needed more definition? Was her collarbone too pronounced, her neck too slim? Or did the problem lie in the brushwork? Was it too hot and heavy for someone as cool as Marianne? The canvas sat unhelpfully on its easel. Marianne offered no clues. I sat down again. And for the first time in my career I didn't know what to do next.

16

'Do you think you were screwed up by your upbringing?'

Marianne's opening gambit on the third morning. I was so surprised all I could manage was a grunted 'No.' I turned away and mixed a gob of cadmium red into some grey on my palette, making clear it wasn't a line of conversation I wanted to pursue. The portraitist should *never* become the subject or a work is guaranteed to fail. Marianne's teeth were as sharp as a rodent's, but her voice was soft.

'All roads lead to Highlands.'

I looked at my palette knife. The cerulean was streaked with titanium white and alizarin crimson for her eyes. The silence grew. I said, perhaps too haughtily,

'I'm surprised you remember Highlands. I didn't think you ever went there.'

'I didn't. But it sounded so weird I've never forgotten it. The mum who never showed any love. The dad who died but who never came home even when he was alive. The brother who was so out of it he thought going to Oxford was a jail sentence. The sister who buried herself in books and never engaged with real life. Then again, I'm not sure any of your family ever engaged with the outside world, except for you. You were their only link to it. Otherwise it sounded like five people living separate lives under the same roof. I always thought the mad house on the moor that you described was the perfect metaphor for isolation.'

I put my palette down on the trolley. In spite of their faults I was protective of my family — there had been times when it felt as if I was the only one trying to keep the show on the road — and I knew I couldn't let Marianne get under my skin. Was she really trying to goad me or was I being paranoid? I glanced at the portrait. The painted Marianne stared down at me, superiority (and contempt?)in her eyes. It was impossible to know. It was as if everything — Marianne in the dormitory, my life, Ed, that woman, Philips, this portrait, our family — had morphed into a single painted accusation. I had to move the conversation on.

'Why did you ask me to come here and paint you?'

Marianne's mouth twitched humorously.

'Because I wanted my portrait painted and you have a reputation.'

'Please.'

'And because I wanted to see you again.'

'You could have called. We could have had lunch.'

'Because I wanted you to paint my portrait. I wanted to spend some proper time with you.'

I was tempted to say she had spent as little time as humanly possible with me, but instead I said,

'Why now?'

'Why not now?'

'Because you were never a 'why not?' sort of person.'

Marianne inclined her head and her nose

flared like a fox sniffing for scent.

'OK, here's why: I always planned to get in touch again, I just didn't know when. I always assumed there would be a time when it would feel right. It was never about showing you how successful I was — I could have done that years ago. Besides, I know that's not what you're about. Then I saw you on the news the other day, losing your cool with that journalist, and I knew now was the moment.' She relaxed her pose. 'I was intrigued. Because the Alice Tenterden I remembered was far too self-possessed to explode like that. And that set me wondering. Stress works on different people in different ways. I see it all the time in business. I wondered what the stress that was affecting you might be.'

'You have children. You wouldn't want Jack to see his mother treated like that.'

'No, I wouldn't. But children survive. They're stronger than we give them credit for.'

'Mine are still young.'

'Sure, but they're growing up, they're becoming who they are. Teenagers are broadly formed. Their characters are set, their strengths and weaknesses. They've turned to their peers for influence. God knows, I of all people should understand that. The fashion industry lives off that insight.'

Her voice was strong but there was a tint of melancholy, an emptiness that is a kind of loneliness. I felt a stab of pity. I was transported back to the dormitory, to the moment her lofty idealism was betrayed by grubby reality. I had always had options she never had. Her life might seem enviable now but I wouldn't swap it for mine.

'Do you miss Jack?'

'Everyone misses their past.'

'Is that why you wanted your portrait painted?'

'I've always wanted my portrait painted.'

'By me?'

'Yes.'

'And now I'm infamous . . . '

'Exactly.'

'I'm flattered.'

'And I wanted to see you again. See how you'd turned out. My guess, call it my intuition, is that you probably don't have any close friends, not properly close anyway. You never did at school, except me, and I always seemed an aberration, the result of my background and your admirable if somewhat ironic dislike of spoilt people. You're not the type to get close to other people, it's not hard to see where it comes from. As I said, I've never come across a family that sounded so disconnected. I suspect Ed is the same.'

'Hardly.'

'In terms of friends. Thing is, I have always found that people marry to type at some subliminal level. They marry attitudes and ambitions they understand. I know his background is nearer mine than yours, but he's an obstetrician and you're a portrait painter. They're vocations, not jobs. They take you into an enclosed world totally removed from your past. In fact, when I found out that's what you had become I rather admired you for choosing it

240

as a career. It's exactly what I would have recommended if I had thought of it.'

'Thank you.' I didn't try to hide the sarcasm.

'It seemed ideal for someone who had watched from behind the sofa as her family fell apart, yet emerged unhurt from the wreckage to go to Cambridge, marry the great doctor and build herself a successful career.'

'Portraiture isn't exactly fashionable. At least, not in oil.'

Marianne gave a dry laugh.

'But you're doing what you want, and, more importantly, you believe in it. To that extent you've never changed. Because the Alice I knew always wanted — always *needed* to believe. So, when you blew up in the street that day I felt something was wrong: I didn't know what it was, obviously, but I wanted to see you again, and I felt that now was the time.'

'I'm touched.'

'And I wanted to see whether my hunch was right.'

'Your hunch?'

Marianne paused, as if for a moment she was battling with herself, unsure whether to continue. We both knew she was posturing.

'That you or Ed or both of you together really did have some connection to the death of that girl.'

She watched me like a chemistry teacher waiting for a reaction to begin. I stared back, blank as an empty test tube, but Marianne simply arched an eyebrow. I shook my head at the absurdity of it.

'That's ridiculous! If there was any doubt the police wouldn't have let us go.'

Marianne cocked her head and looked at me sceptically. I had to move everything on.

'Can we get on with the portrait?'

For a moment I thought she hadn't heard, but then she nodded graciously, said, 'Of course', and re-established her pose. She had a feline quality, mischievous and dangerous. Marianne had lit her fuse. I retreated behind the easel. When I did look up it was only to line her up with a heavy brush and to ask her to tilt her head slightly to the right. She tilted.

We had a long period of silence. I tried not to think about Marianne's accusation but it was impossible to divorce it from the character I was painting. I had to hope we could move on, but as the morning lengthened I realized I was exhausted, deep-down exhausted, cut adrift at sea, oar-less, unable to stop, unable to go on. Forward motion, time itself, seemed buried in the past. I desperately needed a break but was conscious I wasn't as advanced as I needed to be, the result of that wasted afternoon, the first morning spent chatting and Marianne's persistent absences. I thanked God there was no background beyond the orange abstract, which I could paint in my studio. It was simply a case of recreating the amazing orange. I re-cast her nose. It worked on its own with the eyes but in adding her mouth it seemed to have shifted, making her look crafty in a way she signally wasn't. I was dabbing Naples yellow on to the underside of her bottom lip when she said,

'What would you do if Ed had done it?'

I smudged a fleck of umber on her left eyebrow with my finger.

'He didn't.'

It was as if I hadn't spoken.

'If, I don't know, something had happened between them?'

'It didn't.'

I put my paintbrush to my mouth and held it horizontally between my teeth while I picked up another. It's an old trick when you don't want to answer. I raised an angled palm like a hairdresser, motioning her to turn her head slightly left.

'After all, it wouldn't be the first time.'

I mumbled a couple of words, paintbrush-unintelligible, and touched a glimpse of terre verte to the corner of her mouth.

'Middle-aged man meets young woman at a party. Is flattered by the attention. Gets drunk and stays the night.'

I took the paintbrush out of my mouth and wiggled it in the jam jar of turps.

'He only stayed because there were no cabs.'

'Oldest story under the sun.'

'He's not that obvious.'

'Clichés are clichés for a reason.'

I added a gob of cadmium yellow to the grey.

'Marianne,' I tried to sound as light-hearted as possible, 'it didn't happen. It's not possible.'

'Chronologically or temperamentally?'

I dabbed Mars black on to her right ear to create greater weight on that side of her face. Tangerine to soften the black.

'Both.'

'Because he was with you?'

Rose madder for the ear. Only it sucked colour away from the eyes and Marianne shone in her eyes. If I messed them up I hadn't got a portrait.

'Because he was with me.'

'How did I guess?'

I ignored her intonation. Manganese blue for the eyes.

'Hypothetically then.'

'It's not even possible hypothetically. It's too out of character.'

'Well, let's just imagine he did. You're the creative one. Out of character he gets drunk at the party. That's not in dispute. Why? Because you're not there? Because he's knackered? Because a pretty girl hits on him?'

The white disc of the sun blasted through the huge windows, burning the day. The lake shimmered in the haze. I forced myself to stay calm, allowing only the mildest indignation to creep into my voice.

'Are you serious?'

'Let's imagine . . . So they go back to her flat.'

'It wasn't just him. That young guy who was arrested, he was there for a start. So were a whole lot of others.'

Marianne gave a feathery grin.

'OK, so he goes back there with an army. Then what happens? One by one the platoon disperses, falls in, falls out, falls asleep, falls in love, whatever, I don't know, they're young and single, there's no law against it, until it's just him and her, or maybe it's not, but hey, who's counting? No one knows him. You said they were

244

all from London. And he's already done one out-of-character thing that night by getting drunk, what's to stop him doing another?'

'That's not his style.'

'What? Ending up drunk in a flat with a lot of twenty-and thirty-year-olds is not his style?'

'That too.'

'Sounds like he was having a night off from his style.'

'Marianne, you're worse than the trolls!'

She coolly brushed a forefinger against her temple as if it was a compliment. This was how she built her retail empire, pushing forward, never taking 'no' for an answer. How different it was to the tentative, questioning business of making art.

'Put it this way: he went back to her flat; they were drunk; he stayed the night with the other guy; she's dead; the other guy's been released; the police think — or thought — Ed was involved in some way. They must have had some reason. It all stacks up.'

I looked at the portrait on the easel. Was it even possible to capture her remorselessness? I had to treat it as if it was a joke. There was no alternative.

'Now I know you're bonkers!'

'You don't *know* anything.'

What else could I say? That I was amazed and terrified by the ferocity of her intuition? No wonder she could predict what colours and styles everyone would want to be wearing the year after next. I dabbed a flash of viridian where her jacket caught the light. I had to hide behind my easel. Her portrait-eyes were on fire. They needed cooling down. They needed grey. I said firmly,

'Actually I do know one thing. I know Ed. I know what I mean to him. I know what his children, who are not grown up and are not doing their own thing, mean to him. You may never have had a normal family life, but a family is irreducible in a way that's impossible to describe. I've seen both sides too. I know Ed and I know he would never throw his family away.' Marianne smirked triumphantly, so I added meanly,

'A family can't be replaced by a big house or a successful business. It only works with love. How do I know that? I just *know*.'

I turned back to my palette, where I was running short of corn-yellow. She nodded, as if accepting the truth of my words, but then arched her back extravagantly and said,

'Instinct is more powerful than knowledge.'

I gritted my teeth. There was nothing I could say or do. I felt pinned to my stool. When she saw I wasn't going to reply she said softly,

'Do you want to know what I think?'

The answer was apparent but there was no point saying it.

'I think he killed her.'

It was as simple and brutal as that. She scanned my face for a reaction. I tried to look as if I'd never heard anything so ridiculous, but suddenly I didn't trust myself to speak. How long can you defend the indefensible?

'Don't get me wrong, I'm not calling you a

liar. I think you were probably with him whenever you said you were, but I also think he was with her when she died.'

I didn't want to listen. There was white noise in my ears. This was how it felt when your husband was charged with murder. I forced myself to meet her gaze, to give a disbelieving shake of the head, a false, sickly grin at the absurdity of the charge.

'And, you know, I'm not saying he's a murderer.'

'Then what are you saying?' My voice sounded hoarse. There was nowhere to escape in that baking white room.

'I'm just saying that whatever actually happened, and whatever chain of events led to it, I think he is the man the police are looking for.' She scanned my face cheerfully. I was rigid with fear. 'I know people in Bristol, I've got a shop in Cabot's, and I know people at Sotheby's, I put business their way, and from what I can gather Araminta Lyall was one screwed-up lady with an eye for the older man. I think your husband got too close and then, I don't know, there was a fight or perhaps an accident and he couldn't own up or tell the truth because he couldn't prove it wasn't murder.'

I was shaking my head all the while she was speaking and yet I was rooted to my stool in terror. Marianne had been checking the story, understanding that woman, burrowing through her past, probing her motivation. I had no choice. I had to stop her. I said,

'Marianne, that might all sound plausible but

it simply doesn't stand up on the timings. There's not a shred of evidence for any of it. In fact, everything points the other way, that he couldn't have done it.'

'You know, I'm always wary of people who talk about 'facts'. 'Facts' don't exist. Interpretations exist. Perspectives exist. Motive exists. Weakness exists. More than that, from where I'm sitting — and assuming the police are right and Mr Trumble didn't do it — then it seems the obvious explanation, maybe even the only explanation. That's why the police came on to you that day.'

'I don't get 'obvious'.'

'Because you know as well as I do that if you put a drunk forty-five-year-old in a room late at night with a bunch of drunk thirty-year-olds and something goes badly wrong, the wise money will always be on the odd one out.'

I sighed melodramatically, playing for time, but I was going under. She had every angle covered. Marianne was powering on:

'I think he did it for two reasons — circumstantial, I admit, but all the more powerful to my mind for that.' She surveyed me for any sign of weakness. I stared back numbly, incapable of speech. 'First, because everything I've read about Ed and everything you've told me makes it clear he's a gentleman in the old sense. That being the case, there's no way he wouldn't have said something after you were swamped in the road that afternoon. He would have defended you, if not at that exact moment because he wasn't there, then afterwards. He would have taken the pressure off you and diverted attention to himself. He wouldn't have left you hung out to dry, not when anyone could see you were in a really bad place.'

She paused, taunting me, but my heart had exploded because I had a chance to tell the truth and to puncture her self-satisfaction. I almost shouted with triumph,

'He did offer! He did, I swear, exactly that, he offered to speak out, but I refused. I said it would only fan the flames. You're completely wrong about that!'

For a moment Marianne seemed almost conciliatory, but as soon as the look appeared it was gone.

'Then why did you refuse?'

'Because . . . '

'Exactly. Why would anyone refuse after what you'd been through? Unless . . . '

'Unless what?'

'Unless you had something to hide.'

I stared at her. My mouth may have dropped open.

'And the second reason . . . '

She allowed the silence to build for so long that for a moment I thought she'd forgotten what she was going to say. She must have heard my heart pumping. At that moment I would have preferred to be anything — a pillar of salt, a bar of soap — than trapped in the floodlit glare of Marianne's stare. The easel had spun 180 degrees. She was the hunter, I was the prey.

' . . . Is you.'

I was determined not to be drawn but I

couldn't help blurting out,

'Me?'

'You. On the first day here you said you wanted to chat before starting because you had to get to know me again because you knew Marnie, not Marianne. But you were wrong, weren't you? I haven't changed, not fundamentally, and judging by the stuff I've read about you, nor have you. Everything I've read tells me that when you're not being trolled by the press or helping the police with their inquiries you're the same self-possessed and confident Alice Tenterden you were at school, just as sure in your opinions of other people and artists, and of yourself and your work and your place in the world as you ever were. Only you're not suddenly, are you? Not now, not here. So what's changed, that's what I asked myself. What's happened since you were profiled in *Tatler* or *Harper's* or wherever it was and you were sounding off about the 'poverty' — I think that was the word you used — of so much contemporary art and proclaiming your own combination of figurative and abstract, your own brand of realism and truth? That Alice was exactly the Alice I remembered from school, the one who knew her own mind and wasn't afraid to speak it, the one who didn't buy into any bullshit. For God's sake, that's why we were friends! But the Alice painting me is suddenly tongue-tied when it comes to the subject of her husband and some girl. The Alice painting me is relying on 'facts' and 'times', and mistaking 'facts' for truth in a way she would never have done at school, at least not when we were friends.' Her voice dropped into a cartoon whisper, as if she was letting me into a secret. 'The Alice I knew at school always believed in some larger truth; the one painting me can't even muster any self-belief.'

I gave her a look which tried to make out she simply didn't realize how wrong she was. But Marianne had started. And when she started she kept going until she finished. She always had done.

'And you know what? It makes me think maybe I'm not being ridiculous after all. It makes me think this Alice is frightened of something, and maybe what she is frightened of is the truth. I don't know, of course, I can't ever *know*, but put it all together and it seems pretty conclusive. To me, anyway.' She gave a stagey wink. I shook my head and offered a contemptuous laugh but it fell short and hollow. 'But don't worry, darlin', *I* won't tell the other girls. Your secret is safe with me.'

I stared at her in what I hope conveyed disbelief, but I knew I only had one line left. I had to use it to maximum effect. So I spoke slowly, gaining purpose as the sentences tumbled out,

'Ah, I see, I get it, so that's what this is about. I suppose I guessed we'd get here in the end.' Marianne shifted out of her pose, glinting dangerously, but said nothing. 'You deliberately asked me up here to make ridiculous accusations about Ed, and to try to screw me up as a painter or fuck up my reputation to get back at me for what happened at school. That's the truth, isn't it?'

She glided over to the sofa and perched on the arm.

'Ah, school. I wondered when we'd get round to that.'

Her tone was light, playful, but also deadly serious. I stood up. I was looking at her over the easel.

'Because I'm sorry about that, I really am, and I have been since the moment it happened. I tried to apologize at the time but you wouldn't let me, and I understand that. I understood it then too. It was your prerogative. So I didn't pursue you. But don't think I haven't often thought about you and wished things had been different and wondered how everything turned out and really hoped everything would be OK.'

'How very gratifying.'

There was bitterness in her voice. No matter how successful Marianne had been, we both knew countless opportunities had been cut off the day she was expelled for theft. She'd had to make her life the hard way.

'But at least I told the truth.'

'That I was poor and you were rich?'

'That had nothing to do with it. You know that.'

'You mean, if it had been Alice who'd been clutching the tenner they would have dragged you off to the Headmistress without even asking for your side of the story?'

Marianne's jaw was set, her cheeks blazing. There had been no university, no leisure, no self-indulgence, no slow-burn achievement in art, no time to watch her baby grow. Instead there had been work, a warehouse, single motherhood, a shop counter, spreadsheets. An exotic mind in a sunless mall. A young woman tapping an older man for a loan. A boy brought up by his granny. The sun created a lemon wedge of light on the floor. Marianne was looking at me intently, as if she'd been waiting for this moment all her life.

'Well, come on then, what was your side of the story?'

'I came from Manchester.'

'What does that mean?'

'It means they would never have believed me anyway.'

'But nevertheless, the truth was — '

Marianne sliced the air with a horizontal hand, a conductor silencing an orchestra. The sun caught her silver bracelet. I stopped dead, stunned by the venom in her expression.

'The truth was — the truth is — I got back to the dormitory about thirty seconds before you. The ten-pound note was on the floor by Annabel's locker. I saw it as I was going past her bed to mine and assumed it must be hers. So I picked it up, opened her drawer, and was about to put it in when you came in. You saw the open drawer and the money in my hand and even though you were my best friend you jumped to the wrong conclusion. But before I could explain what had actually happened the others came in and asked you what was going on and you just blurted out I was stealing without having ever asked for my side of the story. That was the end of me.' She made a small whirring noise like an arrow finding its target. It had been twenty years. 'I was putting the money back, you see, not taking it out. But if you come in halfway through and you don't know what's happening and you don't bother to ask, then obviously they look the same.'

Marianne was perfectly still, watching me. I laid down my brush. The colours were dead on the canvas. The ceiling came swirling down.

17

I was sitting in the big armchair in the corner of the kitchen, leaning forward, a boxer on the ropes. *Franny and Zooey* lay unopened beside me. Nell was in her room, texting or Skyping or Facebooking or Snapchatting or Instagramming or Tumblring or WhatsApping or messaging or whatever it is she does all day, because it doesn't usually include talking to us. Arthur was killing people at Stan Reynolds' on Sion Hill, hopefully only onscreen. It was the first time he'd walked there alone. My mother would not have approved, but there were mitigating circumstances. The mitigating circumstances were me.

Ed was sitting on a stool at the island in his thin-lapelled grey suit. It was the one he'd worn to Pete's party. He looked exactly how I didn't feel: healthy, bronzed, fit. While I'd been with Marianne he had played tennis, walked to work and bicycled to Bath and back with Arthur. They had swum in the river, jumping off a disused railway bridge, arms rotating, mouths frozen in a silent shout. His blond hair was swept back from his forehead as if he was auditioning for a role in a period drama and the bags under his eyes had completely disappeared.

Despite his aura of well-being, Ed had been visibly shocked when I told him why I'd come home a day earlier than expected, even though he tried to hide it. He knew nothing short of a crisis would have made me give up on a portrait — this was my career, my life — so he tried to take the news calmly, murmuring 'uh-hmm' and 'OK' at regular intervals and attempting to see things from my perspective. Eventually he asked me to fetch the unfinished portrait, which I'd refused to leave with Marianne. 'Not even as a memento?' she'd cooed, ostentatiously tearing up the cheque I'd left to cover her deposit. I propped it up in front of him against the mantelpiece. I could hardly bear to look at it.

'I thought it was an article of faith that you never gave up on a painting.'

I felt puffy and cloud-like, defeated.

'It was.'

'So what changed?'

'Everything.'

He opened his hands like a priest. I was rocking in my chair. I owed Ed an explanation, much as I had owed Marianne one. Hers was easier. She wasn't vain and she had never had any interest in the portrait. Her interest was me, and in Ed, and in some sort of payback for how I had failed her — no, more than failed her, how I had taken her prospects and her life away. The portrait was simply a vehicle to buy time and intimacy. Her job was done. No wonder she released me from my contract with a flourish.

When Ed saw I wasn't going to answer he picked up the photo I had taken of Marianne in pose, flicked its corner, looked across at the portrait and said,

'I think it's perfectly good. More than that, I think it's . . . ' he was shaking his head, struggling for the right word, ' . . . great.' In spite of everything, I almost smiled. Ed could always be relied upon to deliver an opinion with the minimum of drama. He'd learnt it at work. 'Obviously I've never met the woman but from her photo the portrait seems spot on. I don't get what was the problem.'

'Because it's not her.'

He held up the photo next to the portrait.

'You're joking. You must be. I honestly wouldn't know which is the real her. I would recognize her in the street.'

I shook my head.

'Please, darling, tell me this is some sort of game? Tell me you brought this back because you needed to touch it up or work on the background or she had to go on a business trip or there was some other reason for finishing early? Please tell me you didn't really refuse to continue? Because from where I'm standing this is the real deal.'

I examined a knot in the wooden floorboard. It was hourglass-shaped, like Munch's *The Scream*. I knew I could never make him understand, but I owed it to him to try.

'I should never have gone. I wasn't in the right place to do it. I should have known that.'

'But . . . what's wrong with it? Look at it . . . It's great.'

I looked at the portrait like a criminal forced to confront the evidence.

'It's a likeness, but it's not her. It's a picture, not a portrait. There's no essence of Marianne. I didn't capture her. I failed completely. I knew it and she knew it. There was no way back.'

'But I thought you said there was always a way back, that you could always work stuff up, scrape paint off, start again? I don't get why you had to give up on this. I mean, you haven't even started the background.'

Ed was staring at me, willing me to give an explanation he could understand, but I couldn't. I couldn't revisit that huge bare room with its floor-to-ceiling glass, its merciless sun. I didn't want to think about Marianne in her dark suit, or her theories, her remorselessness, the sense I was the one being interrogated, intimidated, analysed, judged, hunted down, captured for posterity.

'Because it's not a portrait of Marianne, it's a portrait of me. At best it's a portrait of us, of everything that's happened.'

'I don't understand. It's self-evidently not you.'

'It's a portrait of me in the presence of Marianne. It's a study of my weakness, my arrogance, my failure to understand and, in the end, my humiliation. You can see it in those drilling eyes. I don't expect you to see it, but I can tell you, that's what it is. It's not a portrait of Marianne. I couldn't do that. I couldn't lay a finger on her. The idea it was me painting her portrait and not the other way round was a joke.'

Ed stared at the painting determinedly, as if by looking at it hard enough he could make some sense of what I was saying. His cheeks were pale. He didn't understand but there was no other way I could explain.

'That's ridiculous! It doesn't look anything like you.'

'Ed, I promise I tried. Maybe it started out as a portrait of her, but it became a portrait of us, Marianne and me, our relationship, our history, and then, because of the way she was, that shaded into my relationship with you, and that woman, and everything that's happened. I didn't want it to, I fought it, I promise I did, but she . . . well . . . she was on home ground and she was too strong. In the end I realized I could no more paint her portrait than run her business.'

Ed turned the photo upside down, sideways, looked at the back, mystified, shaking his head, trying — somehow, anyhow — to see if he could see what I meant. I looked at the Munch-grain in the floor. I couldn't help him understand. I heard a squeak as his stool pushed back and he came over to me, sat on the arm of the chair, placed a cupped hand under my chin, lifted my head until our eyes met, mine reluctantly, and said,

'Darling, you have to try to understand that what we are doing is for the best. For me — yes, of course, obviously it suits me — but also for you and the children. If you can just try and get your head around that I promise it really will make everything a whole lot easier.'

★ ★ ★

It is often said that everyone who was old enough remembers where they were when they heard JFK had been assassinated. I can believe it, because I can remember exactly where I was when I heard Princess Diana had died — the equivalent example of a world-famous person mown down in my lifetime. I was at JFK since you ask, though I've always preferred the airport's original name, Idlewild, a beautiful word which lacks the sleaze-bag connotations that accompany the Kennedys and 'Camelot' these days. That's the land of liberty, though: shiny on the outside, worms within. I was waiting at baggage carousel seven with Robin Seldon, who I trekked round the US with the summer I left school, when the news came through. I always thought Diana's death must have been a welcome release. She had nowhere to go. I'm beginning to understand what she went through.

I heard Ed's news in the kitchen. I was sitting at the island, my brain dead, my fingers hooked into a mug of tea, leafing aimlessly through a copy of *Hello!* that Nell must have picked up somewhere. Its priorities hadn't changed. Simon was on his speedboat with two interchangeable girls. Gwyneth was swimming off a yacht off Malibu. A blonde lady, all boots and bosom and botox, someone I promise I had never seen before, was inviting me into her ranch-style Surrey house to tell me how the death of Joss (her husband? her daughter? her *horse*?) had made her value her privacy more than ever.

I was looking at her bleached hair and leathery skin, her bereft but unbowed expression, but I was thinking of all the cameras and lights and microphones and people and wires trailing across oceans and plains and beaches and streets and staircases, turning real lives into make-believe for the armchair gratification of the unknown. I was thinking of the black-eyed cameras shoved in my face in the road and Isherwood's famous opening line when Ed appeared, momentarily as a ghostly presence beyond the door, then in person, broad and solid. He was in his suit but his tie was loosened, top button undone. There was triumph in the flare of his nostrils. He glanced around the room to check I was alone and said,

'Have you heard the news?'

His voice was excited in a way that was 'sooooo not Daddy', as Nell would have said.

'Gwyneth is in Malibu?'

'No? What — '

'Surprise me.'

His face cracked into a smile. It felt like one I hadn't seen since the Plantagenets were on the throne.

'They've called it off.'

'Called what off?'

'Called the murder inquiry off. The police. They've called the manhunt off.'

His face was so bright, so eager like a schoolboy's, I could only manage —

'Oh darling!'

— before I felt the walls cave in and tears (of joy? of despair? of both?) burst out. I didn't want him to see me cry, so I pulled him to me and buried my head in his chest. I held him tightly for the first time in ages, as if my life depended on it, which is what I should have done all through these past weeks.

'I got an email from that guy Pullen, the DI who pulled you in. You got it as well. Surprised you haven't seen it.' I didn't say anything. He didn't need to know I hadn't opened an email since I got back from Marianne. There couldn't be any good news. 'Said they'd followed every lead and testimony and nothing had led anywhere. So they'd come to the conclusion it was an accident and are going to shelve the investigation unless anything new turns up. Nice of them to let us know. They now think she hadn't taken her drugs — there were none in her body at the autopsy, but apparently there should have been — she was on various prescriptions — and she slipped and hit her head. Case closed. Or, not quite closed, but left in a file marked 'Do not open unless further evidence emerges'.'

I lifted my head and squeezed out happiness.

'Oh darling, that's brilliant news.'

And maybe just for a moment I thought it was and that we could go back to where we had been before Peter Spurling's party. But when I caught sight of Ed's face, I realized he hadn't really heard my words because he was so wrapped up in his triumph and relief and joy, and my pleasure drained away. I could hardly blame him for being ecstatic, but his ecstasy only took account of what he had been through, not what I was still going through or what would be wrapped around us forever. Ed had always looked forward but his unconcealed delight, his apparent deafness, spoke volumes. Everything was all right again and the world according to Edward Sheahan could just roll right on. There was no scope for doubt, no room for justice, no need for truth. No place for me.

'Let's go out to dinner? Somewhere special.' His eyes were alight and his tone expansive.

I disentangled myself. I couldn't face dinner out, not à deux. But I didn't want to rain on his parade so, in a deliberate voice that tried to disguise my despair, I said,

'I'm not sure it's a cause for celebration, even though it's great news. I mean, someone still died.'

It was as if someone had switched a lamp off. There was a pause before he said quietly but firmly,

'Darling, nothing can change the past. But what has changed is the future, our future.'

'Her parents' future?'

He gave a long sigh, frustration written across his face like bankruptcy.

'Darling, accidents happen. Look at the news any night of the week. War, flooding, disease, poverty, drought, death of every kind — it's around us every day. Most of it isn't even an accident, it's a part of life. What's happened today may not end brutality in Somalia and it won't save the NHS, but it saves us and, more importantly, it saves the children.'

'It saves you.' I tried to sound ironic, or playful, but I could see in his look that I hadn't pulled it off.

'OK, yes, and it saves me.'

'And that's a good thing.'

And it was. I reached up and put my arms around his neck. He bent down to kiss me on the mouth. His arms were around my back and they pulled me to him. I felt the softness of his lips swimming against mine and I began to feel guilty again. It wasn't a case of either/or. Binary outcomes belong to the world of maths. This was about people, real people, eating drinking sweating swearing greedy frightened people. Even if these lips did kiss that woman, even if this body slept with that woman and even if as a direct result she lost her life, maybe she really did bring it all upon herself.

Don't we all?

*   *   *

Ed was singing in the bath. His voice wasn't bad, though it wasn't good either. He was singing the sounds of the words of the 'Ode to Joy' but not the words, which he doesn't know because he can't speak German. That makes it sound as if he was singing the tune, but he wasn't doing that either. Really he was just making an 'Ode to Joy'-like noise to tell the world all was well and he was happy with his place in it again.

Next door I lay on our bed staring out at a cyanic sky. Gradually his singing began to get on my nerves. It shouldn't have, because it was entirely understandable he felt reborn, but it did. What could I say? I didn't feel reborn. I felt as if I was lying in a field of black tulips, their heads bowed. My skin prickled and my legs ached. My brain was in a vice. I could see my empty studio, the primed canvas, clean brushes, fresh paint on the palette, but all I could think about was the impossibility of walking up one flight of stairs and starting work, because all I could hear was Ed, his voice blocking out everything.

I had to get up, get out, go anywhere to get away, but the heat was oppressive, my limbs too leaden to move. I couldn't breathe. The air was static and there was no noise from the open windows, only Ed filling the house with his joy. I put my thumbs in my ears and pressed my nose with my fingers, my eyes shut, but he had started repeating 'Freude, schoener' over and over again at full volume. The invasive, unstoppable noise — it wasn't singing, not as anyone halfway musical would consider it — made me feel like Alex in *A Clockwork Orange*, strapped in my chair, driven mad by force-fed Beethoven. I couldn't stand it any more. I screamed,

'Please, Ed, SHUT UP!'

The singing stopped mid-word. I opened my eyes tentatively. Arthur was looking down at me with a worried expression.

'Mum, are you all right?'

'Yes, I'm . . . it's just . . . your father's singing . . . it's so awful.' I tried to fake a smile. 'It always has been.'

'But he was only singing to himself.'

I spun off the bed, Arthur stepping hurriedly backwards, surprised by my sudden movement. If I'd stayed one minute more in the house I don't know what would have happened. It, Ed, the heat, everything was smothering me, wrapping itself around me, summoning my long-stilled claustrophobia. Without a word to Arthur (there was nothing I could say), I pulled on some trainers and headed downstairs, hurrying past Nell, who waved from the kitchen table, which was piled high with revision books. Oh God! I had completely forgotten my promise to text her this morning to wish her luck in her exams. I hadn't the energy to wave back.

I was out the door and halfway down the path before I realized I didn't know where I wanted to go. Should I head down to the river or westwards towards the gorge? On a summer's evening the riverside would be a riot of colour, a *paseo* of dog-walkers, skateboarders and bicyclists, elderly couples taking the air, retirees on balconies, drinkers on quays, their legs dangling over the river. All it needed was Seurat. Scullers would be skimming across the tinted water, windsurfers wrestling with sails, waves scribbling on the hull of the Bristol ferry. A riverbank contains multitudes, as the Walt-man could have said.

That was the problem. I might have met someone I knew. I didn't know whether the police had announced anything but if they had I didn't think I could have handled anyone's presumption of my relief or their belatedly restated belief in our innocence ('Of course, Bob and I always knew . . . '). So instead I decided I'd head towards the Polygon, taking the high-walled tree-lined walkway from Cornwallis Crescent, which was always dark and silent and empty. No sun or sound reaches in. It is a place of perspective and depth.

I opened our gate and there, sitting in an unmarked blue BMW parked immediately outside, window down, was Philips. Our eyes met. I hovered uncertainly. I wasn't going to say anything unless I had to, but before I could decide what to do — clearly I couldn't go back into the house — he nodded slowly, knowingly, at me and gave a serpent smile. I shivered despite the heat. Philips's arrow-eyed stare was a death sentence. Without uttering a word or taking his eyes off me he reached for the ignition, turned on the engine and, after the merest glance in his wing-mirror, pulled out and glided away.

I stood still for a few moments until I was sure he had gone. My first instinct was to turn back to tell Ed that Philips was still on our case, but I remembered the bed and the bath, his singing, my empty studio, and I knew I couldn't go back there yet.

Feeling completely frazzled, I headed for the sunken path and the Polygon, a Georgian crescent of exquisite proportions, where I sat on a bench and thought about Philips. I couldn't bear the thought of his triumph, his gleaming face and ridiculous moustache, the calligraphy on his absurd boots, but nor could I bear the status quo. I was caught in a floating world where nothing was grounded, nothing could be resolved. But I knew I would go mad unless I forced myself to think about things that were unconnected to me or Ed or Philips or justice or news or the Internet. So I conjured up Richard Diebenkorn's 'Ocean Park' series in my mind and thought about his rare balance of colour and line. I walked by Hope Square, up Granby Hill, past the Avon Gorge Hotel towards the bridge and Christ-church Green with its shady trees and grand houses. Couples lay on the grass on Sion Hill as I had but Ed hadn't on the day that woman died. No one watched me pass. Killing time, I wandered down through Clifton Village to Victoria Square where I sat on the low stone wall and felt the warmth of the sun on my face. I watched two small boys in shiny red shirts playing football while their mother or au pair sat on a rug reading *Marie Claire* and smoking a cigarette.

When I had wrung Diebenkorn dry I still didn't want to go home so I tried to remember, as if for an architecture exam, the decorative details of buildings in Manhattan. I started with the Chrysler, my favourite, next the Flatiron, third a brownstone I once stayed in on the Bowery. I was determined not to think about Ed and his secret that in one way had miraculously ceased to exist yet in another had still not gone away. Eventually I stopped thinking altogether and just watched the Square breathe. A man on his haunches was trying but failing to light a disposable barbecue. He looked around irritably, pushed back his straw panama, wiped his forehead and took a swig of beer from a bottle. There was quickness in his movement that hinted at a core of anger. A dyed-blonde in black-jeans-gone-grey slit at the knees and a baggy Homer Simpson T-shirt had kicked off her boots and was lying on her back, a fat paperback for a pillow. Her boyfriend played on his phone.

Finally, I drifted home, time passing as I tried to get my head round the fact — yes, *the fact*,

Marianne! — that if Philips didn't get us I was going to have to live with Ed's lie forever. Would that affect my art forever? All art is a quest for truth, every picture a set of problems that has to be solved with integrity. I sat on a bench on the parched grass on Clifton Hill staring out over the haze of south Bristol. There was no solution. In the end I had no choice but to walk back down the hill home.

For some reason, before I opened the front door I looked through the window into the kitchen. Immediately I wished I hadn't. Ed, Arthur and Nell were sitting around the island eating roasted salmon with pesto, Nell's favourite, roaring with laughter. Arthur was literally bent double. He'd pushed his plate away and his forehead was on the side of the island and his shoulders were rocking. Nell was giggling the way she did when she couldn't stop; every time she slowed she'd catch Ed's eye and start again. She leant into him. His arm was around her. He pulled the levers. Whatever he'd said, Ed was beaming, his place in the centre of his family secure once again, the unqualified love of his children assured. I stood outside for more than a minute watching them laugh at their private joke.

The laughter faded into an embarrassed silence when I entered the kitchen. No one had heard the front door.

'Hi.' I tried to sound relaxed, as if the fact they were having a full-on belly laugh after I had stormed out didn't mean anything at all. 'You're obviously having a good time.'

My bonhomie sounded as hollow as it was. There was a stifled giggle from Nell. Arthur pulled his plate towards him. Ed said,

'I hope you don't mind, you were gone so long I did the salmon. Nell's choice.' He glanced at Nell, who pulled a face to stop herself laughing again.

'So I see.' I didn't want to sound irritated.

'Did you have a nice walk?'

It was obvious he was only being polite but there was eagerness in his voice. Ed wanted everything to be as good for me as it was for the three of them, the clock turned back to a time before Peter Spurling's party. I could hardly blame him. But you can't reverse time.

'Fine.'

My downbeat response did nothing to affect his demeanour.

'Anything you've forgotten?' he asked cheerily. Arthur raised an eyebrow at Nell and gave a brief final snort. Ed gleamed with pleasure.

'Um . . . ?'

'Book club?'

Book club! The first since the night that woman died. I could see from his face he hadn't made the connection. To stop myself saying anything I might regret, I glanced at the kitchen clock. Twenty past eight.

'Yup. Geraldine rang to see where you were.'

For a second I wondered whether I could face book club, but even as I wondered I knew it was preferable to this room with its sawn-off joke, a supper suspended by my presence. It would be better for everyone if I went.

'God, I better go.'

I looked around for my bag.

'On the sofa. And there's a card for you on the table.'

I could hear the relief in his voice. I grabbed my bag and the pink envelope, mumbled, 'Thanks, see you later', and headed for the door, acutely conscious I was taking my atmosphere with me. There was silence until I shut the front door. I imagined an explosion of laughter accompanying it. To take my mind off the scene I was leaving, I pulled open the envelope and took out the card. There was a hand-drawn vase of unidentifiable flowers. They were in bright colours, as if it was a primary school project. Inside, in big loopy handwriting, was written: *Dear Alice, You sing beyond the genius of the sea. Matt has told me lots. Hopefully we will meet. I can never thank you enough. Love Jo.*

18

Geraldine had lived alone in a flat-fronted Victorian cottage in Redland since her divorce. Her husband, also a GP, ran off about fifteen years ago with a younger GP at the practice where he and Geraldine were partners, leaving her and their three then-teenage children. He was in his late forties when he cut, exhausted by the hamster-wheel of paying the mortgage and school fees, taking two holidays a year, never having any spare money. As if she wasn't. He'd found someone, much younger as it turned out, who he said *understood* him, who loved him for who he was rather than what he could provide. One tired cliché, six lives repointed, the children damaged in some structural but indefinable way. Geraldine's eldest, already a mum, had started a new family, but the emptiness would be as hard to fill as an echo. When I told Ed, he'd shaken his head and said, 'How can you do that to your own kids?' Those were the days when he — we — could afford to take the high road.

Book club was purring along on familiar lines when I finally arrived. John was in charge, as usual. Diana was absent without apologies, as usual. Peter was drinking too much, as usual. Neil was Neil, with his margin-notes in green ink, though I did catch him giving me a funny look. Fiona was as waspish as ever. She was wearing black Lycra with yellow Day-Glo safety stripes. Sarah was silent. Geraldine clucked around pouring Australian Chardonnay and Chilean Merlot and cutting thick slices of homemade bread to go with her Keralan fish stew. She'd said, in her fading Morningside accent as she opened the front door, 'I thought about you. I was going to call. But I thought it was probably the last thing you'd need.' It reminded me that, to everyone else, Ed and I were still the local stars of Bristol's best-known murder manhunt, even if it had been downgraded to a simple inquiry into whether a woman had taken her pills or not. Unexpectedly, I felt a lump in my throat and struggled to get out the words 'Thank you'.

Franny and Zooey — my choice — was not a popular one. The universal view was that Franny was a spoilt brat who needed a good shake. Peter, holding his wine glass with the base on his palm and rolling it around in a circular motion, said, 'I even felt sorry for that berk she was with. What was that lovely line he had about having to be dead or bohemian to be a poet? Or being some clown with wavy hair? Love it!' I didn't have the energy to defend her, though I'd loved the book ever since I read it in a single sitting at Didcot Parkway waiting for a delayed train to Oxford to meet a boy. To me, Franny had always been an idealist who wanted nothing more than for the world to be perfect and was struggling to understand why it couldn't be, and that hurt.

We left in ones and twos, hooting our goodbyes and enthusiasm for the next meeting. I found myself on the pavement with Neil as the door closed behind us. He pulled out a packet of cigarettes and offered me one. I shook my head. I hadn't smoked for years. If I started again doing the job I do, I would be on fifty a day within a week. His match flared as we headed towards our cars. A pair of female students in matching sports vests staggered past, giggling, supporting each other, fresh out of The Kensington. Neil shifted to snatch a second look as they passed, blew a smoke ring which rose and widened and flattened and said,

'Everything OK?'

'Yup, thanks.'

'What with the police and all?'

'Yup. All done. Not that there was anything anyway.'

'Only you were a bit late. For dinnertime.'

I stopped dead. Where had I heard that word — 'dinnertime' — before? I suddenly remembered and immediately recoiled.

'Oh my God! It was you, wasn't it?'

'Me? What?'

I hissed, 'Who told them.'

'Told who what?'

He glanced at me sideways.

'Who told the police you'd seen Ed in Stokes Croft on the night of the murder, the accident, whatever they now think it was, on the night that girl died. It was you, wasn't it? At dinnertime. That's what you said to me.'

The micro-pause, his eyes glancing upwards, looking for an answer. There wasn't one. I'd nailed him.

'You fucking idiot! Why did you do that?' Neil

had taken a step back. I obviously looked as if I meant violence and certainly I was pent-up enough, but his naked fear brought me to a halt. In a softer but still compulsive voice, I said, 'You did, didn't you?' He tapped his cigarette nervously with a finger but said nothing. The ash fell on to the tarmac. 'Why? Why did you do that rather than come to us? Because we might have killed you?' He didn't answer, just looked at the road. 'For God's sake, we'd had a bad enough time as it was, without some guy turning up on a Saturday afternoon trying to force me into some sort of confession just because you'd said you'd seen Ed when you hadn't.'

Neil looked as if he was fighting some internal battle. After a few moments he said quietly,

'I did see him.'

'You couldn't have done.'

'I've thought about it a lot. It was definitely your husband.'

'It's not possible. Anyway, you hardly even know what Ed looks like.'

'I've met him a couple of times at yours on the book group. I googled him after you were arrested. His picture was in the paper.'

'Twice? And googled. Oh, right, well, that's definite then.' Neil looked slightly ashamed. 'And we weren't arrested. They just wanted to ask some questions.'

To my surprise, Neil began shaking his head and looking squarely at me. He had a renewed confidence that made me nervous.

'It was him. I know it.'

'It can't have been.' I had to nail this now.

'Why not?'

'Because I was with him at six o'clock, on Brandon Hill.'

Neil gave an involuntary squeak of triumph. His face was weaselly.

'Then why didn't you say that? When I told you originally that I'd seen him you should have said I couldn't have done as you were on Brandon Hill together. The fact you didn't say that was what made me tell the police when I saw in the paper Ed had been arrested. I thought it was important evidence.'

I was almost hyperventilating, but it was more out of anger than fear now. What sort of stone had Neil crawled out from under? At least I'd wrongly Judas-ed Marnie to her face. I said as coldly and deliberately as I could,

'Because you said you'd seen him 'at dinnertime'. Those were your exact words. But we were eating our supper at Sarah's when you said it. So naturally I assumed you used 'dinnertime' to mean 'lunchtime'. If I'd thought you meant 'dinnertime' as being six o'clock, of course I would have said you were mistaken.'

Neil's crime-fighting glory dissipated. It was replaced by a half shrug and a grinding jaw. Sherlock with aviators but no deerstalker. He dropped his cigarette into the road, crushing the glow with his shoe, frowned, ground his teeth but said nothing.

'So next time you want to accuse my husband or anyone else of murdering someone who it transpires has in fact died by accident, please will you at least have the decency to accuse him to his face? People like you make me sick. Goodnight.'

I turned my back on him and walked away. But as I did I was sure I heard Neil say, as if he was confirming it to himself or repeating into a hidden microphone for the benefit of someone listening in, 'I know it was him.'

★ ★ ★

I was sitting in the car thinking about Neil because I didn't want to go inside. I didn't want to talk. I didn't want to see Ed. I didn't want to be reminded of the suppertime scene, the aborted joke. So I parked outside our house and just sat, watching the dimming outlines of the treetops and the lights along the river.

At midnight I switched on the news to take my mind off my own insoluble problem. My life, this problem, was so removed from the global stage. Out there in the unreal world a bank was reaching the point of no return. If it couldn't do some sort of deal, it was toast. They played a clip of the CEO protesting he was good for his debt and asking for time to sort out his lines of finance. He sounded a hard man, someone who would do whatever it takes. He must have done whatever it took to become the boss of such a hornet's nest of ambition and greed. And he had taken whatever he could. Maybe that's why the market was taking everything back. Or maybe it just didn't trust him. That was sad. Because when families and children depend on someone, you need to be able to believe in them.

The car door clicked on the passenger side. For a terrible moment I thought I was going to be attacked but Ed's head appeared, pale and ghostly. He wiped away the hank of hair that flopped over his forehead.

'Darling, are you all right?' There was real concern in his voice.

'Yuh. What are you doing out here?'

He slid into the passenger seat, the door open, left leg dangling over the road like a child on a bike without brakes. I could hear his breathing and my heart pumping, feel his physicality beside me. At that moment I wanted to be anywhere in the world rather than in a car with my husband. Ed put his hand gently on my arm. I stiffened. I couldn't help it. He sensed my discomfort and his arm dropped on to the gear stick. He was wearing the beige shirt with breast pockets he bought when we went on safari.

'I was worried. I wondered where you'd gone.' He leant forward and, hand poised over the 'off' button of the radio, said, 'May I?'

I shrugged.

'Book club. You knew that.'

'Not this late. I was worried.'

I looked out of the windscreen at the back of the car in front. It was a Volvo estate. Such is normality.

'Please. I know you're stressed, my darling. It's been a very hard time for you, I know that, for both of us, and — believe me — I'm really sorry and I really appreciate your support and everything you've done and put up with.'

For a long time I didn't reply. I didn't know

how to tell the truth. Eventually, to avoid it, I said,

'Philips knows.'

'What do you mean, Philips knows? Who's Philips?'

'One of the policemen who interviewed me. The one who came round asking questions that Saturday afternoon. He was sitting in his car right outside the gate when I went out.'

Ed looked paler than usual in the light of the streetlamp.

'What did he say?'

'Nothing.'

'Nothing? Then how do you know he knows? It may have been a coincidence.'

I was staring at the steering wheel.

'He knows. He was waiting for me. God knows how long he'd been there. When I came out he just looked at me, nodded and drove off. Effectively he was saying they might have called off the hunt officially but he knows we're guilty and he isn't going to let it go. That's what he wanted me to know.'

Ed thought for a moment.

'Don't panic, darling, we only have to sit tight. Think about it: if they had anything at all on us they wouldn't have called it off. He's bluffing, I promise. Seeing if he can throw you.'

'And Neil knows.'

'Neil?'

'From book club. The one who saw you on Stokes Croft on the night she died.'

'But he hasn't got any proof or he would have gone to the police.'

'He did. That's why Philips came round that Saturday.'

'And then they called it off. Because they didn't have any way of proving it. We were on Brandon Hill. You have to think positively, darling.'

'But if they both pretty much know, and Marnie's worked it out, who else does? What are we going to do about it? I'm not sure how long I can go on like this.'

'There's no 'like this', darling, they haven't got anything.'

'It doesn't feel like that from here.'

'Even though the police have officially — '

'Even though.'

There was a pause so long I thought he might have got out of the car. A welcome breeze wafted through the open door.

'My darling, I promise everything will be OK. You just need some time to get your head round things. You should go away for a while, relax, de-stress.'

'Go away?'

'Yes. I think it would do you good. I think you need some time out.'

'I don't need any time out. What I need is to deal with this . . . this thing, one way or another.'

'I know. And if you get away for a while I think at some moment it will hit you that this really is the best thing that could have happened for all of us. For the children.'

'Where do you want me to go?'

It sounded more defensive than I intended.

'Anywhere you want. Somewhere nice. Take

the kids if you want. Leave them here if you want. Go with friends. Go alone. Whatever you want.' He paused to see if I would brighten up. I didn't. 'Forget painting, forget everything, just go away and enjoy yourself. Spend some time on you. Take a girlfriend. Whatever you want, my darling. You'll be amazed how much good it will do.'

His profile was hard but his voice was soft, encouraging. I suddenly wanted to hug him. He did understand what I was going through and, so far as he could, he wanted to make things better. I looked through the windscreen again.

'With you?'

He shook his head. 'Best not.'

He really did understand.

'For how long?'

'As long as you want.' I squeezed his arm.

'Where shall I go?'

'Wherever you want.'

'Europe?'

'Anywhere.'

I thought for a moment. Should I go where I had been happiest or somewhere I had never been? Where had I been happiest? A reel of images unspooled. Hazy mountains and dusty roads, turquoise sea, lemon trees, olive groves. I had been happiest on holiday with Ed and Nell and Arthur. I never liked the 'rent-a-villa-with-eleven-others'-type holidays, men showing off, girls jockeying round the pool. Matt, who agreed, once said, 'There's always someone no one likes, and if you can't work out who it is, it's you,' which probably tells you more about him than anything else, but I had never forgotten it. Who should I go with? Not the children. They were the question at the heart of everything. A friend? Which one? Marianne was right. There was no one I could share this with.

Ed was right too. I had to go away. It was our only chance. I needed to miss him. I had to make myself realize once and for all that I couldn't live without him. But it was a high-risk strategy, because what if I found that I could? Ed was not a high-risk man. So for him to be taking this chance told me everything I needed to know about how he was feeling.

And suddenly I knew where I would go. I would go alone. I would go somewhere I already knew, where the memories were cider-tinted, somewhere from before I met Ed that was redolent of paths not taken, unadorned possibility, a different future. Even as I thought it, I knew I wouldn't be able to explain to Ed why it had suddenly become the place I wanted to go to more than any other. It was a place of unfinished business, from where I had originally placed my trust and hope in the world outside. I had to renew my vows. I said,

'I'll go to Highlands.'

'Highlands?' Even Ed couldn't keep the surprise out of his voice. 'Are you serious?'

I nodded.

'Don't you want to go somewhere more glamorous? Somewhere hotter?'

'I want to go home.'

'Really? Not anywhere in the world without your mum? Money no object.'

But in that moment I had never been surer of anything. What I wanted was to go home, the one place in the world I had always felt alone, no matter who or how many people were there. I wanted time to roam across the moor, swim in bone-chilling streams, clamber over boulders, climb crags and tors, buy crumbly white rolls in the village shop, snooze in green hollows. I wanted to return to my childhood, that solitary landscape of stories, where I had thrilled to tales of escaped prisoners and brave children. It was there I had become a reader and because I became a reader I became a painter of portraits, because what is a portrait if not the opening up of a character, the physical manifestation of the story of a life?

19

I reached Highlands at the end of a long drive. It's always a long drive, wherever you come from, because after you leave the M5 and A30 you have to pick your way high up on to the moor, where the roads are windier, bridges narrower, tractors heavier, streams deeper, fords wider, dry-stone walls less forgiving, passing places less frequent and, for those who don't know their way around from birth, signposting less obvious.

As my old Golf climbed on to the moor I began to breathe more easily. Every mile was taking me away from Ed. Every mile was taking me towards a place I used to call home. If I didn't feel any better with the window down and pure moorland air rushing through the car, at least I felt a tiny sense of hope that didn't dissipate as it usually did when I reached the moss- and lichen-covered, weather-battered gatepost with its rusty legend, 'Highlands'.

The house was Victorian and grey, slate-roofed, Gothic-windowed, a city of chimneys and empty rooms. If you didn't already know how bleak it could be inside, the architecture offered early indication. An elbow of outhouses containing old scythes and rusting car parts that would never be used again stood to one side. Alice Sheahan's First Law of Agriculture: 'The profitability of any farm is in inverse proportion to the number of unidentifiable rusting objects half-buried upon it.'

Mother, who had been watching and waiting or heard the car on the remnants of gravel, opened the side door and waved at me to come in that way. She has never met me at the front door, not once in my whole life, even though she always greeted Matt out front, no matter what state he was in — often when he would have preferred to sneak in the back way. Not that I mind. Who's counting? Anyway, the back door befits a crafts-woman, a portraitist, a seeker of the reality behind the painted façade. You don't find that when you arrive at the front door or are welcomed into a tastefully decorated hall as artificial as stage flats. Rembrandt never used the front door, especially the old impoverished Rembrandt, author of the greatest self-portraits of all. Has anyone anatomized themselves and their failure so brutally?

The back door opened to reveal a familiar inky rectangle. I had spent so much time with my nanny, Maud, back there that I could navigate my way into the kitchen blindfolded. The worn brick passage dipped past the larder and there were three low stone steps up to the kitchen, smoothed and bowed from footfall. The larder had a whirring fan, a hospital-blue light behind a wire mesh and a dangling flycatcher, an analogue piece of cardboard manufactured circa 1970. It was possibly the latest gizmo in the house. I would slip in after primary school and dip my finger into the lemon curd that Maud made, or lift the gauze fly-resister off a half-eaten leg of lamb and tear off a piece to dip in mint jelly, always dodging the mould. At least, I did until Mother caught me. Stealing was not tolerated. I've never eaten lemon curd since.

She shielded her eyes from the sun. Mother was as erect as ever, her tweed coat too formal and surely too hot, a salmon scarf wound around her throat. She looked older and smaller, her strong straight nose capable of sniffing out children being children at a hundred yards seemed less well defined but her thin lips were still primed to condemn. There was a prickle of teeth when she smiled. She was always harder on me than on Matt or Bridgey because I was the one who fought back. Matt just took the pain and glided away, further into himself. Bridgey's nose wasn't out of a book long enough for her to be in trouble or to realize she was in trouble. Their pliancy made me bolder. It was as if one of us had to stand up for childhood. But it also gave my mother strength. She was fleshier around the jowls than I remembered and her hair was snowy, but although she was smiling it was not obviously with welcome. She'd never had a mummy's face.

No matter. I wanted to be here. I was pleased to see her. I hadn't been down since Christmas. Her mouth moved as if she was practising speech, trying it out to see what it was like. She had lived alone too long.

'Mother.'

'Alice.'

We hugged. Her skin felt cold and papery. She disengaged a moment too soon, as if human touch was alien, and said,

'Why don't you take your case up to your room and then come down for dinner?'

'I thought I might go for a walk first if that's OK? Stretch my legs a bit.'

She nodded and gestured me into the house and we lapsed into silence. She has never managed small talk. I walked down the passage, past the wicker basket with ball-stained cricket bats and tennis rackets in wooden presses, listening to her rickety steps behind me. The familiar smell of apples mixed with coconut matting. The kitchen was painted a colour so faded it had become indeterminate. A four-barred wooden clothes-rack was hanging from the ceiling, lowered by rope and pulleys. It had probably hung there since the Boer War. The thin-legged Formica table stood in the centre, laid for two. There was no tablecloth. It reminded me of a long-gone boyfriend, Tom Carbine, and the question he asked on his first trip to Highlands, one that had resonated down the years: 'Why does your mum want to live in 1950s Budapest?'

We reached the hall. I stopped at the foot of the stairs.

'What time would you like to eat?'

'Seven fifteen. If you would like a sherry I will be in the library at six forty-five.'

'Is there any of that lovely local cider?'

'No.'

Welcome home.

★ ★ ★

I didn't have much time so I headed straight for the place we called 'the bracken stream', even though it was the widest part of the river on our land. I planned to spend the day there tomorrow if the weather was good, take a picnic, swim, read, snooze in the sun, *think*, but, first things first, at that moment I simply wanted to see it again, dip my fingers into it, lay my face to the soil, feel the moor beneath my feet. If you fell asleep at the bracken stream and woke with the sun slanting golden-green through the trees and playing on the water you'd think you'd died and been reincarnated as Laurie Lee. It's the place that meant most to me here. More than my bedroom, which never felt safe with Mother and Joy the joyless cleaner coming and going; more than the old playroom where I would sit drinking tea with Maud until Mother found us and found tasks for us to do; more even than the treehouse in the woods, which wasn't really a treehouse at all, just a hollow in the trunk of a great beech, and was Matt's place anyway. It was always full of his pipes and bongs and Rizla papers and the dope he kept in the transparent plastic bags he was given cash in by Mr Sawter, the old bank manager in the village. Mr Sawter never did work out why Matt always asked for his money in coins.

Our old worn path through the fields had long since disappeared, swallowed by nature, but I could still take the right lines, every boulder and tree a landmark. I reached the river quickly, luxuriating in my freedom and solitude. The bank was shaded by oaks and willows and ash, the evening sun poking through, dappling the translucent water. Silver-black fish glinted and twisted in the shallows. Smooth pebbles shone on the river bed. A spider spun its web between ferns. I found my old grassy hollow. It was a couple of yards back from the stream. I lay down and looked up at the sky where the evening sun — the planet's obstetrician — poured down on to my face. The ground was warm and moulded to my curves, exactly as I remembered. It was as if I had only been here yesterday, as if I was the same shape as when I was a teenager.

I was lying there like a farmyard kitten, my mind a beautiful blank, when I heard whistling on the breeze. I pressed into my dip, praying whoever it was wouldn't stumble over me. This part of our land had no right of way. It couldn't be Jim, the farmer, because he always went home on the stroke of five, even though he never wore a watch, and no one else would come down here, except maybe a poacher. I felt a moment's fear for my mother. Were gangs roaming around the house while she sat in the library doing the *Times* crossword and nursing a thimble of sherry?

Keeping my head down, I turned on to my front. On the far bank an unshaven man in dirty jeans and a tatty sweatshirt was heading towards the river. He was wearing a black LA Dodgers cap with gold piping, the peak pulled low. A fishing rod and a canvas bag were slung over his shoulder. He looked in his early twenties but beneath the peak and the stubble it was hard to be sure.

I glanced at my watch. Ten to six. I had fifteen minutes at most before I had to head back if I was going to change for dinner and catch my mother in the library, which I ought to do tonight if no other. I lay motionless as the man prepared his bait. He worked smoothly, efficiently, familiar with his business, comfortable in his private landscape, a natural man in a natural world, fishing in the way man had been doing for thousands of years. I felt the tension draining from me, as if I could lie happily in my green bower forever, simply watching him set up his rod, lay out his hooks and bait, catch his fish.

And suddenly I knew what I had to do. I had to paint him. Immediately the idea excited me and I felt an artistic stirring I hadn't experienced since Ed's confession. This man, whoever he was, offered an escape from everything unnatural that had happened. He could be my bridge back into art and into life. It would be a non-psychological work, a portrait of an everyman going about the hunter-gathering business of killing to put food on the table to feed his family. Doing what men do. I didn't need a Marnie or a Marianne, or even a Julie. I didn't need someone I had to psychoanalyse down to their last fingernail. I just needed some way of pouring my soul into someone wholly alive in a landscape I loved. It was as if I had stumbled upon a single chance to reconnect with an elemental truth that was part of us all.

As he worked with his bait I marked out the composition in my mind. I would paint him here in his natural element, low in the water, casting his line. To paint him in a studio or from photographs would destroy the thing that made him *him* and here *here*. I wanted to paint the Dodgers cap. I wanted to paint the bracken stream. I wanted to paint the whispering trees. I wanted to paint my solitude. The title would be *A Thousand Years*.

The man cast with a lazy flick of the wrist, the hook hooping out over the water. A hawk hung high in a pink sky. Slowly I got to my feet. I didn't want to disturb the fish. I called across the water.

'Excuse me?'

He looked up, pushing the peak of his cap up his forehead, squinting across the river into the sun. There was grime on his face and his cheeks were hollow. It took him a moment to register.

'I'm sorry to disturb you.'

He didn't respond.

'But can I ask you a favour?'

He wiped his hand on his sleeve.

'It may seem a bit odd . . . '

I couldn't read his look. All I could hear was my voice booming across the lazy river.

' . . . but I was wondering . . . if I could paint you? Your portrait?'

He stood perfectly still. Then, as if the word portrait unleashed some prehistoric poacher's fear of identification, he flicked a strong supple wrist and hooked his worm out of the water.

'No, hold on a sec! You can keep fishing.'

As smoothly and efficiently as he'd unpacked, and never taking an eye off me, he reeled in his line and threw away the bait.

'Please don't go. You can fish here. There's no problem.'

He paused for a moment but then continued. Oh why was he on that side of the fucking river? Why couldn't I get up close and show I didn't want to cause any trouble?

'Look, honestly, I don't mind. I could get you fishing rights here whenever you want.'

He stopped for a moment and looked across at me, but even as he did I realized I'd made a mistake. I'd established ownership. I was the class that punished poachers.

'Please talk to me. I just want to paint you. Nothing else. I won't be any trouble. Please?'

I was almost shouting. It didn't matter. There was no one around to see how mad I looked, pleading with a poacher.

'Please! I'll pay you.'

He slung his canvas bag and rod over his shoulder. He shot me a short final stare like an urban fox and turned his back, starting away over the moor as without thinking I leapt into the river and began wading across, struggling against the flow, keeping my balance on the polished stones, the icy water swirling around my hips. He stopped, glanced back and started to jog in the direction of Okehampton. I stopped midstream, soaked, knowing I would never catch him, not with two-thirds of the river between us. My legs were freezing. The river was up to my waist. I knew how ridiculous I must look but he didn't turn around. Soon he was nothing more than a distant speck, taking his rod and his cap and my last hope with him.

The room we called the green library was painted Chelsea blue and didn't have any books in it. There was a mahogany roll-top bureau where Mother wrote her letters, a small, gull's-egg grey sofa with a dark wine stain the shape of Tahiti that has been there longer than anyone can remember, a nest of tables with cork coasters, two silk-covered single chairs and two leaden-skied landscapes of indeterminate quality, British, late 1940s, signed illegibly. It always amazed me to think they were painted at the time Abstract Expressionism was exploding in New York. Nothing symbolized the derivative, unambitious nature of so much British art better. Mullioned windows looked out to the steep moor at the back of the house.

I accepted a glass of sherry in a pre-war cut-glass thimble whitened by time and washing and asked about Bridgey and about Matt's visit. I had long ago learnt there was no point asking directly how my mother was because she would just say she was 'fine', as if it was rude to ask. Like any dictator, she asked the questions. Bridgey had taken a job teaching comparative literature at Middlesex University, which Mother supposed was 'an old polytechnic'. I didn't tell her I had met Matt at Temple Meads on his way back from Highlands. He definitely wouldn't have told her. She said his new business venture wasn't going well but made no reference to the request for money, or to Jo. Knowledge had always been power for Mother. She didn't make it sound very hopeful and she was probably right. Matt was many things, at his best a lovely fragile poetic man, but he wasn't a businessman and history showed he wasn't good at staying clean. Only Jo stood between him and his demons.

We moved into the kitchen where Diane had left a fish pie big enough for six on the hot plate. I uncorked the bottle of Chablis I'd brought. I served Mother her fish pie and poured us both a large glass of wine. She gave a mouth-turned-down look at the size of my glass but drinking was the best way through supper at Highlands. Mother didn't drink on her own — 'Only alcoholics' — but would tipple away like a Trojan whenever she had company, presumably because that's what had been considered 'proper' in 1952 or whenever it was. We ate the fish pie with purple broccoli from the walled garden. The potato was fluffy and the fish was chunky and tender and fresh. Diane's husband had caught it. I had forgotten how delicious simple fresh food could be.

'Is everything all right?'

My fork paused halfway to my mouth like a cable car in high winds.

'Yup. Ed's well, the kids are well. Nell's working hard. Arthur isn't. No change there.'

'I meant about the police.'

I chewed a hunk of fish pie. It was creamy and I could taste the mackerel.

'Oh that, yuh, that's fine.'

'It must have been awful.'

I gave a half-laugh to show it had become a

family joke, a tale to tell the grandchildren.

'It wasn't great. But it's just one of those things. Mistaken identity. It's done now.'

'And those photographers in the road. Frightful.'

'You saw that?'

Mother was always in bed by ten o'clock.

'Peggy Marshall showed me on her iThingy. She told me Ed stayed a night with the girl and that's why you'd been taken in.'

'That's right.'

'Then it wasn't mistaken identity.'

I ate a mouthful of fish pie to give me time to regroup. Mother instinctively homed in on the difficult truths. Was I going to have to tiptoe my way through conversations forever?

'Well, no, not entirely, though it was in the context of Ed not being there when she died.'

'Why did Ed go there?'

'Long story. It was after a party.'

'Where were you?'

'Painting a portrait. In Suffolk. They now think no one was there when she died.'

'It was suicide?'

My mother had barely touched her food. She has a gnat's appetite when she gets her teeth into a subject or, more often, someone.

'No. They think she didn't take her pills. Or she took too many. They think she fell over and hit her head.'

'Surely they did an autopsy?'

I made a mental note to concentrate. Mother had not lost her sense of smell. There had been times during childhood when it seemed all she wanted to do was catch us out, while displaying utter indifference about almost everything else in our lives.

'They did. She hadn't taken her pills.'

Mother looked dubious. Her hair was thinning at the crown, a pink-blue scalp showing through.

'Would that have made her hit her head?'

'I've no idea. I'm not a doctor.'

'But you're married to one.'

'Oh yes, so I am.'

She looked at me sharply. She disliked sarcasm.

'And you must have discussed the case.'

Coming here was beginning to feel like a mistake. I could have been lounging by the pool in some Tuscan hilltop hotel but instead I was nursing a glass of warmish white and answering questions on the one subject I was trying to forget about. As always, she made me feel like a little girl again.

Was that why I'd come?

'Of course we have. Only the police didn't tell us what pills she was on when they saw us, presumably because they thought we were guilty and therefore didn't want to give us anything to go on.' Mother looked straight at me, trying to detect sarcasm in my tone. Eventually she gave a nod and pronged a tiny amount of mashed potato. 'There was no way for Ed to know whether not taking the pills contributed.' She coughed once but continued eating. 'And as you know, he's not a man to give a diagnosis without knowing the facts.'

'That was always his problem.'

Mother often moved from the micro to the

macro in a single leap, a tiny blemish — forgetting your keys, bringing mud into the house — became symptomatic of a major character deformity. She was like a Hollywood thriller in which the ordinary-Joe hero stumbles upon a neighbourhood murder only to find the CIA, the FBI and the White House ranged against him.

I didn't rise. Instead I topped up her glass as, artfully late, her hand feigned to wave the bottle away. We ate in silence, cutlery clinking as if we were in a provincial B&B. After the fish there were raspberries from the garden and my mother dug out a knob of bone-hard cheddar and some stale biscuits. Mould crept around the corner of the cheese. I drank another glass of Chablis and began to feel light-headed. I told her about Nell and Arthur and gave a brief and partial account of my trip to paint Marianne, whom she'd forgotten, if I'd ever even told her about her. There was silence. Mother doesn't return serve.

'Are you all right here? Not lonely?'

She gave me a wary look. Maybe she thought I was hinting she should move out and we should move in. I wasn't. Much as I loved it, I couldn't think of anywhere I would like to live less than on top of Dartmoor. Sheep are sheep and people are people and I know which I prefer. But old people are paid to be cautious. They have a nasty surprise ahead.

'What I mean is it's not too big?'

'It hasn't got any bigger,' she said coldly, turning the cheese knife upside-down and stabbing a triangle of cheddar with the prongs.

'But you're not getting any younger.'

Mother gave a contemptuous snort.

'There's Diane who comes in, and Jim's obviously around. Joy still comes on Tuesday, though she's actually past doing anything useful, just drinks coffee and dibs at the silver. Helen does the cleaning now.'

'Helen?'

'David's niece.'

'David?'

'David Seaton.'

I looked blank.

'David was the woodsman we used. Unfortunately he was not an honest man. Your father kept using him far too long. I'm afraid that was one of his weaknesses. He was too kind, even when people didn't deserve it. It always cost him in the end.'

Mother looked slightly flushed. She was rarely so garrulous. I took a sip of wine and — out of nowhere, because this was not Mother's kind of conversation — asked,

'Do you miss Dad?'

She picked up her napkin and dabbed her lips as if a thought had crossed her mind for the first time for so long she had forgotten it ever existed. She turned to look at the dresser. Her profile was less dramatic, her brow less an agony of frozen formality than I remembered, forehead wrinkled like shallow contours on an OS map.

'I always missed your father,' she said, and put her hands on her lap. I assumed that was it and was thinking about another line of conversation when she added, 'even when he was alive. He was a good man. He just couldn't see it himself.'

It was the most intimate thing she'd said to me about him in the thirty years since he'd died.

'In what way?'

She looked out across the empty paddock to the dark hills beyond. Her triangular cut of cheddar was untouched on her plate, Diane's squat jar of homemade pickle unopened. There was a long pause, a silence passing back through the years.

'He didn't understand things weren't perfect. That they never could be.'

I thought there was going to be more but her mouth opened and shut like a fish. I had never seen my mother in such a reflective mood. Maybe she really was getting lonely. Maybe it was Matt setting out on another doomed expedition — this time on the Yorkshire coast but it could have been anywhere, the ending always the same — that had dislodged her memory. Maybe it was having me at Highlands without the membrane of Nell and Arthur to turn the visit into an arm's-length exercise in logistics rather than flesh and blood or raw emotion. Whatever the reason, I sensed she was feeling more open, perhaps more vulnerable, than I'd seen her before. I topped up her glass. Maybe she'd had more sherry before dinner than she should have. She took a sip without seeming to notice it had been refilled.

'Was he like that when you met?'

'Yes, though it wasn't as obvious as it became.' There was a lengthy pause, as if she had to wait while long-buried emotions re-formed. 'There was a sort of grandeur in the beginning, a yearning for a better life, an indifference to the world as it was. Initially it was very attractive, that doomed youthful romantic sensibility of wanting more from life than it could ever deliver. Unrealistic, yes, but very attractive in a young man just down from Oxford. He was good-looking too.'

There was another pause while she picked at her cheddar and memories. I didn't say anything. It would be fatal to interrupt her flow. These thoughts might never resurface.

'Of course he never found it. And a sense of failure sort of hardened in him. It wore him down. He never liked the City. Never wanted to work there. There were so many like that in those days, young men who didn't want to follow their fathers into family businesses or on to estates or into the City or the army, but they did because they'd been brought up to do what their fathers wanted. It wasn't like today. There were some very unhappy young men around in those days. They were at all the best parties. Grandpa Tenterden had always got what he wanted. That's where your father got his expectation, only he didn't have the power he needed to satisfy it. Grandpa had the power. It's a lesson I tried to teach you three: expectation breeds disappointment.'

'You certainly did.'

'Bridgey understood. I'm not sure you or Matthew ever did.'

There was an obvious point to be made about the world not moving on without the expectation things could be better, but now was not the moment.

'What should he have done?'

'I don't know. A job away from his father. Something in the theatre perhaps. He always loved the theatre. But Grandpa would never have allowed it. A sailor even. He always loved the sea. You remember he kept that boat at Brixham? Not that we ever went anywhere on it, mainly because he was never here and I was totally uninterested in boats. But then we got married and he needed to make money for you three and there was this place to keep up.'

There was a ting! of steel on china as her knife slipped on the cheddar. I thought of Matt in Whitby with Jo, with their wonderful love and impossible fishing net business. Outsiders are drawn to the sea.

'And he was on his own when he died?'

She nodded dreamily.

'Mmm. I sometimes wish I'd been there. You never know. It might have been different.'

'But you never went to London with him.'

'I did go. Not often. You were too young to remember.'

'Anyway, you always refused to drive in London. That's what taxis and buses were for, you said.'

'Not drive in London? What's that got to do with it?'

She stared at me as if I was mad, and in that nanosecond I realized something was wrong. This was more than a cross-purpose conversation. An idea began to form in my peripheral vision, shrouded in darkness but definitely within reach.

301

'Well, you wouldn't have been driving.'

'No. I know that.'

'So why would it have been different if you were there?'

'Because . . . '

She stopped and glared at me.

'Because?'

'Because . . . oh nothing! Alice, this is boring. I'm tired.'

I shook my head because . . . something long-buried was surfacing, becoming clear.

'Because he didn't die in a car crash.' It was not a question.

'It was an accident.'

There was residual hauteur — thirty years of power — but it was fading fast. I focused on her like an electric beam.

'But it wasn't an accident in a car, was it?'

'It was.'

'It was what?'

'It was . . . ' Mother was never at a loss for words. She looked bewildered for a moment, ten years older, before her shoulders slumped.

'Mother, how did he die?'

Silence. She stared at the tablecloth. My eye was caught by an orange in the wire-mesh fruit bowl. I waited. I was here for as long as it took. Eventually, she said in a voice so soft I could hardly make out the word:

'Suicide.'

A single key on a piano. A solitary note of acceptance and defeat.

'Suicide?'

The bible and gun? The razor blade and the

hot bath? Whisky and the pill? The rope and the chandelier? The open window, an unforgiving pavement?

He'd always loved the theatre.

'But why? Lots of people are unfulfilled at work. Why did he do it?'

Mother looked down again. She'd aged twenty years in two minutes. I wasn't sure I could bear it.

'Because he was homosexual.'

She gave a bitter look as if to say, 'You asked'. It was true. I had asked. I had dredged up all the unhappiness — and I was glad I had. It was as if someone had switched on a light. For the first time I could see everything clearly.

'He was gay?'

'Yes.'

'Bi, I guess.'

'If it makes a difference.'

'But no one kills themselves just because they're gay. Not since the 1950s anyway.'

She pursed her lips.

'And he couldn't think of anything he wanted to stay for?'

A single shake of the head.

'Or anyone?'

Another shake.

'What about us?'

'Well, he wasn't much use as a father, as you know. I don't actually think it made much difference to you three.'

'But there must have been another way. So he was gay? He could have played the field in London and the family man in Devon. I don't

303

get why he had to kill himself.'

'Word was going to get out.'

'So? It was the 1980s, not the 1880s. Apart from you, Grandpa T was probably the only person who mattered. And he didn't exactly do gossip. I shouldn't think he even knew where Soho was, or anywhere outside the City or St James's.'

'You don't understand.'

'What don't I understand?'

'He'd been arrested. He was going to court. It would have been in all the papers.'

'Arrested for what?'

'He never told me exactly. I didn't want to know. A young man . . . a public lavatory.'

'Don't tell me: a policeman.'

She winced. I wanted to reach out and hug her but she turned away. Mother was not built to receive sympathy. Neither parent knew how to take it, or to give it. Neither knew how to touch. She was twig-wristed, paper-skinned.

'Oh, poor poor Dad. And poor you. Did he leave a note or anything?'

A quivering finger scratched the table, long nails, picking as if it was an old wound. A microscopic nod.

'Have you still got it?'

She wasn't looking at me but at the sideboard behind my head. The sun was dipping beyond the hill, bathing the kitchen in a flycatcher light.

'What did it say?'

'That he was sorry. That he loved us all. That it was the only way the rest of us could continue as we had. It wasn't long. He'd scrawled it on a seaside postcard, a picture of Beachy Head. 'Explore Wonderful Beachy Head' it said.' She gave a wistful-angry-sarcastic puff and I found myself wondering how cold she must be that she'd been able to keep everything to herself all these years. 'They found it in his car.'

'Did he mention us?'

'He said he loved you three more than anything in the world and he hoped one day you would understand why he had done what he had done and find some way to love him. He hoped your lives would work out better than his. That was it.'

Poor man. Mother's lie meant he had never been granted his last wish to be understood. There had been no acceptance for his restless soul. I looked across the table at her hunched figure, rocking gently on her chair. What right did she have to play God, to reshape our lives, pulling them away from the truth?

Poor poor man.

What he had been through. In the police station when they pulled him in and said they were going to charge him and ruin his life. Homophobic coppers smirking, knowing they'd hooked a press-worthy fish. Lying in bed thinking about the shame he had brought on everyone. Wondering how he could tell Grandpa T and his wife. It was hard to think of two people one would be less inclined to confess to.

'How did he do it?'

'Jumped.'

Her voice was so quiet I could hardly hear. I didn't want to know but I had to. After all these years. It was my life too.

'Beachy Head?'

She nodded. She was staring bleakly at the mould on the side of the cheddar.

'He drove all the way to the south coast from London? What's that, maybe a couple of hours grinding through South London and so on, knowing he was going to commit suicide?'

She shrugged. She'd had to deal with this every day for thirty years. I pictured Father in his brown Peugeot, stationary in South London traffic, sucking in sounds and colours, the radio silent. There was no news he wanted to hear. In one way the fact he drove made it better. It wasn't a mistake. It wasn't a rash decision made after a bad day at the office. Every day was a bad day at the office. A big tear formed in my right eye. They always started there. I tried to blink it back.

What must it have been like standing alone on the edge, wind ruffling his hair, winter trees as bare as coat-stands, feeling he had let everyone down so badly there was no way back, believing there was no love left for him anywhere in the world? I wiped my face with my handkerchief. It was stained by tears and make-up. He had no one to share his pain. He obviously thought that with this one act he could atone for everything, for all the things that were his fault and all the things that weren't, that with this one gesture, this self-sacrifice, he could make life whole again for everybody else. He was so proud. He must have realized if he was out of the way the storm would be stilled and his wife and children

306

spared. There was honour in his ending.

I imagined him standing in his dark coat with its smart velvet collar, a striped City shirt and a narrow tie, crested cufflinks. I could see him raising pale eyes to the horizon, clearing his mind of everything and everyone, hearing nothing but the sound of the waves crashing against the rocks below. He wouldn't have glanced down before he stepped off into the sound of the wind and the empty future.

★　★　★

'Why did you lie to us?'

We had moved back into the library. The air was still. Mother seemed diminished, slumped in the corner of the sofa. I knew I should go easy but I remembered all the times she seemed so tall. She looked around the room as if safety might be found in those dreary British landscapes or bulbous china figurines, the Toby jugs depicting tricorn-hatted Dickensian men. God knows where we got them or why we got them. Eventually, with an effort that required almost more than she seemed to have strength for, she said,

'You were too young.'

'Too young to know the truth?'

'Yes.'

'Are you ever too young to know the truth?'

She glanced at the bookshelves, as if wondering which leather-bound volume held the answer to one of life's biggest questions.

'Yes.'

'Was Matt too young?'

'Yes. Especially Matthew.'

There was iron in the voice. She wouldn't go down without a fight. I should have known. She'd had time to rationalize the decision she made and she had an instinctive understanding of weakness.

'And when we were old enough?'

There was another long silence, the cadence of another time.

'It was too late. There was never a right time.'

'Too late to tell your children the truth about their father? We wouldn't have loved him any less. We would simply have understood him, and maybe each other, a little more.'

'I took a decision not to tell you straight away because what happened raised so many questions I felt you were too young to comprehend.'

I picked up the near-empty bottle of Chablis from the drinks trolley and poured myself a splash of wine. There was only a dribble left. I canted the bottle neck rhetorically towards Mother but she shook her head. I emptied the dregs into my glass. I felt the same, tipped up and emptied out, my life's narrative drained of its true meaning.

'And having not told you originally it became harder to do so, even if I'd only told a white lie for the right reasons.' She turned away, in order not to catch my eye. 'I suppose I thought that in the end time would bury it.'

'But why did we never get a hint? If the trial was going to be in the papers, surely the suicide was? How come no one picked up on it?'

'After he died it was different. Grandpa T was a powerful man. The establishment looks after its own.'

I remembered standing beside the open grave in Highgate Cemetery as his coffin was lowered into the ground. Four burly undertakers, black top hats against a brilliantly blue January sky, the green stacked turf as bright and unreal as a greengrocer's, every sod in sharp relief. I had hardly dared to breathe in case I fell in.

'Believe me, Alice, there hasn't been a day, not one single day, since it happened when I haven't thought about how to tell you or what to say. Now I wish I'd told you everything straight away. And if I had my time again I would have, of course I would, but I didn't, and I — we — have to live with that. Life's not perfect. It's a mess. We all make mistakes. There never seemed to be a right time and then suddenly you were older, Matthew was an adult, Bridget was away at school and you were all in different places and had different lives and different problems and it just seemed to be from a different age, an unhappy time, and what was the point of raking over the past when it wasn't going to make anyone happier? And then Matthew had all his problems and after that it was always too late . . . '

'Telling the truth is not 'raking over the past'. Maybe that secret was part of Matt's problem? Have you ever thought of that? Maybe even it was the root of it? Maybe Matt overheard someone talking, or sensed he hadn't been told everything, but had to bottle it up because he had no one to talk to? Maybe that's why he's had all the issues he has?'

She shook her head. Thin white hair.

'Matthew's problems were evident before your father died. Children are resilient. They take the world as they find it. They grow up as they are. Whatever happens to them feels normal — it *is* normal for them. You lost a parent and you lived.' She shifted on the sofa. 'Matthew lost a parent and he lived.'

'In a manner of speaking.'

My tone was harsh, too critical. I knew immediately I had gone too far. Mother wasn't going to take any more. She stood up, using the arm of the chair for leverage. I watched her walk across the room. She paused at the door, almost seeming to bare her teeth, and said in the clipped tones I knew so well,

'Matthew has lived the way he was always going to.'

20

Ed was waiting in the sitting room. It's the smartest room in the house, the only grand room in the old sense. There's a high ceiling, a cornice with intricate plasterwork, three tall windows giving on to a wisteria-entangled wrought-iron balcony with a lead awning and a wide view over the rooftops to Ashton Court. Two long sofas face each other across a low-slung oak coffee table we were giving as a wedding present. A smoky mirror in a carved gilt frame from Highlands hangs above the fireplace. There are three portraits — Ed, Matt, me — on the opposite wall. They are three of my best.

From everything I've said, you might expect me to fight shy of self-portraits, the ultimate self-exposure, but I don't. Although a self-portrait has the capacity to get closer to the truth than any other work of art, it is only for public consumption if the artist wishes and doesn't require the painter/sitter to open themselves up to anyone else. Self-portraits have a storied history revolving around the impoverished artist unable to afford a model but desperate to descend into the silent depths of humanity. Some of the greatest paintings in the history of art are self-portraits — think Dürer, Velázquez, late Rembrandt, especially late Rembrandt, even Samuel Palmer. It's not surprising. The painter knows the sitter better than he or she will ever know anyone else. Some critics argue that every painting, like every novel or film, no matter the subject, is a self-portrait of the artist or writer or auteur. I don't buy it. Art is about objectivity. It is essential to separate the life from the work. The self-portrait in the sitting room was painted soon after Nell was born and although I seem ecstatic about my new-babe joy that is the surface working. Look deeper and you'll see a sort of sadness in the shallow curve of my mouth and an elusiveness in my eyes. It seems to hint at connections not made, as if I already knew a mother must give up everything for the happiness of her child.

Ed was fiddling on his smartphone when I arrived. He was wearing the black dressing gown with Chinese-style patterning I bought for him in Torque on Westbourne Grove a couple of years ago. Ed doesn't like staying up late and told me pointedly when I called from the car and woke him to tell him I was on my way home and wanted to talk that he had a hard day the following day. He said going to Highlands had been a bad idea from the off and whatever it was, surely it could wait until the morning. He must have detected the strength in my reply because he didn't say it again. Ed thought I should have been tucked up in a Tuscan hotel taking the sun. He was wrong. Highlands was exactly the right place to go, even if I didn't manage to stay a whole night. But he didn't know that because he didn't know about the decision I had taken there. He didn't know how that decision had freed me from the weight that was dragging me down.

He shifted on the sofa when I came in and glanced at his watch. Twelve forty-five.

'Good trip?' His voice was thick with irony.

'Yes, thanks.'

After Mother had left the library I hovered in the kitchen tidying up before I went to bed. I couldn't face running into her again. I knew her contempt for weakness, how she could home in on it from fifty yards, and I was too angry and upset to trust myself with her. If I saw her I would scream or cry, for my father first of all, but also for all of us, for what she had done, for a family that didn't exist any more, if it ever had done. For a family built on a lie. I remembered Marianne's comment, 'I've never come across a family that sounded so disconnected.' Was that the inheritance I was bequeathing to Nell and Arthur? It was so different to the simple laughing love Ed had experienced as a child and offered as a father.

So, just to be certain she had gone to bed and wasn't padding around in the corridor, I spent a few minutes looking at the generic prints of wild Dartmoor flowers — foxglove, flax, sedge, orchids — hanging in the passage beyond the hall. They were perfectly done, perfectly *rendered*, but they lacked individuality. Sometimes I thought it was extraordinary I ever became an artist having grown up at Highlands. Mother had no interest in art. She would have hung a Kandinsky beside the Tiverton Parkway train timetables. My artistic streak must have come from Dad, not that he lived long enough to know.

I went up the back stairs and, for no reason other than I was at that end of the house and I hadn't been there for years, I looked in on Matt's old bedroom, the 'graveyard slot'. To my surprise, it was exactly as he'd left it twenty years before, with its *London Calling* and *Clockwork Orange* posters, old school desk, vinyl record collection, his sunken armchair, overflowing bookcases and stack stereo with its large black wooden speakers, headphones still plugged in. The only thing that had changed was the curtains were open. I thought of mine and Bridgey's bedrooms at the far end of the house, guest bedrooms from the day we left university, no trace of our personalities remaining, and I realized that in her frozen way Mother had always loved her son and heir.

It was while I was lying awake in the spare room thinking about Matt and Dad, the desperate loneliness of his end — his silk handkerchief and delicate wrists, the wounded sky — and the way my mother had stolen his truth from us, how we had never been able to forgive or grieve properly, that I understood I didn't have a choice any more. We had reached the place we were always going to reach. Highlands had done its job. I didn't need to spend any more time with my mother and she didn't need to spend any more with me. So I got out of bed and sat on the window-seat taking in the cool, moorland-scented air, rolling my decision around in my mind, and when I was certain, I dressed, repacked, crept downstairs and left a note on the kitchen table saying I had to go home. She would understand.

'Ed, we have to talk.'

He raised a laconic eyebrow. Why else had I asked him to wait up? He seemed admirably cool given I was unlikely to be doing anything at this hour except creating trouble. Ed put his mobile on the arm of the sofa and, leisurely as Drake, reached down to pick up a glass of water I hadn't noticed by his feet. He took a sip, leant back on the sofa and crossed his legs, cool as you like. I perched on the arm of the sofa opposite, leaning forward, my feet barely touching the floor.

'Fire away.'

'We have to deal with this. We have to tell the children.'

He closed his eyes and made as if he was counting to ten. When he opened them he said,

'Haven't we been through this?'

'Not so as we've reached a conclusion.'

He gritted his teeth, simultaneously expressing frustration that the subject hadn't gone away and his determination to remain patient.

'Darling, it would be completely unfair on them. You know that. They'd be forced to keep a secret they need never have known. There's no upside for them at all.'

'Other than our relationship with them would be honest. That's some upside.'

'Our relationship with them is based on the fact that we are their parents and we will always love them and do the best for them. That's the parent — child contract. It doesn't change. There's nothing in it that says they need to know everything about our lives, just as we don't need

315

to know everything about theirs.'

'That was certainly the view my parents took. And look where it got us.'

He examined his fingernails for a moment.

'Darling, I really don't think going round in circles is going to get us anywhere.'

My stomach churned. I felt unexpectedly nervous. There was a dead fly at the foot of the curtain.

'That's the problem, though, can't you see? We have to get somewhere, because I can't go on like this, not forever. I can't work. I can't *breathe.*'

'O-kaay.' His tone was slow and thoughtful. It was the voice he used when one of the children couldn't grasp a basic concept in their homework and he was going to have to think of another way of explaining it. He uncrossed his legs and leant forward, tapping the tips of his fingers thoughtfully against each other. 'So what's the alternative? We ruin our children's lives by telling them a secret that brings them no benefit but demands an incredible amount in terms of keeping it?'

I shook my head. He pursed his lips and frowned as if preparing to explain a simple principle for the umpteenth time to someone who was very stupid indeed.

'I thought we were sitting here because you say you are finding it impossible to live with the secret and need to tell them. You're saying you can't cope and you can't work and you have to have a valve. Why should it be any easier for them?'

I shook my head again. He'd missed my point. 'What then?'

I didn't answer. I couldn't bring myself to say it. I couldn't articulate the ending. He was my husband and a good man and in spite of everything I still loved him. But it was a different kind of love. Life had intervened. Death had intervened. Betrayal had intervened. I waited for him to understand. His mind was in circular motion, until finally, slowly, his eyes narrowed Clint-style, and he shook his head slowly.

I nodded, equally slowly.

'Oh no.' The emphasis was on the first, drawn-out syllable. I didn't say anything. I didn't want to break the chain. He leant back on the sofa, shaking his head slowly like a poker player passing a hand. 'I don't think so.' I didn't reply but never took my eyes off his. 'No. No way, darling, it's not going to happen. I promised. Day one in Arthur's bedroom.'

I nodded. His voice gained a harder edge.

'I'm not going to fuck up their lives when I don't have to.'

'There's no alternative. Not if we're going to stay together, as a family.'

My voice was cracking. I was trying to sound controlled but underneath I was bubbling like microwaved soup. I knew I had to stay calm. Otherwise he would dismantle my arguments, pull me apart bit by bit. He tried to keep the irritation out of his voice, not entirely success-fully.

'Why isn't there? There's every alternative. The police have done their stuff. The game's over. All we have to do is never mention it again. Never even think about it again.'

He reached down and picked up the glass of water. Although he seemed in control I could see he was dry-lipped. The vein that stood out on his forehead when he was under pressure had sprung a tributary. I didn't want to go through this any more than he did, but I knew if I was ever going to work again, if I was ever going to breathe again, if we were ever going to be a proper family again, I had to hold firm. Leaving him, running away, couldn't be the solution. It never is. We had to deal with it tonight. I said,

''All we have to do . . . ' I can't believe you can be so cold about it. And anyway, whatever the police do, that has nothing to do with us, as a family.'

'Meaning?'

'Meaning we can't go on like this, covering it all up.'

'Why not? It's over. There's nothing left to cover up.'

'There's everything left to cover up! We need honesty in our lives. I can't live with this . . . this lie hanging over me. I can't take it any more.'

He tilted his head, as if gauging the strength of my will. I felt a cool breeze and, from somewhere, the smell of nutmeg.

'So I go to jail for God knows how long and Nell and Arthur hang their heads forever as the children of a killer because you are finding it hard to work? I thought the whole point of art was that you solved problems. You take life as you find it and distil it into your work, the good and the bad, the ugly and the beautiful.'

I didn't answer. He took the opportunity.

'And how do you think Nell and Arthur will view their mother in years to come? As someone who defended their childhood and their innocence or someone who took them away?'

'I didn't kill anyone.'

'Nor did I. It was an accident.'

'I didn't sleep with anyone.'

'Jesus, Alice, please, be reasonable, it was a mistake. I have apologized for that and I will go on apologizing. I can't believe that I did it, and I hate myself for it, and I'll do anything you want, anything I can, to make it up to you. But this isn't some art project. This is real life and real people — the people we love more than anyone in the world — will be brutalized. I didn't murder Araminta Lyall. So what's so honest about me sitting in jail for fifteen years? Because I slept with her when I was too drunk to remember? You really want to put Nell and Arthur through what you went through that afternoon in the road? Just imagine what it's like to be the child of a killer. Maybe you change your name and move to Sussex. Maybe you emigrate to Australia. But if you do they'll still be the kids of a murderer, it'll get out, and they'll never see their dad, and if they do it will be in fifteen-minute bursts after a five-hour drive to some godforsaken, depressing, windswept, impossible-to-get-to visiting room with a warder listening in and saying what we can and can't say to each other. Wherever they are, they'll have to spend their whole lives denying who they are, which means they will have to stop being who they are. For God's sake, where's the honesty in that?'

He glanced around as if the answer was hidden in the room like a chocolate egg on a rainy Easter Day. I looked at the floor, the surfboard-shaped grain, and thought about that woman, the weight of his head on her pillow, my father at Beachy Head, his deep-dyed honour. I looked at Ed. This was the man who through his dedication to his work had taught me it didn't matter what you didn't do, it didn't matter what you thought, it didn't matter what you said, it only mattered what you did. I said,

'It'll be manslaughter at worst, especially given the character witnesses you'll have and the good you can do when you're out.'

'I assume I can quote you?' There was no humour in his tone.

'You know it will.'

'What I know is the police will see I had a motive, that I lied to them, that you did too, and they'll go for it. Why not? High-profile case, big-cheese doctor, society portrait painter wife — you've seen how the papers lap it up, the web. What I also know is I will never work again afterwards.'

'Of course you will!'

Ed's face was gleaming.

'How many convicted killers do you know who have passed the NHS integrity test?' I swallowed. It sounded like thunder in the silence. His jaw was set, the muscles in his cheeks strained. 'Or there's another way. We can carry on and put things back together unless you choose — yes,

Alice, unless you *choose* — to run a knife through me, through the children and through everything we've built up.'

'There's a fault-line running through it.'

'There's a fault-line running through millions of things. That's how the world is.'

'It doesn't have to be.'

He snorted contemptuously.

'That's the difference between us.'

'Alice, please think it through, all of it. Because once you've done this it's out of our hands, however big it gets and however it goes in ways you may not have expected. There's no turning back. I mean, what if they arrest you as an accessory after the fact or for perjury? What if you go to jail too? Where do the children live then? With Bridget? With your mother? With *Matt*?'

I didn't answer. It wasn't a question of logistics. It was a question of truth, of being honest with ourselves and our children. There was no future for us as a couple, a family, or myself as an artist or maybe even a human being if I didn't go through with this. We had reached the point of no return. There was no way to cope with an infinite lie. There had to be an ending. That was what I knew. The rest was just talk.

'We have to do the right thing. In the end it's the only way the children will respect us.'

'Oh, for fuck's sake listen to yourself!' His voice was low and controlled, which was scarier than if he shouted and screamed. 'When did you get to be so perfect? OK, so you're the great artist and you deal in universal truths. Well, not

321

all of us are up to that. Some of us are only human. We make mistakes — yes, I admit it, terrible mistakes — and there are accidents, things we can't turn round, and we have to learn to live with them, often for the sake of other people. This is one of those times. It's about Nell and Arthur as much as you or me, and they aren't going to thank you or respect you for fucking up their childhood, their whole lives, in the name of some ridiculous artistic ideal!'

For a moment I hesitated, thinking of the shape of their heads wrapped up in their pillows, Nell's cat's-lick, the curl of hair around Arthur's ear. They didn't deserve this. Who did? But the decision had been taken at Highlands and the moment I'd taken it I'd felt liberated, as if someone had opened a cell window and I had climbed through it into an empty square of sky. I had floated back to Bristol like a heroin-drenched saxophonist, needle dancing around a hundred, wheels scarcely touching the road. Ed's anger and frustration were inevitable but it only made me more determined. Whose fault was this anyway?

'Children survive. They're resilient. Whatever happens becomes the norm. They live their own lives.'

'That makes you feel better?'

'Better than our relationship with them and each other and everyone else being built on a lie? Yes. It does. They have a right to know and to understand.'

'They'll understand that their childhood, maybe their life, was wrecked because their mummy was too wrapped up in herself to think about them and their needs. You're the one pulling the plug. This will only happen if you want it to. Not because you need it to or they need it to but because you want it to. No other reason.'

He blew out air and turned away angrily, momentarily staring at his reflection in the inky glass. I hated the way it was going but I had to hold on to see it through. If I wavered everything would be over.

'Ed, it's about who we are, the people we want to be, the example we want to set to Nell and Arthur, them knowing what we stand for, what we believe in. It's about them knowing the truth, understanding the narrative of their lives. Honestly, there's no other way.'

'Of course there's another way. It's just that you don't want to take it.' He ground his teeth angrily as if he'd suddenly understood an angle he'd missed all along. 'And the reason you don't want to is because this isn't about me at all, is it? And it's not about the children either. It's about you. It always has been. Maybe everything always was.'

I was shaking my head, that was ridiculous, but Ed continued, his tone desperate and bitter, gaining weight and force.

'No one has ever matched my perfect wife before, because she's always been the prettiest most talented loveliest cleverest smartest most creative person in any room and all the men have only ever had eyes for her. But now her husband has slept with someone else, someone younger, maybe as pretty, perhaps as clever, by all accounts as talented, maybe even more so, and, forgetting everything that happened afterwards, she can't handle that because she's never had to. A world that has always and only ever revolved round her has suddenly had to expand to include someone else. No wonder all my apologies are not enough. I should have known they never could be. Because this isn't about me at all, it's about you.'

I couldn't believe what I was hearing. How could he twist the truth like that?

' 'Forgetting everything that happened after-wards'?' I couldn't keep the derision out of my voice. 'That's magnificent! If nothing had happened 'afterwards', we wouldn't be having this conversation.'

Ed leant forward. His voice was bitter, his pale cheeks aflame.

'Oh yes, we would. We were always going to have this conversation one day. If it wasn't about this it would have been about something else.'

I almost laughed out loud.

'Do you mean 'something else' *like* sleeping with someone and killing them?'

It was as if I hadn't spoken. He carried on like a battering ram.

'And the reason we were always going to have it is because you've been so fucking self-obsessed all your life that you can't cope when something happens in the real world that affects real people and that isn't about you. Well, it did. I didn't mean it to, but it did, and I have to deal with it. I can't theorize it away. I can't just paint it in pretty colours. That's what's happened here and deep down you know it.'

I looked away. How had he made it sound as if the whole problem was all to do with me? Maybe she had been right and his sleeping with her was an expression of things being subliminally wrong between us? When he saw I wasn't going to reply, he continued:

'Oh, it's not just you. It's all of you, your whole family, probably has been for generations. Look at your dad. It didn't suit him to spend time with his family so he stayed in London. Your mum? What has she actually done for anybody, ever, including her children? Particularly her children! Bridgey? She always pretended life happened between the pages of a book. Matt? I mean . . . Matt? Please! Has he ever thought about anyone but himself? Oh yes, of course, poor misunderstood Matt, he's always been dealing with his issues and doing 'his thing'. Only his thing turned out to be nothing. Have any of you ever loved anyone else? Have any of you ever come down off your mountain and actually taken responsibility for something? Have any of you ever engaged with real life?'

I didn't even try to answer. I could have told him about Matt and Jo but this wasn't about them and I certainly wasn't going to defend myself or my family in this kangaroo court. The decision had been taken and the way he had reacted almost served to calm me down, which meant I knew I could see it through. I could sit here and take the abuse for as long as he needed to dish it out, and — don't get me wrong — I understood why he needed to. I could see why he was bitter. I would have been if I was in his place. But this time I was going to engage with life. This time I was going to do the right thing.

21

It was quarter to four by the time I reached the police station but I wasn't tired. Not at all. My adrenaline was running so hard I could have gnawed off my hand and not felt a thing.

There was no one behind the counter. I rang the bell and waited. I was more nervous than when they brought me here in the back of a police car. Then there was a chance, hope, a game to play. That had been extinguished. I wondered how it would pan out. Would I be held here while they picked up Ed? What about the children? Would they wake to find a policeman in the house? Maybe I should have thought of all that, but I knew I had to get out of the house and do it in case my nerve failed. If I was held overnight I could always ask the police to call Bea. No need to hide from Radio Bea-for-Bristol now. The world would look completely different in the morning.

I'd never seen Ed as angry as he was when I wouldn't budge. He simply didn't get it that I had to do it for all of us, that in the end there was no way I — we — could live forever under the strain of the infinite lie and therefore risking being apart was the *only* way we could stay together as a family. There was a moment when I did wonder whether there was a sliver of truth in his accusation that this was only happening because I was jealous of that woman — a younger version of me! — and it was the adultery rather than the killing driving me. But I was sure in my heart it wasn't.

'What if you get there and the police arrest you because someone has just rung in anonymously and said you killed Araminta?'

'No way.'

Ed stared impassively at me.

'It wouldn't be the first time. Wife jealous of mistress and wants to save her marriage. There's motive.'

'Ed, please.'

'As far as we know, no one saw you on Sion Hill that evening, and you obviously weren't spotted on Brandon Hill.'

'That's totally ridiculous. I didn't even know about her at that stage. She was just some woman who owned a flat where you crashed after a party. You were never going to see her again. Why would I care?'

'Because you found out what had happened between us? You worked it out. The flowers. The weird call. The blue ribbon. Changing my mobile password. There were plenty of clues. In some ways I'm amazed you didn't pick up on them earlier.'

'I trusted you.'

'But say that you did. Say you were a typical wife, wondering why I needed to go on 'overseas charity trips' and 'medical conferences'. A lot of wives would have. The reason you didn't is because you were so wrapped up in yourself and your art it never occurred to you. But say it had. Say you found out. So you went to her flat to confront her, to tell her to back off your man, but things turned ugly, you argued, she pushed, you pushed, she tripped . . . it's your word against a dead body.'

'I've never been in that building.'

'Tough to prove a negative.'

'No fingerprints.'

'Gloves.'

'In May?'

'Took care not to touch anything, rubbed down what you did.' He wiggled his fingers as quotation marks. ' 'I left our house at six to go to lie on Sion Hill and then went straight to book club.' In other words, unaccounted for between six and eight. Murder time? Between six and eight. Did anyone see you? What do you say — remembering anything you do say will be taken down and may be used in evidence against you?'

'That's ridiculous.'

'Stranger things have happened.'

'I'd tell the truth.'

'What is the truth if it's unprovable?'

'You'd never get away with it.'

'Don't tempt me.' Ed's jaw was set. 'It's no more ridiculous than what you're proposing. Let the genie out of the bag and no one knows what will happen. Maybe you should think about that?'

And so the argument had rolled on into the night, one step forward, half a step back, but the outcome was no longer in doubt. It couldn't be. The status quo was untenable.

There was the poster at the police station

warning me to look after my valuables. Surely that was the one place they might be safe? It must be true what they say about bent coppers. I had to ring the bell twice. Bristol criminals can sleep soundly in their beds at night. A policeman finally appeared. He was in his late fifties, the size and shape of a Big Mac with a complexion like Monterey Jack and a rugby prop's ears. He tried unsuccessfully to look as if people showed up of their own volition every morning at 3.45 a.m.

'What can I be doing for you?'

His head was as bald as a cannonball and twice as large, but he had kind eyes which he rubbed with a big red knuckle as if he'd just woken up. He'd been doing this too long. A low-slung tie formed a slack Y below his bowl-shaped jaw and his sleeves were rolled up above the elbow. He had arresting forearms. I momentarily lost my nerve as he pulled a clipboard from under the counter and looked around hopefully for a pen. I felt myself shaking.

'I've come about the death of Araminta Lyall.'

There. I'd done it. There was no going back. I felt like a long-distance swimmer in sight of land, but Mac was having none of it. He didn't holler 'Hallelujah!' He just grunted and frowned and wheezed through his nose and looked like a man who wished I'd shown up on someone else's shift. He stole a look at his watch. Was someone wasting police time?

'I know it's an odd time to come. But that's how it is. I know who killed her.'

A grunt and a suspicious frown. My voice

sounded reedy. The wannabe-famous crew would be well known here.

'And you are?'

'Alice Sheahan.'

He looked at me as if the name was faintly familiar.

'Right then, will you step this way?'

Big Mac moved heavily to the far end of the counter and lifted a flap. I dipped my head and went through, looking back briefly at the empty foyer — a copper's-eye view of humanity in its lowest moment — as he pushed open a door that led into a cream-painted corridor with olive doors on the right at regular intervals. It wasn't the corridor I'd been taken through for questioning. You get a better class of room when they think you might help.

'Can I get you anything? Coffee? Tea? Water?'

'A glass of water?'

'No glasses in here. Here we go then.' He opened the first door. 'Make yourself comfortable. Back in a minute.'

The room was small and square and the bricks were shiny. There was a wooden table and three wooden chairs. From inside, the glass in the door was opaque, one-way. Make yourself comfortable. He'd cracked that one before. I sat in the single chair facing the door. I should have been exhausted by my mother's revelation, the long drive, the argument with Ed, but my heart was pumping like a big-game hunter closing in on the kill.

The door opened without a knock. Big Mac stood aside to allow a lean man in his early thirties to come in. He had liquorice hair and self-regarding sideboards tapering into a point. His Prince of Wales check suit and natty boots looked out of place and time, as if he'd been called from the racetrack to identify a dead aunt. He seemed almost comically self-assured. He favoured Mac with a superior nod as he entered.

'Mrs Sheahan?'

I pushed my chair back. My confessor was younger than I was. I wondered how Ed would take him.

'Yes.'

'Don't get up. Inspector Sladden. Pleased to meet you. Thank you for coming in.' His tone was briskly efficient. 'I'm not normally around at . . . ' He glanced at his watch and winced. It was important I understood how fortunate I was he was here, that I was not talking to some duty sergeant; 4 a.m. is when the low grades, the Macs of the force, beat time. 'PC Baker here tells me you have information concerning the death of Araminta Lyall.'

He pulled one of the chairs towards him and sat down, resting an ankle on a knee. He was wearing snakeskin boots. Baker emerged from behind him and handed me a paper cone of water. The design team hadn't improved since my last visit. The water was warm and went down in one. He lowered himself gingerly on to the other chair as if uncertain it would take his weight. He was no advert for the frothy cappuccino that had appeared in his bear-sized paw.

'That's right.'

Sladden inclined his head. This was his show. Nothing could surprise him in his business.

'Shoot.'

Did he really say that? I shot.

'My husband Ed Sheahan slept with Araminta Lyall on the Saturday before she died and then — '

Sladden was holding up a palm.

'Can I stop you there?'

I paused, more out of surprise than obedience. Not many policemen stopped someone halfway through a confession. Normally their pens scratched away for as long as it took.

'I think you'll find that he didn't.'

'Didn't what?'

'Didn't sleep with Araminta Lyall.'

'I can assure you he did.'

Sladden was shaking his head. He had soft lips and a patronizing look that hovered between humour and regret.

'Shall we hear what the lady has to say?'

Sladden stopped looking at me long enough to throw Baker a contemptuous glance. Baker pushed his bottom lip out and blew air, counting the days to retirement. His name was on every case, his heart in none. Sladden turned back to me.

'We may not know everything about the death of Araminta Lyall — though we are satisfied in our own minds that it was an accident, hence the case is closed unless further evidence emerges — but we do know for a fact that on the night of Peter Spurling's party your husband did not sleep with the deceased — '

'Look, I can promise you — '

' — because we know who did.'

I stopped — dead. Even if I had wanted to speak I couldn't have done. Not because of Sladden's punch-me-in-the-face smugness but because he had just blown my world apart. He leant back in his chair, enjoying the effect of his words, master of all he surveyed. I knew I mustn't say another word until he'd told me everything.

'Unless, of course, your husband is Johnny Trumble?'

I shook my head. I could barely focus on what he was saying. What did he mean, Ed hadn't slept with that woman? More importantly, what did it mean if Ed *hadn't* slept with her? There was no time to come up with any answers because Sladden was continuing, silky-smooth,

'Johnny Trumble, the art dealer we pulled in after you two . . . ' He paused to check I wasn't about to interrupt. I definitely wasn't. 'He had an alibi for the night Miss Lyall died. He was at the Young Vic watching a play with friends. But he did tell us everything about the time at Miss Lyall's flat on the night of Dr Spurling's party, when he and your husband went back with her to Montpelier.'

'With the others.'

'Others?'

'There were six or seven of them who went back, I think.'

Sladden was shaking his head.

'No. It was just the three of them, Mr Trumble was very clear about that. So was your husband.'

There was too much to take in. If Ed hadn't slept with that woman then everything afterwards should never have happened. But why had he said there were six or seven who went back if there were only three? Two men and one woman, at least one of whom was plastered, is an entirely different dynamic to a group of random people. Had he added the others for my benefit? And why had he pretended he had never heard of Johnny Trumble when it was announced on *News at Ten* he had been arrested? If only two men had gone back with that woman, surely he would have recognized the name?

I said a cautious 'OK', because I couldn't think of anything else and I needed him to continue.

'Mr Trumble slept with Miss Lyall that night. The following morning they went next door to Café Kino on Stokes Croft for coffee. There, according to Mr Trumble, he told Miss Lyall it had been a terrible mistake, he had a girlfriend, had drunk too much, very sorry, all the usual, but there was no prospect of them entering a relationship. It seems Mr Trumble had been playing the flute. It happens between consenting adults.'

I didn't say anything, which he took as an invitation to continue. Why did the policeman who should have been asking questions only want to give out answers?

'According to Mr Trumble, your husband was flat out in bed having drunk far more than was good for him. Apparently he collapsed in a chair pretty much straight away.' Sladden paused for effect, relishing the chance to dig into a celebrated obstetrician. 'Mind willing perhaps, but the flesh . . . Mr Trumble said they tried to rouse him but nothing doing, so Miss Lyall generously suggested they put him in her bed as it was longer than the one in the spare bedroom. It seems Mr Trumble and Miss Lyall hauled him into her bed and then slept together in the spare room. Your husband was still asleep when Mr Trumble and Miss Lyall went for breakfast, and as Mr Trumble picked up a cab at the rank and went straight to Temple Meads he didn't know what happened afterwards, but assumed your husband would have simply let himself out. From how Mr Trumble described him, I think it would have been pretty unlikely he and Miss Lyall . . . how shall I put it . . . could have . . . if you get my meaning.'

'I see.'

And I did see. I saw everything. Suddenly I had 20/20 vision, hindsight, foresight, laser-eyes, you name it. I had the best vision on the planet. I saw because I remembered Ed telling me what Pete Spurling had said, too late as it turned out, that he should watch out for that woman because she liked older men, especially married men, and she had the history to prove it. She had slept with Johnny Trumble, been jilted at breakfast and returned to her flat to find Ed, an attractive successful older married man passed out in her bed with no memory of what had happened the night before. So she clambered in and claimed they'd slept together. And why not? She was thirty-two. She had nothing to lose.

Chasing him, pushing him, lying to him, trying to snare him and wreck his family might waste a week of her life, but nothing ventured . . . Only she had been wrong. She had had something to lose. She had her life to lose.

In that moment I understood that not only was Ed not a murderer, which I had always known, but that he hadn't betrayed our marriage either. More than that, I realized with a terrifying burst of self-knowledge, he may have been right in the sitting room when he said that the sex was the grit in my eye as much as that woman's death or my inability to work. It was a possibility I had to face. For if it wasn't, why did I suddenly feel so light? But if he didn't sleep with her then Ed was the victim as much of me and my pride as the deceit of that woman, maybe more so. If she didn't deserve to die for her duplicity, he certainly didn't deserve to swing for me. Neither natural justice nor our family would be served by Ed going to jail.

Of course this burnt through my mind in a fraction of the time it takes to read, and I felt a tear forming because I instantly saw how close my husband was to suffering a terrible injustice. I realized how close I had come — and still was — to ruining everything. My first job was to get the hell away from the reptilian Inspector Sladden as quickly as was politely possible. Thank God Philips wasn't here. There was no way he would have let arrogance or power or simple showing off cause him to miss the target. I tried to sound flummoxed and added,

'In which case, Mr Sladden, there seems to

have been a mistake.'

One chink, one false move . . . He grunted. I beat on hurriedly, trying not to allow a pause for thought or questions.

'Or maybe I'm the victim of some sort of practical joke.' I tried to appear as calm as possible. 'Ed is a bit of a joker when the surgical gloves are off. I'd better get home and find out exactly what's been going on. I do apologize for wasting both your time.'

I pushed my chair back and started to stand. Sladden glanced at Baker but didn't move, though he cased me like airport security. Suddenly he smiled, for real.

'No problem. That's what we're here for.'

'That's very generous at this hour.'

I picked up my handbag. Sladden still hadn't moved. I wanted him to stand up. Until he moved I couldn't take another step without looking too hurried and anything could give everything away. Sladden picked at some dirt on his boot heel and without looking up said,

'And then?'

I knew immediately what he meant but tried to look quizzical.

'Sorry?'

He gazed evenly at me.

'And then? You said 'And then'?'

'Did I? Just then?'

'No. At the beginning. Before I told you about Trumble. You said, 'My husband Ed Sheahan slept with Araminta Lyall on the Saturday before she died, and then . . . ' I was wondering what happened next.'

Oh my God.

'I don't remember . . . '

I pressed my bag against my hip. I needed physicality to counter the disorientating words swirling around me. He leant forward. He was trying to look relaxed but he knew he had missed a trick by interrupting. Baker flung him an 'I-told-you-so' glance that spoke of ancient forests and cunning yeomen.

''And then' what?' He was trying to recover ground. 'And then . . . he professed undying love? And then . . . he slept with her again on the Sunday?'

I shook my head, playing for time.

'I'm really sorry, I can't remember what I was going to say.'

'My husband Ed Sheahan slept with Araminta Lyall on the Saturday before she died, and then . . . he killed her?'

'No!' My indignation was genuine, but not as genuine as my fear.

'And then . . . what? Please try to remember, Mrs Sheahan.'

I focused on his sideboards. They were pointy on his cheek.

'I'll try to remember. I think it must have been my husband slept with Araminta Lyall on the Saturday before she died and then kept it quiet until tonight.'

'But tonight he admitted to a crime he didn't commit?'

'We were having an argument. He's obviously done this to wind me up.'

'Got his wife to go to the police over a crime

he didn't commit but which he's already been brought in for questioning for, just to 'wind' his wife up? Is that how he normally behaves?'

Every minute I spent in that room increased the danger. Oh why hadn't I trusted Ed? I had the straightest husband in the world and I'd failed him. I had tried to betray him even though I knew he hadn't killed her. What did that say about me and my motivation? I leant against the table, feeling the corner pressing into my thigh. I had to slip through the gap created by Sladden's arrogance.

'No. But these aren't normal times. Not since we were brought in for questioning. Any woman whose husband is taken in for questioning about the death of a girl in whose flat he spent a night would have some doubts, I think. Don't you? We're all human. I haven't been able to concentrate on my work. Some horrible things have been said about us online and in the papers. He thinks I don't trust him, which I do, completely, but we have had arguments, I'll admit. So no, it's not been easy and I guess things came to a head tonight. We had this argument and it all boiled over and . . . I guess . . . I guess that's why I came, because of everything . . . '

I trailed off. Forget the Footlights, this was my RADA, LAMDA, West End, Broadway and Hollywood audition rolled into one! Sladden leant back in his chair, nodding, assessing, processing the information, turning it this way and that, probing for the chink. Had I got a place? After what seemed like forever, and with my heart beating like a tom-tom (surely they could hear?), he flicked a glance at Mac that clearly said, 'What do you do with bonkers women?' and his face softened.

'I understand. It can't have been easy.'

I wanted to punch the air like a Wimbledon winner but I remained demure, my bag clasped tight in a sweaty mitt, shoulders hunched like a midnight-homesick schoolgirl. Sladden contemplated me for a moment longer and added, 'Well, I hope this has put your mind at ease. If it has at least it's served some purpose — if maybe not one worth coming out at four in the morning for.' He glanced at Baker. 'It can't be easy being married to one of those types who admit to crimes they didn't commit. What's it called?'

'Dunno.'

I said, 'Munchausen's by proxy.'

Sladden started to stand. 'That's the one.'

I smiled, gracious to a fault, happy to help. I was ready to walk out of the harsh light of the police station into the velvety arms of darkness.

22

I knew what I had to do. I walked out of the police station as slowly as I could, resisting the temptation to dance and leap and holler like a chorus girl and plant a giant smacker on Baker's great curve of a cheek. He offered a sweet 'Goodnight, best of' as he held the flap up so I could pass out into the empty reception. I bobbed up on the right side of the law and caught sight of a photofit of a man wanted for armed robbery stuck to the wall. He looked like Ned Kelly in his armour. Where do they get the guys who put these things together? It would take about two minutes to find someone if they actually looked anything like that, and they'd be guilty. You couldn't look like that and not have a motive. Ned glowered down from the wall, unable to believe I'd got away with it when there were more holes in my case than his armour. I just about managed 'you too' in reply to Baker, even though my mind was sliding around like a loose cargo in heavy seas and my mouth was so dry I could hardly articulate the words.

My hands were still shaking so hard it took two attempts to hit the 'unlock' button on the Golf and when I did the whole car seemed to light up like an attention-seeking Christmas tree.

Luckily it started first time. I didn't want anything to draw attention to me now. Moments later I was cruising along an empty road towards the centre of town at 29.99 mph, every yard taking me closer to a new and shinier future. My original plan was to go home and wake Ed with the news, but as I reached the James Barton roundabout I realized I had unfinished business I needed to deal with first.

So, instead of heading up Park Row towards the university and Clifton, I turned right under the 5102 apartment building, the Cerberus that guards Stokes Croft, and rolled north towards the Carriage Works. The abandoned pubs and industrial clubs were shut or had never opened. Gigantic canvases for graffiti artists and urban activists. I touched the brake as a police car glided out of St Pauls. It was as silent as a shark, all gleam and menace for the desolate figures silhouetted against the dirty windows of caged off-licences and late-night grocers, the men in vests, like drummers. A match flared, the orange tip of a cigarette swung in the air. No problem. It was my road now.

I cruised on and parked opposite the TV-familiar apartments with their Byzantine arches and stylized brickwork. For a few moments I sat in the car staring ahead at the empty road, trying to take everything in. That woman's motives were clear. The narrative made sense.

I pushed open the door, which felt as heavy as lead, and got out. My legs were hollow, still shaking. The air was cool, autumnal for the first time in weeks, and a drum-roll of thunder in the distance barrelled through the night. It held the promise of cleansing and renewal. It had been too hot for too long. I walked around to the passenger side and looked up at the building. There was a faint smell of tar as if the weeks of heat had melted the road. I had a stabbing desire for a cigarette. The building had security lights (but no cameras!), an empty foyer behind the central arch on the ground floor, darkened windows. For some reason I had expected them to be ablaze, lit up like a toy. Fifteen metres downwind a taxi snoozed against the pavement. I looked up at the three infamous windows on the third floor — argument, attack, accident — but they were dark. It was impossible even to tell if there were curtains. The sky was prehistoric. I felt I'd lived a thousand years.

I pulled my mobile out of my jacket.

Was Ed lying awake in our bed, staring at a sliver of light on the ceiling, waiting for the squad car to pull up, the doorbell to ring? Or was he dressed and prowling, fear pitting his stomach, defeat burning in his nostrils? Ed understood how to shape the present to create the future. He saw it every day at work. There was no more running now.

He would be ready. He always was. He would be wearing his charcoal suit, a crisp white shirt, the Hermès tie I gave him for his birthday. It was his smartest tie. Ed never lost his dignity or his sense of place. He would be roaming the house, committing humdrum objects to memory, writing letters of love and explanation for the children. Not for me. Not even Ed could write to the wife who had failed to trust him.

I switched on my mobile. I hadn't taken it to

Devon because I'd wanted to get away from everything and everyone. The children could call me on Granny T's number if they had to. The screen lit up and I typed in my password. I just wanted to whisper 'You're safe' and 'I'm so sorry' and 'I love you', but I knew my voice would crack. Not because the sentiment wasn't true, quite the reverse, because it was too keenly felt.

There was an email waiting. I was about to ignore it and carry on with what I had to do but opening an email was easier than deciding precisely what to say to Ed. I clicked on the icon. The title, 'Sunday morning, 1.45 a.m.', and the sender, Marianne Hever, sprang into life. It had been sent while I was at Highlands. Marianne? Why would she be emailing me? We hadn't exchanged a word since I left Bow House, hurrying to my car with my eyes down, my head burning under that inescapable sun, Marianne watching impassively from upstairs, with an unspoken but irredeemable sense we had reached the end and would never speak again. I opened the email. There was one sentence. 'Instinct is more powerful than knowledge.' That was it. No signature. I stared at the words, wondering why she had sent it and how they related to the email's title, until I realized there was an attachment below. I clicked on it, waiting restlessly for the opening circle to complete and, finally, the attachment to open.

It was a photograph of a building — the building I was standing in front of at that very moment. More than that, the photo had been taken from almost exactly the spot across the road where I was leaning back against my car door.

Why had Marianne sent me a photo of the Carriage Works? I hunted around the photo looking for a clue. There didn't seem to be anything. It was a super-clear image of the building I was looking at, the photograph taken at night, presumably at 1.45 a.m. on an unspecified Saturday night/Sunday morning, with a powerful camera.

It had to be to do with her flat. I expanded the image and homed in on the three arched windows on the third floor, staring at each in turn, but there was no mysterious figure looming out of the gloaming, no glint of steel, no mouth frozen in an unheard scream, no one retreating guiltily into the shadows. I scrolled down to the front door and scanned the foyer. It was also empty, brightly lit but clearly empty. What on earth was it she was trying to tell me? I cursed the fact I only had a mobile but there was no way I could drive home before I'd worked out her message. Marianne was not a person to do anything, let alone send a photograph to someone whose husband she had accused of murder-maybe-manslaughter and who had just walked out halfway through painting her portrait, without a reason.

I contracted the image as far as it would go and scrolled from one end to the other. It was panoramic, stretching southwards from the junction of Stokes Croft and Picton Street past the Carriage Works towards the centre of town.

Other than a few parked cars on the far side the street was as empty as a Sunday morning Edward Hopper. I scanned up and down the pavement and — hey! — there was a figure walking along the pavement, a silhouette passing in front of Café Kino where a Parisian brasserie-style globe lamp above the counter gave out barely enough light for definition. The figure, definitely a man, was leaning forward as if he was hurrying away from the Carriage Works in the direction of Picton Street.

I homed in on the figure. What was the date of the photo? It didn't say. It couldn't have been taken on the date of the accident. That had happened in the early evening, not the early morning, a Wednesday not a Sunday, and there was no way Ed would have returned later that night to the scene of the crime. He would have told me if he had. It couldn't have been the night of the party, as although he must have arrived around 1.45 a.m. he would have been with Araminta and Trumble, and he didn't leave until the morning. Whoever's account one believed, Ed wouldn't have been the one sent out to buy drink or cigarettes as he was already too far gone. Besides, if they did need stuff, why wouldn't they have stopped off on their way back in the cab to stock up?

It was only after I had run through all these questions, scanned the real windows for a few moments trying to work out exactly what had happened in that dark flat over those two nights and looked back at the photo that I realized the figure on the pavement wasn't Ed. Whoever he

347

was, he was too short, a dash too stocky, and his hair was thicker on the top of his head. As I looked at him I realized he could never have been Ed. I had only assumed he was because there was no one else and I couldn't think of any other reason why Marianne had sent the photo. She was playing games with me again, only this time with my perceptions and expectations. It was as if she was daring me, the portraitist who failed to paint her, the best friend who failed to trust her, to look properly, to see. I re-scanned the rest of the pavement, moving slowly left to right, to see if there was anyone else, anyone at all I might have missed, but the street was empty. There was no one else.

And that's when I got it. How could I have been so blind? The moment I focused on the cars parked in a row to the right of the Carriage Works, the nearest one less than ten yards away from the front door, I saw.

The cars I had taken to be parked weren't ordinary cars. They were taxis, and there were five of them. Marianne was showing me Ed could easily have found a taxi on the night he went back to Araminta's after Pete's party because there was a cab rank right outside her building and at 1.45 a.m. on a random Saturday night/Sunday morning it had five cabs on it. What's more — I glanced at the time on my phone — even at 4.37 a.m. on a Wednesday night it had one cab on it. In other words, Marianne was telling me Ed went into Araminta's flat after Pete's party because he wanted to, not because he had to in order to call a cab. Two drunk men and one drunk girl who barely know each other is a different end to an evening than an older man reluctantly joining a group of friends.

And suddenly, from nowhere, I remembered what Pete had said on the phone the day after the party when I called to ask if he knew where Ed was: 'Last I saw he was talking to a girl who's an art student down here, Araminta Lyall, and a man who's a picture dealer in London. It all looked quite involved.' It seemed a long way from Ed's claim that he didn't know who Johnny Trumble was and his line in the bathroom that he'd only spoken to her when he was 'too drunk to remember anything'.

My shoulders slumped back against the car. I was completely drained, the elation I had felt on leaving the police station entirely dissipated. If there was any positive to be drawn it was that she had said our secret was safe. But could I trust her? Marianne didn't owe me anything. That she hadn't gone to the police yet didn't mean she might not go sometime. And what about Philips? Or Neil? In different ways and with varying levels of conviction they had all intuited the truth. There was nothing I could do about any of them. Marianne would do what she wanted. She always had. Maybe we'd been foolish to think we were ever going to get away with it. Someone always had to pay.

What should I do about it? That was the question she was posing. Forgetting Araminta for a moment — 'forgetting everything that happened afterwards' — Marianne was asking me what I was going to do about a husband I had been through fire for but who had never told me the whole truth and so I could no longer trust. Was I going to confront him? Was I going to walk out on Ed as she had Rob and I had her on that long-ago afternoon? Should I go back to the police and tell the whole truth to punish him for his dishonesty? Did I have the energy to go back and re-open all the questions and put my finger in the livid wound? Would he tell the truth anyway and how would I know if he didn't? Did it even matter what he was thinking when he was drunk? He was unlikely to get himself into that state again for a while. Or was I going to take the view that whatever he may have been thinking when he accepted the invitation to go back to Araminta's he hadn't done anything wrong and there is as yet, fortunately, no such thing as thought-crime in our country, and if every man who drank too much at a party and fancied another woman but did nothing about it was booted out there wouldn't be many marriages left?

Did it matter if the distinction was between 'fancied' and 'fancied and wanted' and 'fancied and wanted and would have had if he hadn't keeled over'? It was impossible to tell and, as nothing had happened, was there even any real difference between them?

Did the fact he had lied about his motives on the first occasion he went to her flat mean he had lied about what had really happened the second time he went there? Did it mean he had lied about other things I wasn't even thinking about?

Did he do charity work in the Third World or jet-set to conferences in the First?

Had he gone back because he secretly fancied Trumble?

Was I going crazy or did I know anything about him at all?

Could I believe in him without knowing?

Could I remain married to him or ever work again without believing in him?

I was leaning against my car contemplating the building and Marianne's email and my options when a gauzy rain, so thin and warm and soft it seemed unconnected to the pitiless heatwave or peals of thunder that had rolled across the city, began to fall. It fell lightly on my forehead, my bare arms, and when I ran a hand through my hair there was a gossamer film, damp to the touch. And it was while I was standing there on Stokes Croft, looking at the Carriage Works, thinking about everything that had happened, everything I had thought and believed, everything I thought I had known or understood, thinking about questions that couldn't be answered, thinking about the way the truth changed according to one's perspective, and about how things leak into things, how they shift and fluctuate, that I finally glimpsed the choice Marianne was showing me.

★   ★   ★

The studio was washed by the first light of a grey dawn. For a long time I stood in the doorway surveying the mess of paints and brushes and palettes as if seeing it for the first time. The canvas on the easel was primed but bare. I'd been unable to paint since I got back from Marianne's. I couldn't bring myself to analyse a physical object, much less any human being.

A stack of canvases leant against the wall. The one facing into the room was a maroon and purple abstract, imagined moorland, unnerving and indistinct. Beyond, Marianne's abandoned portrait stood alone, facing the wall. I hadn't known what to do with it. I couldn't bear to look at it and I couldn't live with it forever, but equally I hadn't been able to summon the nerve to throw it out. That would have been the final admission of failure, not only of that portrait but of everything in which I had invested so much. I wasn't quite ready to take that step, though on more than one occasion I'd almost picked it up, determined to haul it out and drive straight to the dump. Yet each time I'd paused, as if it — she — had cast a spell. Letting it go would have been the end of me as an artist, a rejection of everything I'd always believed. I was trying to get my head around that.

I looked at the back of the beige canvas tamped to the wooden frame, the horizontal crossbar with its tiny nails and knotted grain. When I was ready, I picked up the painting and carried it over to the table where I left work I wanted to study or assess or live with or simply look at from a different perspective. I turned the portrait round so it faced outwards and leant it against the wall. I fetched the wooden chair and pushed it across the floor until it was directly in front of the table and sat down. Then and only then, sitting directly under the single harsh spotlight, not knowing what to expect, I raised my eyes to Marianne.

She stared down at me, her cool, detached look emphasizing the scale of my defeat. In her self-confidence I saw the shape of her triumph and my failure, our history, my weakness, her strength. Whichever way I looked, there could be no doubt Marianne had remained beyond my grasp. I hadn't been able to put my arms around her. I didn't know her. I wanted to turn away but I forced myself to look at it and to think about Marianne the way I had outside the Carriage Works when I had the first inkling of the choice I faced, and eventually I understood.

Instinct is more powerful than knowledge.

Don't paint what you see, paint how you feel.

I thought back to that afternoon in the dormitory. Dust dancing in shards of light. A misperception unchecked, a question unasked. It had taken more than twenty years for Marianne to force me to take responsibility for what I had done, and to show me I had been wrong about absolutely everything I thought I knew. It had taken her three days (and one email) to undermine fifteen years of trust.

I sat there a long time, staring at the portrait, absorbing Marianne into me, contemplating the reality of my failure and the fork in the road ahead. When there was nothing more to take I reached forward and laid the portrait flat on the table, its face up. A distant boom of thunder rumbled through the dawn and rain began to fall, fat silver tears on the windowpane. I crossed the studio and from an old Campbell's tomato soup can (my nod to Andy) picked out a black marker pen and a large pair of specialist-sharp artist's scissors. In the middle drawer of the filing cabinet there was a wad of thick brown paper and a roll of bubble-wrap, a stray postcard perched on top (Matisse, one of his cut-outs, vibrant, ultramarine). I brushed the master of colour aside and took the paper and bubble-wrap and, from the bookcase, a postcard with our address printed on it, industrial-strength tape and a ball of string. I carried my booty over to the table and laid it out beside the portrait.

The painting was so large I had to wrap it in three sections. First, Marianne's slender legs disappeared into the bubbles and paper, along with a cursory outline of the base of the orange abstract, that never-painted emotion. Next, I wrapped her torso, from the top of her thighs to the bottom of her neck, admiring her slim figure in its smart black suit, her lithe posture, the resilience and confidence that had taken her all the way. All that remained was her head. As I cut the final sheaf of bubbles I looked into her eyes, diamond-black holes I would never comprehend. They sailed on unknown seas, marched to a private music. I had not known Marianne or understood her or captured her in paint. My failure was the sense I had of her, and that alone was true.

After the portrait was wrapped and addressed — Marianne Hever, Bow House, Ashton under Lyne, OL6 — and neatly tied with string, I

354

reached for the postcard, which lay face-down on the table and squared it in front of me. I picked up the marker pen and without a pause for thought I wrote: 'It's finished.' There was no kiss. No cross to bear.

★　★　★

When everything was done I parcelled the portrait and left it on the landing before I slipped quietly downstairs. I deliberately didn't look in on Ed in case he woke up and we had to go through another futile argument. I knew I was betraying him but there was no other way. We couldn't live and work and trust each other against the backdrop of an infinite lie. Nell and Arthur might not see it like that but that was the chance I had to take. At least as adults they would never be able to say to me, as I had said to my mother: 'Why didn't you tell us?' Even if I had failed them in everything else, even if my work had taken precedence and I had refused to trust their father, I wouldn't fail them in that. As I said to Ed in my studio the day after I was hounded by the press, I would always know I shot for the sun.

The route was familiar. Soggy Clifton backstreets, student terraces, Queen's Road and the Union. The RWA. The last clubbers stumbling home from the Triangle. Wills Tower and the university buildings, a reminder of the money that built Bristol, tobacco fields, slaves, port wine. Park Row rolled downhill topographically and socio-economically, past the BRI with its coloured hoops, the atmosphere increasingly transient, law courts and bus station, Subway, Tesco Express, every side-street tempting me to reconsider, every set of traffic lights offering a pause for thought.

My hands were steady on the wheel. The James Barton roundabout was washed in a silent moment of dawn. I could have turned left towards the Carriage Works and shimmied in amongst the row of idling cabs. Instead I swung right at Cabot Circus towards Temple Meads before gliding up the ramp beside the underpass, following signs to Kingswood. Biscuit-coloured buildings. The glint of fresh rain. A town exhausted in the pale light.

The reception area of the police station was empty, except for Ned, of course. He stared down glumly from his wall, surprised to see me back so soon. For a split-second I was tempted to bolt, but the feeling evaporated as quickly as it arrived. This was the only way forward. There was no way out. Marianne knew, Neil knew, Philips knew. The dam was cracked. It would break eventually. This was the only way I could take control and do justice to everything that had happened and everyone it had happened to and to ensure that one day as a family we could begin again. The lino squeaked under my feet. I was about to press the bell for attention when Inspector Sladden appeared from a door behind the counter. He was wearing a knee-length leather overcoat and a black trilby. When he saw me he frowned.

'What is it now?'

He didn't try to conceal the irritation in his voice.

'Um . . . ' My voice sounded simultaneously frail and huge in the silent reception. ' . . . I need to tell you something.'

Sladden sighed and leant back against the wall. He had the look of a man who couldn't wait to get home to a place where things were what they seemed to be and people behaved as they were supposed to.

'Can't it wait? It's five-o'-fucking clock and I've been here all night.'

'I know. I'm sorry.'

He clicked his teeth irritably.

'You know we charge people for wasting police time?'

I nodded. Still he didn't move, just surveyed me sceptically from beneath his hat. I nodded towards the door to the interview rooms but he shook his head.

'Here?'

'Here.'

I understood. Who wouldn't want to go home? I had used up my goodwill. There were no offers of coffee or cones of water, no Big Mac with a tiny pen in a giant fist to watch over us, bringing a slice of beefy humanism to proceedings. Sladden shoved his hands into his pockets. He watched me carefully across the foyer. He didn't take his hat off or show any sense he expected to be there for more than a minute. I felt exposed, standing in the middle of the floor under the harsh lights with no chair or table for a prop, but for once it didn't worry me. I wanted exposure.

He flipped open a pack of gum and popped a pillow-shaped piece in his mouth. I didn't expect him to offer me one and he didn't.

'You remember when I was here earlier and I said, 'My husband slept with Araminta Lyall on the Saturday before she died and then . . . '?'

I waited for him to reply but he simply nodded.

'But you told me he hadn't?'

I paused, waiting for him to acknowledge, but still he didn't speak.

'And then later, at the end, when you asked about that sentence I backtracked and said I hadn't said 'and then', that you must have been mistaken?'

He yawned and glanced ostentatiously at his watch.

'And eventually you let it go?'

Sladden wanted it to be clear that he had a low threshold of boredom and I was crossing it.

'Well, there was an 'and then'.'

He breathed in deeply through his nose.

'What I should have said was . . . '

I glanced at the floor as if for encouragement, or maybe the truth, but neither was to be found on the dirty lino. Sladden was still slouched against the wall, showing no interest.

'My husband slept with Araminta Lyall on the Saturday before she died and then — '

My voice cracked momentarily. Despite himself, Sladden leant forward. His lips were moist. They quivered imperceptibly.

'I killed her.'

★ ★ ★

The cell had a camera high up, a caged bulb, a steel door with a peephole. The smooth-edged table was fixed to the floor.

I sat on the chair facing the door. My handbag and necklace and the silver bracelet Ed had given me on our wedding anniversary had been taken away by a policeman barely old enough to be out of school, also the laces from my pumps. He seemed almost embarrassed to be asking for them. I made it as easy for him as I could. I was exhausted and yet sitting there, waiting for the circus to begin, I felt whole, free in a way I hadn't since the moment in the Soho burger bar when I sussed the identity of ML xxx. It was as if I had finally landed and at last I could relax. Everything was calm, everything still. After all the tears and the talking, the bitterness, the shouting and despair, the silence of the cell was oceanic. There was nothing left to hurt me. I had paid my debt to Marnie. I would never paint again. Not in prison. Not whenever I got out. Not ever. There was a time when that would have been the life sentence, but that time had gone. It had cost too much. I couldn't handle the failure that every portrait, every painting, every work of art must be. Hope crushed anew. I had had my turn on the wheel.

What had Ed said? 'Sometimes there is no right and wrong. Sometimes there's no possibility of a perfect outcome.' He understood. He always had done. Would Nell and Arthur ever understand why I had taken the blame for Ed? Would they accept that one of us had to go down, that for all of us this was the better way and in the end for me it was the only way? Life isn't only what you see in front of you. It takes place in the margins, in the lines between the squares. They would survive. Teenagers are more resilient than their parents want to believe. I saw them again through the kitchen window eating at the island, Nell leaning into Ed, his arm around her, Arthur's forehead on the wooden top, rocking with laughter — the ease, the self-sufficiency, the love.

I pictured my father alone on the cliffs, silhouetted against the horizon, light spilling off the water, a piercing wind, the humbling sea. What had he written on his Beachy Head postcard? That it was the only way the rest of us could continue as we must, the only way we could live the lives we had to live. He had taken responsibility, as had Matt in his own fragile way. They understood love.

My hands were on the table, palms facing up. Which was my lifeline, reaching out for happiness? There was so much I didn't know. Why do caterpillars become butterflies? How far can a woman run? None of it mattered any more. The only truth is that the colours fade. But there is relief in powerlessness. It absolves responsibility and gives wings to imagination. It rejects tragedy.

A door banged. A rumble of voices moved down the corridor. The key turned in the lock, smooth as pearl. Sladden, hatless, but still in his natty coat and snakeskin boots, was followed into the cell by a policewoman with a notepad. I nodded at her but she didn't respond. Sladden waited by the door, gazing at me, saying nothing.

It was as if he wanted to frame this last moment of peace, the face of a killer before the carnival began. I stared evenly back as though I was sitting for my portrait. I could be generous with my time. Eventually he sighed, pushed a hand through his slicked hair and said,

'Prove it.'

I closed my eyes and took a deep breath. In the tender darkness I saw the colours that shine, a kingfisher that flew.

Acknowledgements

Many people, advertently or otherwise, contributed to the writing of *What Alice Knew*. Prime amongst them is Susanna Wadeson of Transworld, who not only picked up the novel, but has proved to be a brilliant editor and guide, a character and narrative obsessive. Lizzy Goudsmit has been equally incisive and long-suffering, similarly cold-eyed. This novel would not be whatever it is without them.

I would also like to thank Becky Hunter, who has been a whirlwind of energy and sound advice. She is part of the wonderfully talented and welcoming team at Transworld. It is hard to imagine better publishers.

Next there are my work-in-progress readers, too numerous to name but you know who you are, who read and critiqued not only *What Alice Knew* in various states of undress but also previous unpublished work. Without your insight, encouragement and generosity, this ship might never have set sail.

Finally, I would like to thank Emily, whose belief may have wavered but whose support never has, and Martha, Madeleine and Louis, who give me more than they will ever know.

THE ORPHANS

Annemarie Neary

Eight-year-old Jess and her little brother were playing at the water's edge when their parents vanished. For hours, the children held hands and waited for them to return. But nobody ever came back. Years later, Jess has become a locker of doors. Now a lawyer and a mother, she is determined to protect the life she has built around her. But her brother Ro has grown unpredictable, elusive and obsessive. When new evidence suggests that their mother might be alive, Ro reappears, convinced that his sister knows more than she claims. And then bad things start to happen . . .